C000203833

ANTHONY BURGESS

The Right to an Answer

HUTCHINSON
London Sydney Auckland Melbourne Johannesburg

Hutchinson & Co. (Publishers) Ltd

An imprint of the Hutchinson Publishing Group

17–21 Conway Street, London W1P 6JD

Hutchinson Group (Australia) Pty Ltd
30–32 Cremorne Street, Richmond South,
Victoria 3121
PO Box 151, Broadway, New South Wales 2007

Hutchinson Group (NZ) Ltd
32–34 View Road, PO Box 40–086,
Glenfield, Auckland 10

Hutchinson Group (SA) Pty Ltd
PO Box 337, Bergvlei 2012, South Africa

First published by William Heinemann Ltd 1960
First published as a Hutchinson Paperback 1983
© Anthony Burgess 1960

Printed in Great Britain by The Anchor Press Ltd
and bound by Wm Brendon & Son Ltd,
both of Tiptree, Essex

ISBN 0 09 153391 0

To

GOODRIDGE MACDONALD

'Go and be hanged!' said Scopprell. 'How can you have the face to make game of matrimony?'

WILLIAM BLAKE:

An Island in the Moon

I

I'm telling this story mainly for my own benefit. I want to clarify in my own mind the nature of the mess that so many people seem to be in nowadays. I lack the mental equipment and the training and the terminology to say whether the mess is social or religious or moral, but the mess is certainly there, certainly in England, and probably in the Celtic fringe and all over Europe and the Americas too. I'm in a position to smell the putridity of the mess more than those who have never really been expatriated from it – the good little people who, with their television, strikes, football pools and *Daily Mirror*, have everything they want except death – because I only spend about four months in England every two years now, and I get the stench sharp in my nostrils (widened by warm air) as soon as I land and for about six weeks after that. Then, gradually, the corruption creeps up, like fog round the boat-train, and, yawning over the television in the front room of my father's semi-detached, arriving at the pub sometimes five minutes before opening-time, I can feel damnation being broken in like a pair of shoes, myself becoming a citizen of the mess, and I'm only saved by having to get on the B.O.A.C. plane at London Airport or, which shortens my stay in England, taking the P. and O. – *Canton, Carthage, Corfu* – from Southampton.

I feel at this moment as though I have a sandwich in each hand and don't know which to bite first. I want to tell you a little more about this mess and I also want you to know how it is that I have (for so I'm often told) such an enviable life – two years of sun or, at least, of the exotic and not too much work, followed by four months of civilisation with enough appetite to chew away at the big rich pudding which is the exile's dream of home. This big rich pudding has nothing stodgy about it – it's all fruit and no flour. It's the long catalogue of shows in the *Evening Standard*, the trip – warm brown ale in the boat's bar – from Richmond to Westminster, afternoon drinking in underground clubs the size of a Singapore lavatory (glint and tinkle of endless new rounds, my rounds, under the strip lighting), the married women dancing to the juke-box, ready for a lark till their taxis at six (hubby home to a casserole from a time-controlled electric cooker) and all the rest of it. Anybody, by the way, who envies me this enviable double life, anybody young enough, anyway, is very welcome to try it. The colonial civil servants are moving out everywhere, but the trading companies are still anxious to recruit bright young men (a good school not obligatory, but the right sort of accent wanted and, preferably, fair hair) to sell brilliantine, cigarettes, Lambrettas, cement, sewing-machines, outboard motors, airconditioning plants and W.C.'s in those sunny lands which have just achieved a perky independence. I am no longer a bright young man, but the Company evidently still finds me useful. (I'm literate, I read fairly widely. I can turn on the charm, I can hold anything I drink.) Even to and from Tokyo I'm allowed a first-class slumberette every two years. (I'm over forty now and do the 'old man's tour'.) In a few years' time I'll retire, though God knows where to, with a very fair pension. My name, incidentally, is J. W. Denham.

And now the other sandwich, but this is harder to get one's teeth in. I shall nibble round the edges, because my teeth aren't so good. The post-war English mess that hits me on arrival, in the smoke of the boat-train and the laughter in the airport bar. It's a mess that's made by having too much freedom. That may sound a stupid thing to say when you consider how little freedom is left in the modern world, but I'm not thinking of political freedom (the right to curse the Government in the local pub). I don't think political freedom's very important – not, anyway, for more than about one per cent of the community. It's amused me in the East to see citizens of newly independent territories scampering off to places still groaning under the British yoke. They don't want freedom; they want stability. And you can't have both.

I don't want to preach, I want to tell a story, but I have to make this point. You definitely can't have both. What makes for stability is neither here nor there, but once you lose it you suffer. I think Hobbes had this idea, but I mention that name very diffidently because of the usual stupid misunderstanding in the club the other night when everybody thought I was talking about cricket. You suffer from the mess, the great democratic mess in which there's no hierarchy, no scale of values, everything's as good – and therefore as bad – as everything else. I once read a scientific article which said that perfect order can only exist in matter when the temperature's low. Take your food out of the deep-freeze and it soon goes bad. It's escaped the grip of the cold which gave it a pattern; now it becomes dynamic enough, seething like a political meeting, but you have to throw it away. It's a mess. But the horror is that you can get used to rancid food, used to a mess. It catches up on you, however. Mithridates must have been the only poison-eater to die old. Those who blaspheme against stability don't last very long.

At the beginning of my story I was on leave in one of

3

the suburbs of a rather large smug Midland city. My parents had gone to live there after my father's retirement (he'd been a printer in North Wales) chiefly at the request of my sister, whose husband ran a school a few miles out of the city. My mother had died suddenly in the middle of my tour (I was looking after the Company's branch in Osaka) and I hadn't been able to get home for the funeral. My father and sister had never really cared for each other, Beryl being very much her mother's girl. My mother had never really liked me since the time she caught me in the potting-shed, in North Wales, when I was sixteen, with a girl who lived three doors down. The shame, the disgrace, etc. Anyway, Beryl got my mother's estate of eight hundred pounds odd and put down the money for a phony cottage in a commuter's village twelve miles away from her poor old widower father. I never could stand the woman. I once learned by heart a poem written by some modern poetaster about a similar sort of woman, called Ethel, and substituted Beryl's name. I remember two verses:

> Beryl is the daughterly daughter:
>   The rankest filial piety oozes
> From the flesh that she washes in greasy water
>   And the pallid pie that the cat refuses.
>
> Mother and womb must come to dust;
>   That gone, what else can compensate?
> In sheer devotion then she must
>   Inherit the entire estate.

I'm not really bitter. I've more money in the Hongkong and Shanghai Bank than Beryl will ever see. I mean that. She'll undoubtedly outlive me, but she won't outlive me on any of *my* money.

My widower father was stuck with a suburban house he

4

didn't like very much, cooking for himself, leaving the other chores to a sharp-nosed weekly woman who breathed deeply while shaking the mats. He had no affiliations in the region. But it seemed pointless for him to move elsewhere. His great oak desk could only be moved from its upstairs 'den' through the window, and that seemed too big an undertaking – even vicariously – for a man at his time of life. He'd arranged his books carefully (there were some limited editions that he'd had the printing of), though he never really liked reading books. When he said that some book was 'a lovely thing' he only referred to the typography. He'd rawlplugged his pictures (Millais, Holman Hunt, Rosa Bonheur) deep into the walls. He might as well stay there as anywhere. Lately he'd taken up golf again. A small factory-owner, a man in the local Co-op, a traveller in medical supplies – these used to pick him up on Sunday mornings for a game. On Monday afternoons he did nine holes with the High Church vicar. He'd got into the habit of going to the Black Swan every evening at nine for a pint and half of bitter beer and a talk with his golfing friends about the sports programmes on television. The High Church vicar only appeared in the pub on Sunday evenings – after service, still in his vestments – to knock back a pint and say, 'Christ, that was thirsty work.' This, I suppose, was to show that he was High Church.

The Black Swan was what was known locally as a 'Flayer's ace' (a house run by Flower's of Stratford-on-Avon, presumably). Most appropriately, the landlord was an Arden from a village not too far from Wilmcote where, of course, Mary Shakespeare, née Arden, had been a farmer's daughter. You only had to look at Ted Arden to see that William Shakespeare had got his face and forehead (if not what lay behind the forehead) from the Ardens. A strong breed, the Ardens, while the Shakespeares must have been as weak as water. Ted had the fiddle-shaped brows, the early baldness, the big-lidded eyes of the best-known Shakespeare portrait; he had also a kind of charm which, despite the strong Midland accent and the near-illiteracy and the broken teeth, could obviously get him anywhere—the Arden charm which Shakespeare himself must have inherited. People liked to do things for Ted: commercials would bring him jellied eels from London: odd liqueurs and sets of beer-mats would come back from Continental holidays; ragged men in the public bar would give him rabbits, already gutted. ('Look at the fat round them kidneys,' Ted would say, admiringly.) Charm had got him a wife who was every inch, as far as one could tell, a lady. Veronica Arden had a patrician voice that rang clear at closing-time. Thin as a boy, no grey in her blondeness at forty-six, she was as exophthalmic as a young poet. She suffered from odd ailments which made her tired, she had had certain obscure operations. When she appeared behind the bar in the late evening (just before the rush of the last hour), men who were sitting at the tables wriggled as though they felt they ought to stand up—she had that effect on people. Dressed for the Licensed Victuallers' annual ball, jewelled in an opulent gown, her fur coat over her shoulders, waiting for Ted to bring the car round, you felt she was doing you too much honour: if an extra two-pence had then and there been clapped on the draught beer, I doubt if anyone would have complained.

They made that pub. When they were out for the even-ing, the bars left in charge of an innocuous man in a green bum-freezer, the place reverted to what it really was—a tavern for dreary drinkers with loud mouths, the outside lavatories a fair walk in the rain, a reek of fish in the 'best room' from the private quarters upstairs, for Ted was very fond of fish and cooked it for himself every day. When he

6

was there, the fish-smell was glamourised — it was Rabel-
aisian or evoked rollicking sea-ports. When he was absent
it was just vulgar — a fart from the lips or an old Roman
sign, lingering like a stuck note on an organ. Fish was
another present that Ted was always getting from the
customers — Dover soles, halibut, bloaters ('Not seen any
of them for years, me duck.') I once took the pair of them
to dinner at a hotel in Rugby and I introduced Ted to
scampi. He was awed: a new world had opened. With the
coffee and brandy he said, 'Them scampies was bloody
marvellous.'

'Really, Edward,' rebuked Veronica. 'You're not in the
public bar now.'

'Sorry, me duck, but they really was.' And, going back
in the car, 'I'll be on the blower first thing in the morning.
Bloody marvellous. I'll get some of them scampies for me
lunch.' It was a pleasure to do things for Ted. He was
always so appreciative. You could see how Shakespeare
had managed to get in so well with the Earl of Southampton.

The Black Swan stood in a pocket of decaying village,
the dirty speck round which the pearly suburb had woven
itself. The village had shrunk to less than an acre. It was
like a tiny reservation for aborigines. From the filthy win-
dows imbeciles leered down at the weed-patches; cocks
crowed all day; little girls in pinafores of an earlier age
shnockled over stained half-eaten apples; all the boys
seemed to have cleft palates. Still, it seemed to me far
healthier than the surrounding suburb. Who shall describe
their glory, those semi-detacheds with the pebble-dash all
over the blind-end walls, the tiny gates which you could
step over, the god-wottery in the toy gardens? The wind
cut through the spaces between, the wind of the old hill
buried in macadam, striking like the edge of a wet towel.

It stirred up a grey broth over the red roofs and, swirling in the soup, was the alphabet pasta of the television aerials – X, Y, H, T . . .

It was a Saturday evening. My father and I sat in the front room, poisoned by the gas fire, adenoidally gaping at the television screen. My father now had two pro- grammes to choose from – a recent innovation – and we were riveted not to the B.B.C.'s parlour-game but to some American glorification of police violence on the commer- cial channel. My father had refused to have a special aerial installed but, as the commercial transmitter was not very far away, its effusions slid down the original one-channel aerial smoothly enough. The only trouble was that every- thing came out in duplicate; each character had a *Doppel- gänger* that stood a step behind. This, so the local electri- cians had said, was because of the church spire in the village: like the transmitter of some enemy country, it jammed and scrambled and confused. The electricians did not actively resent the church spire: they just advised people to get another aerial. My father, having a High Anglican golfing friend, did not mind very much; more- over, his sight was failing.

The film of police violence ended with an epilogue spoken by a tough police chief in a trilby hat. He told us that the State Troopers were our friends and it was our duty as good American citizens to help them in their arduous efforts to wipe out the traffic in cocaine. Then some monkeys advertised tea, there was a brief soap-flake ballet, a stupid girl with a pony-tail engulfed a whole chocolate and went 'Ooooo'. The gas-fire was making me delirious: I was convinced that my Japanese servant tapped me on the shoulder and said, 'Master wake up now.' I shook myself free of the new England and, as a gloriously imbecilic lady announcer said, 'Right now you're going to see him in the

8

flesh. So, over with Harvey Greenfield to . . .' I switched off. The lady announcer's voice jetted out, and her image turned over like a playing-card. My father nodded, coughed with his whole body (this seemed, somehow, to squash him like a steam-hammer) and went to get his hat and raincoat. The hat was an old pork-pie and the raincoat pockets bulged with half-empty cigarette-packets, match-boxes, dirty handkerchiefs. He clearly needed someone to look after him. I went into the dining-room to get the cigarette-holder I had recently begun to affect, and he came in, ready, to see if I was ready. The quick of a cigarette was already close to burning his lips and a long drooping ash was about to drop on the carpet. This was a mystery I had never been able to fathom: he could go out of a room cigaretteless and come back a second later with a tiny end scorching his mouth. It was like a bad piece of continuity in a film. Perhaps he had a guilty passion for mere butts, one that he didn't like to admit to by being seen lighting them. I don't know. My father was part of England, and England is perhaps the most mysterious country in the world.

We went out silently, leaving ash on the carpet and a hot yellow cave in the fireplace, the barometer banging against the wall as the wet suburban air blew in. My father locked the door with fussy care and then put the key under the mat, panting and creaking like the old man he was. We turned into Clutterbuck Avenue, passing the letter-box that spoke of a bigger world, walked against the drizzle wheezing slightly, for it was a slight climb (it was queer to reflect that Clutterbuck Avenue was really a hill), then turned sharp right to a cobbled path which led to the old village. The old village accosted us like a prostitute as we turned the next corner. Then came the Black Swan or Mucky Duck, a Flayer's ace.

9

The ritual sweat and discomfort of Saturday night pub-life hit us hard in the eyes and throat. The week-end waiter, a handsome milkman in a bow-tie and green mess-jacket, keen on the dignity of service, was bringing a tray of Babychams to a table near the door. My father coughed hard, as if to clear the room, and a violent storm-ripple passed over the fizzy pear-juice. But he was greeted heartily enough.

'Evening, Bert.'

'Evening, Mr Denham.'

'Ow are yer, me old sport?'

'Telly were a bit of a wash-out to-night, eh, Bert?'

The golf-players were at a table near the door, frequently refreshed by blasts of cold air brought in by newcomers like my father and myself. The better, central tables, and the roasted tables by the fire had filled up as early as opening-time. My father sat tight up against his cronies on a little stool that had been hidden under the table, and I squeezed in between strangers on the settle that ran right down one wall. The waiter who was so fanatical about service swooped, and I ordered for the whole table. That was right, that was proper. I was the returned nabob. The golfing traveller in medical supplies said, 'If it's all right with you, old man, I'll have a Scotch. Beer's a bit off to-night. Must be near the end of the barrel.'

'A double?' I said.

'If you say so, old man.'

I smiled to myself, thinking of the suburban glamour of 'shorts'. In my parts of the world beer was fast becoming the rich man's drink: I'd paid seventeen-and-six for one bottle in Calcutta.

I sipped at my half of bitter dutifully, trying to convince myself that I really liked it, the warm beer of old England. The exile's dream of frothy tankards was a convention.

('And the first bloody thing I'm going to have when I land is a bloody big pint of draught Bass. God, what wouldn't I give for one now.') I knew that soon, my leave only being a month old, I would be back on lager and 'shorts'. Something to do with the blood getting thin, perhaps, or the digestion getting weak; I felt guilty about disparaging British beer. I found that my father was calling across the table to me. I couldn't hear: the tray-clatter, glass-clink, coughs, laughs, twittering of women got in the way.

'What's that, dad?'

'Mr Winter, next to you. He's in the printing trade.'

'Oh.' Mr Winter the printer, I thought, and made him comic almost before I looked at him. He was in his early thirties, fresh-faced, spots burning on his cheekbones from the heat of the room. His chin was round, weakish, the small mouth had no real shape to it – like his suit, not well-cut. The eyes were hazel, speckled, hunted – fine eyes, I thought – and his nostrils were set in a fixed flare (like a woman re-entering a room, noticing a smell that was not there when she went out). His hair was straight, too well-brushed, creamed, the strawy hair it is such a shock to meet again after the rich raven of the East.

'How do you do?'

'How do you do?'

'Will you have a drink?'

'Oh, thank you, I've got plenty here still.' There were about three inches of beer in his glass: he was evidently not a drinking man. But you could tell that too from his voice – light, without resonance, unwarmed by phlegm or hearty laughs from the belly. I wondered what he was worried about: his eyes kept turning to the door, to the bar, to the men back singly from letting some out, the women – after a more elaborate ritual – back in giggling groups.

'My father was a printer,' I said.

'Oh, yes, I know. We often talk about it.' His eyes were not with me; he kept looking at the bar, as though some figure or figures would appear there, having risen from a cinema-organist's cellar or materialised in ectoplasm from the nostrils of Ted Arden. Then he would look at the door, as at a less probable source of appearance. Ted, I noted, was very busy – at the pumps, at the glasses behind, the bottles below, the merrily ringing till, like a percussion-player in some modern work who dashes with confidence from xylophone to glockenspiel to triangle to wind-mach-ine to big drum to tambourine. But Ted had time to accept, with charm, presents from customers who stood manly, one foot on the rail, or the less lucky who stood behind, without counter or table, needing three hands if they were to smoke as well as drink. In the short time between my entrance and the cry of 'Last orders' I actually saw Ted accept a dressed fowl, a jar of home-made chutney, some chrysanthemums, and what looked like a religious tract. At this last he roared his head off, saying, 'That's good, isn't it? Now isn't that good? Bloody funny, that is.' Veronica was in the public bar, too far away to rebuke. (I discovered afterwards that the pamphlet was entitled 'What the Tories Have Done for the Working Man' and that all the pages were blank. Ted would have laughed just as loud, no louder, if it had been the Labour Party. He was very like Shakespeare.)

Winter the printer distractedly accepted a drink from me, his eyes still roving. I had the foreigner's right to ask questions where an Englishman would have to be silent. 'Is something the matter?' I said. 'Are you looking for somebody?'

'Pardon?' he said genteelly. 'Oh.' The flushed points of the cheek-bones glowed brighter. 'Yes, as a matter of fact. My wife, as a matter of fact.' And then he really blushed.

For some reason I got the impression then that his name wasn't really Winter but Winterbottom, and that he'd suppressed the 'bottom' because rude men or boys had called him Coldarse. It was just a hunch I had.

'I'm sorry,' I said. 'Perhaps I shouldn't have asked.'

'Oh, no,' he said, 'that's quite all right. Really.' He sank his blush into the pint I'd ordered for him. The *stretto* of the Saturday night fugue was coming. The women chattered more, laughed more shamelessly; men talked about the War and what they thought of them Wogs—Egypt, India, Burma; cars were discussed; football talk grew more acrimonious; drink-buying became urgent, but Ted did not noticeably favour the present-givers. And then Winter the printer said, 'Oh. She's there,' and blushed again.

He had been right to concentrate on the bar rather than the door, because—trick photography rather than bad continuity—a foursome had suddenly appeared from nowhere and, to make the whole thing more mysterious, they already had drinks in their hands. They were very gay. Winter had evidently willed one of the women to look his way, and, when she did so, he waved and smiled shyly and she, with a far bigger confidence, raised what seemed to be a Pimm's Number One in a sly toast. She was an appetising woman with a full-cheeked smile, about thirty, a Nordic blonde but not icy, though ice was suggested in its tamed winter-sport aspects: the flush after skating, log-fires and hot rum and butter, fine heavy thighs, that would warm your hand like a muff, under a skirt that had swirled in a rink waltz. Her beaver lamb coat was thrust back from a green suit: solid charms, thoroughly wholesome, were indicated. I know little about the women of my own race—they're genuinely exotic and mysterious, while Eastern women are, to me anyway, very straightforward. I don't think, looking back, I've ever been intimate in the *News of the World* sense with an Anglo-Saxon woman (Celts are different, more like the East). My general image of physical contact with Englishwomen is of somebody else's wife on my lap in somebody else's car, coming back from a country pub under a hunter's or Christmas moon, frost on the Triplex glass, part of the rich pudding I digest after leave. This woman, evidently Mrs Winter, joined in imagination those brief incumbents – I had, in a flash, so firm a tactile image of her body – and then I saw that it was her married name (registered subliminally) that had started off the icy, cosy associations. For some reason I had a passionate desire to know her maiden name, and then, as I realised that nothing could possibly be easier to find out, the passionate desire ebbed.

She had greeted her husband; she turned back to her escort now. He was curly and brown, a games player if ever there was one: automatically I posted him East to wear an open shirt and shorts the year round – the hidden wealth of healthy, hairy leg, wasted in cold, clothed England, would have graced any tropical bar-stool. His trade? I wondered, and decided he must be an office man who only began to live after five o'clock. He must, I thought, leap from the bus as from bed, to weights or spring chest-expander, a bolted lunch on Saturdays but no dyspepsia in the rugger scrum. But, of course, keep-fit people are no good in bed, and this man was obviously good in bed. I said to Winter the printer, without thinking first:

'What's his trade?'

'Eh?' His face went almost black as in a bad newspaper photograph, the knuckle-bones on the pint-handle sharp and creamy. 'What do you mean?'

'I'm sorry. I just thought I'd seen him before somewhere. Playing football or something.'

'Who?'

'Him. That man over there.'

'He's an electrician.' He said that almost shamefacedly, as though it explained a superior virility, a power (like 'He's a poet' or 'He's a professional tenor') of attraction cognate with a particular vocation. 'It's Jack Brownlow.' And the flush and mumble there would have better suited an errant daughter confessing her crime.

'Oh.' Prudent, I made no further enquiries. But Winter now began to gush information, just at the moment when youthful mouths would be starting to gargoyle out a Saturday surfeit of beer on to the flags of the yard behind the public bar. Did my combination of healthy bronze and the sedentary figure inspire confidence, or else my mad Eastern look?

'That's my wife, you see, and that other woman there, see, is Jack Brownlow's wife.' She was the kind of low-browed compact brunette called cuddlesome, would give off warmth like a convector. 'And the other man is Charlie Whittier, you see, but he's not married. The trouble is, you see, I don't play tennis, I don't like tennis.' He said it with passion. 'And they play tennis.'

'But not now,' I said foolishly, 'surely? Not at this season. Winter,' I explained and then (the cliché is unavoidable) flushed beneath my tan, turning my head to look at Charlie Whittier again. For Winter silly little booby-traps evidently lurked everywhere. Charlie Whittier, I noticed, was a sort of scooped man from the chin down. His pull-over was sucked into the concavity of his chest, his viscera had been spooned out, leaving a flat rind. His body, in a brown-bread-coloured suit, was approaching the two-dimensional. His nose and jutting brow had discovered this too late and protested ineffectually to the air. I could see him on the tennis-court — animated laundry, irrelevantly parrot-beaked, very fast, cartwheeling.

'Not now, no,' said Winter. 'But I won't do it, you see, I won't play any of their games. Charlie Whittier,' he added, taking a bold swig, emerging to sneer wetly, 'the fast talker, the big lover. But I won't have any of it. It's not a game, whatever they say.' Yes, I could see the peculiar erotic *usefulness* of Charlie Whittier, that body coming down like a great spoon of a hand. But why pick on him when the other man — Jack Brownlow — was whisper-grinning down at Winter's wife and she smiling and biting her lip? Perhaps Charlie Whittier was the walking scooped metaphysic of this cynical suburban love, surely already out-of-date, cast-off Noël Coward?

'What is Charlie Whittier?' I asked. In this pub you could play real Happy Families: there were plenty of good solid trades, little of your vague something-in-the-city.

'*What* is right,' said Winter. 'A thing, that's what he is. An ice-cream butcher. That's what the real butchers call him.' I knew what that was: a man who sold meat but knew nothing of the poetry of the slaughterhouse. An illiterate bookseller; an off-the-peg tailor. A butcher and no butcher, not like the man that Ted Arden's ancestress married. He surely could tan hides and make gloves, and young William Shakespeare played the game of 'killing the calf', didn't he? At this moment Ted Arden began to call time. He tingalingalinged a sort of Lutine bell, calling with a jocular desperation: 'Oh, come on, me ducks, all of yer, you'll lose me me licence, oh, let's ave them glasses, oh, oh, what a to-do, I didn't make the laws now, did I, come on, any more for the front, the police car's round the corner, ain't yer got no omes to go to?' The customers were remarkably good-humoured: they choked over their glasses and pint mugs, anxious to please Ted, who, indeed, rewarded the fastest drinkers-up with smiles of great charm and compliments like 'Lovely, lovely, me duck, I'd give me right arm for a swaller like that.' Then Ted began to escort his customers to the front door, giving smacking kisses to the prettier wives, whose husbands smiled with delight. Ted Arden was no ice-cream butcher.

Then Mrs Winter came over towards our table, greeting my father – rather to my surprise – with an almost daughterly tenderness. My father, rosy with heat, beer and coughing, said, 'My son. Uh uh uh uh. Back from foreign parts. Uh uh uh uh uh.'

'Coughing better, Bert,' said one of his golfing friends, and he banged my father on his back. Glasses tingalinged in collecting hands. 'Time' echoed from the public bar.

'Pleased to meet you,' said Mrs Winter. Then to her husband she said, her head shaking in humorous sadness, her lips fondly smiling, 'Oh, Billy, Billy, you *are* a silly, you know.' Winter flushed and his lip trembled. Then his wife was folded into the crowd, and the crowd was swiftly kissed and fondled and cajoled out by Ted Arden. Winter the printer sat there, saying nothing, looking with blind eyes at the wet towel that drooped over the beer-pumps. Then he went out the back way with a good-night to nobody. Nobody noticed except me. My father said, 'Roland's going to give me a lift back,' and he coughed again.

'All right,' I said. 'I'll see you there.'

'Sorry there's no more room, old man,' said the golfing traveller in medical supplies. 'It's only a Ford Prefect.' He gave me a bitter leer, knowing I had, somewhere back in the mysterious and lucrative Orient, a car far bigger complete with driver. I tried to look apologetic. When I started to leave, Ted Arden put his arm round me and whispered, 'No need just yet if you don't want to. Ave a little arf with me and the missis. Just wait till these buggers is gone. This, I knew instinctively, was a very high honour. I bowed my head as if it were already Sunday.

2

There are no free gifts nowadays: everything has to be paid
for. And time, which costs nothing, costs the most. Why
should I really regard it as a privilege to be asked to stay
behind after closing to buy little arves for him and the
missis? I could afford to stock my father's house with all
the vulgar drinks of Ted's pub, instal a small bar in the
front room, drink at leisure and in comfort and not be
beholden to anybody. But it is recognised in England that
home drinking is no real pleasure. We pray in a church
and booze in a pub: profoundly sacerdotal at heart, we
need a host in both places to preside over us. In Catholic
churches as in continental bars the host is there all the
time. But the Church of England kicked out the Real Presence and the licensing laws gave the landlord a terrible
sacramental power. Ted was giving me grace of his free
will, holding back death – which is closing-time – making
a lordly grant of extra life.

Still, I didn't really like paying for it by sweeping cigarette-ends on to a shovel, panting as I bent down, and washing lipsticky Babycham glasses. This was houseboy's work.
Not that anybody actually asked me to do it; I just felt
that it was somehow expected of me to volunteer. Cedric,
the week-end waiter, had taken off his green mess-jacket
and danced about with a broom, showing natty braces,
whistling. There was a kind of imbecilic helper in the
public bar who washed glasses with ghastly speed, his

idiot's spectacles filled with light. And there was a flabby man with a ruined boxer's face who wore a wasp–striped sweater. He growled to himself like a dreaming dog as he swabbed the public-bar counter. Veronica emptied the till and counted the takings, and Ted did obscure things with dipsticks in the cellar. It was a long time before I got a drink. I said a couple of times, 'Perhaps now you, Mrs Arden, and these gentlemen here wouldn't say no to a glass of something.' (I was not yet on Christian-name terms with her.) But Veronica merely nodded distractedly over her counting, the boxer growled, and the idiot showed me his open mouth and flashed light at me. I got a horrible feeling that perhaps none of them really liked drink, that they only liked to sell it. But at last the host came up and the warmth of his real presence beamed over the bar.

We drank at the public-bar counter, literally little arves of washy mild beer, which Ted drew himself and elevated to the light with pride. 'Lovely,' he said. 'A good publican's always judged by his mild beer,' he added sententiously. 'It's the mild-drinkers what brings the money in. Them's the ones you've got to look after.' The potions were drunk with reverence but, I thought, little pleasure. Then I asked if I might be allowed the privilege of buying a round. Veronica said she would have a port-and-brandy, the idiot asked for a black beer, the boxer for a rum-and-lime, Cedric for a whisky mac. It was as though I were a sort of genie, sprung from an Eastern bottle, ready to grant the most hidden and fantastic wish. Then I looked at Ted. He twitched his nose like a rabbit. He said :

'There's a bottle up there on that shelf there, right at the top, and I've always wanted to know what's in it.'

'Doesn't it say on the bottle?'

'Funny writing, me duck. Nobody ere can't read it. We showed it to one of them Indians what come round selling carpets, and e couldn't read it either. But,' said Ted, 'I always knew e wasn't a real Indian.'

'Why don't you get the bottle down?' I said.

'Yes,' said Ted, 'you've come from foreign parts, a long way away, so you ought to be able to read it. Ere,' he called, 'Selwyn.' Selwyn was the imbecilic one. 'Not so daft as e looks,' said Ted, 'are yer, Selwyn?'

'Am daft as ah thinks on ter be,' said Selwyn promptly and obscurely. The voice was like a slack bass string.

'Climb up to that top shelf, me duck,' said Ted, 'and fetch down that bottle with the funny writing.' He turned to me and said, 'Bought it in a job lot when the Crown was burnt out. Lot of odd bottles. Ere, me duck,' he said to Selwyn, 'use the chair'. But Selwyn had mounted the counter, reached out over space with a big black block of a boot, and now seemed to be climbing the shelves. He reached ceiling-level, grasped a bottle, flashed his glasses onto it, and said, 'This woon?'

'That's the one, me duck. Watch yerself coming down.'

'Catch.' The bottle hurtled through the air into Ted's fielding hands. It was colourless liquor, the label in Cyrillic lettering. 'Am coomin dahn,' boomed Selwyn, as from a clock tower. And down he came, neatly enough, the black boots clanging on odd bottles.

'This,' I said, 'must be a kind of vodka. You know, Russian stuff.'

The boxer growled. 'I reckon the Russians is as good as what we are. What is this Communionism? It's everybody doing their best for everyone else, the way I see it. Isn't that right?' he challenged Cedric.

'Please, please,' said Veronica, in a breaking E-string voice. 'No politics at this hour, if you please.'

'In a way,' said Cedric. 'Everybody's the same. No higher and lower. Nobody waiting on anybody else, as you might say. Now, I don't think *that's* right.'

'Please,' said Veronica more sharply. 'Not in my house, if you don't mind.'

'Yer dint think ah could do that,' said Selwyn, nudging me hard, looking up at me from blind electric-light eyes and open mouth.

'Oh, yes, I did,' I said, smiling, anxious to please. 'Look,' I said to Ted. 'Open it up, and we'll drink it with tomato juice and a drop of Worcester.'

'Never eard of that before, me duck.'

'A Bloody Mary,' I said. 'Vodka in the red. A lot of people drink it.'

'Ow could yer doon?' said Selwyn, nudging me harder. 'Ow could yer known ah could do that when ah not doon it afore?' He opened his mouth wide in triumph to the gloomy boxer. 'E couldn't a doon, Cecil,' he said. This was too much: Cecil, Selwyn and Cedric: this was going too far. Cedric said:

'Swearing's worse than politics, Mrs Arden. I should have thought swearing's one thing you wouldn't stand, especially from a stranger.' He gave me a prim look.

'E's Bert Denham's lad,' said Ted, 'back from foreign parts. Yer seen im in the smoke room, earlier on.' He gouged the bottle-cork with an expert wrist-twist, mounted the bottle like a horse, and strained to open it. A loud costive noise came from his throat.

'He said "bloody",' persisted Cedric. 'That's swearing.'

'That was one of the queens of England,' I explained. 'She was called Bloody Mary because she burnt Protestants alive.'

'They're all the same,' said wasp-sweatered Cecil. 'R.C.'s and C. of E.'s. Meself, I was brought up Primitive Methodist.'

'Let's have no talk of religion, please,' said Veronica. 'My head's splitting.'

21

Out came the cork. 'Is it, me duck?' said Ted, tragic with solicitude. 'Yer never said. Ave a couple of aspirins and I'll bring you a nice ot cup of tea up to bed.' He put the bottle on the counter. Fumes gushed from it, fumes of aniseed, meths, carraway, acetylene. My head swam. Selwyn tottered. Cedric said, 'That *does* smell strong.' Ted enfolded Veronica in loving arms of helpless compassion. 'Me poor old duck,' he said, lips against her bony forehead.

Veronica's large blue poet's eyes grew misty. 'It's not too bad, really,' she said, smiling with woman's 'silly-boy' tenderness. 'But I *will* go to bed.'

'Aspirin, me duck?'

'No, they don't do any good, really. It's just the old trouble.' Everybody nodded sympathetically, as if they knew what that was. 'Don't be too long, Edward.'

'No, me duck. Just one little un, that's all.' Veronica said good-night and went off, slim as a blade in toreador pants. Everybody relaxed. 'Aaaaah,' said Ted, pouring out generous slugs of the colourless spirit. 'Tomato juice, eh?'

'Tomato juice,' I said. 'And salt. And Worcester.' Everybody looked on with intense concentration, as at a dangerous chemical experiment. Ted encarnadined the spirit and seasoned it, stirred with a long spoon, stood back, looked at the glasses as though he first had to consecrate them. Then he said, 'It looks bloody all right.'

'How much?' I asked. I always had to re-learn this English habit of paying for drinks as I ordered them. 'And there's Mrs Arden's port-and-brandy which she hasn't had.'

'She'll ave it to-morrer, me duck. Let's see, we'll call that five bob and we'll call these three bob each and five threes is fifteen and fifteen and five is twenty. One quid exactly, me duck, and thank yer very much, sir.' He took my pound and then gripped his Bloody Mary by the stem. We all gripped ours firmly, except Cedric. Cedric finger-and-thumbed his like an exotic flower. I drank off half of mine and at once had a sensation of levitation. My skull swelled under the pressure of pumped-in helium. The room minced delicately round, tilted, rocked and then settled. Whatever the liquor was it was not vodka. Cedric coughed and sprayed us. 'Keep it to yourself, Cedric,' said Ted. 'Oh,' said Cedric. 'Oh, it's strong.' Selwyn said, red on his lips:

'Ah wus born between the nart and the day.'

'All right,' said Ted, 'we've eard all that before.' He calmly finished his Bloody Mary and said, 'That tomato juice is a bit off. Been in the tin too long.'

Selwyn nudged me very hard. 'Ah wuz born with a thing arahnd my ead.'

'Yes,' I said. 'A caul.' I finished my glass. Really, it was not bad at all, whatever it was.

'Call be boogered,' said Selwyn loudly. 'It were a thing arahnd my ead and my moother sauled it fer six an a tanner.' He drank more, without comment. Then he said, 'Ah can see things wot oothers caaan't. I seen a man with no ead walk through a wall, and it wuz in broad daylart in Parkinson Street.' He turned to Cecil. 'Ah, Cecil,' he said. 'It wuz week afore Carter got knock dahn.' Cecil was taking his Bloody Mary in quick sips, like a very thirsty man with hot tea.

Cedric didn't look well. 'I'll have a glass of water,' he said, 'if you don't mind. Funny stuff that is, whatever you call it.'

'And,' said Selwyn, 'ah can see things rahnd pipple's eads. A green un rahnd Cecil's and blue un rahnd Ted's and noon rahnd Cedric's and a kind of a dirty pink un rahnd yours, mister.'

'Perhaps there's a kind of aura laundry somewhere,' I said. 'I'd better send it there.'

'We'll try it on its own,' said Ted. 'That tomato juice is a bit off.'

'Awrer be boogered,' nudged Selwyn. 'Like a thing all rahnd yer ead.' Cedric drank some water and immediately spluttered. Whatever the liquor was, it didn't like water.

'I think I'd better go round the back,' said Cedric. 'I had a fried egg for my tea, and the missis said it didn't smell too good when she broke it and . . . Oh dear,' he said. He looked in horror at my left lapel, seeing the fried egg distinctly. Then he ran off very fast.

Ted grinned, showing many bad teeth. 'This is just you and me, me duck,' he said. 'Others isn't ready yet. Cheers.' And down it went, and mine too. It was really all right; I was getting a taste for it. 'That,' said Ted, 'will be six bob, me duck.'

I dug out a mound of silver. 'And these gentlemen?'

'Ah can teck anoother er them,' said Selwyn. He pushed over his red-flecked glass.

'Nine bob,' said Ted.

The last drop sang down Cecil's throat like a drain. He put down his glass slowly and said, 'Not much to it. What I really wanted was a rum-and-lime.'

'Get it yourself,' said Ted. 'That'll be eleven and a tanner altogether, me duck.'

Cecil served himself and came very seriously over to me. 'Where you've been,' he said, 'do you have blackies?'

'Some have been black, some brown, some yellow,' I said. 'It depends where you are, really.'

'Old Jackie Cox,' said Selwyn. 'That were the woon. E ad a yeller un rahnd is ead. Yeller as yeller, it were. Like farmahse booter.'

'No, no,' said Cecil, 'what I mean to say is, have you been with black women?'

'Well, yes, once,' I admitted. 'That was in Lagos.'

24

'And what was it like?' asked Cecil.

'Well,' I began, and everybody leaned on the counter, breathing hard. But at that moment Cedric came back, looking fresher but puzzled. 'Came up clean as a whistle,' he said, 'egg and all. Look,' he said, 'that chap's sitting there in the W.C. Just sitting there, trousers on, coat on. With the door open. He won't go away.'

'What chap?' asked Ted.

'The fellow who works at Rawdon's. Winterbottom.'

'Winter the printer the sprinter the splinter,' I suddenly said and was shocked. That liquor was starting already. 'Sorry,' I said.

'Poor bugger,' said Ted. 'Poor old devil. She's gone off with the key and e can't get in. Locked out of his own ouse,' he said. 'It's a bloody crying shame, that's what it is.' The drink was getting him too: there were tears in his brown eyes. 'Bring im in ere,' said Ted. 'E can't stay in the petty all night, poor little bugger.' He poured out for himself and for me. 'Six bob, me duck,' he said distractedly. And then, 'There's too much of that going on in these parts. Swopping wives. Swopping usbands. It's not right, whatever way you look at it. Would you do it?' he asked Selwyn. 'Would you do it?' he asked Cecil. 'Would you do it?' he asked me. 'Of course you wouldn't. You've done it,' he said to Cedric.

Cedric looked less pale. 'It was only once,' he said. 'After the outing. There were three coaches and everything sort of got mixed up. I didn't really *want* to do it.'

'But you did it,' said Ted. 'Catch me letting that sort of thing appen with me and my missis. Idle minds and idle ands, that's what it is. Aven't got enough to do. No kids in the ouse. Cheers, me duck,' he said to me. 'That'll be six bob.'

I wasn't now sure whether I'd paid or not. If they were

going to try and make a monkey out of me, I thought, just because I'd come back from the East, they had another think coming. I tried to say this. I said:

'Monkeys of every shape, size and texture in the jungles of Borneo.' I said it in a curiously refined finicking way, quite unlike me. Ted said:

'Fetch im in, poor little bugger. Mr Denham ere will push the boat out. Let im ave a drop of this ere.' And then he recited, his eyes fixed on the coloured picture of a girl in her underclothes advertising cider, in a strange mechanical voice like a sibyl:

'Friends, Romans and countrymen, that is the question.
England, with all his faults I love im still.
And passing rich on forty pounds a year.'

Eagerly he said, 'What shall I bring down, me guns or the old man's books? Thousands e ad, old uns, me duck. Best collection of guns I got ere in the ole of the Midlands, What shall it be, eh?' But then Winter the printer was brought in, looking small and miserable in his raincoat, mauve with outside-lavatory cold. 'Come in, me duck,' said Ted loudly. 'Come and get warmed up. Mr Denham ere's just going to push the boat out.' And he began to pour again, lavishly, from the strange bottle. What the hell. I slammed down a bunch of silver that clanked and rattled like a coil of chain. Now it was Selwyn's turn. He said:

'Old Billy Freeman, im that ad draper's afore Peabody's took o'er. Is fess were pressed ard agin that winder.' His electric spectacles flashed steady at the vision. 'In is grev ten year boot there e were lookin stret in.'

'All right, Selwyn,' said Cecil, smelling of rum. 'None of that now.'

'Ah sin im,' said Selwyn. He nudged me, less accurately

than earlier on, and said, 'Ah wuz born between the nart and the day.' Winter the printer spluttered over his glass of Iron-Curtain liquor. 'Too strong for him,' said Cedric complacently. I drank mine without spluttering but saw the room swing like a punch-ball. When it had swung back to rest I saw delectable words dangling like grapes above me. I took one and it turned into a text. 'Adultery,' I said. I settled myself to a sermon. Damn it all, it was my money, wasn't it? I was entitled to my congregation, wasn't I? 'In the common sort,' I said, 'excusable. But Winter is a printer. My father too. God rest his soul.' I seemed to have decided, for the purpose of the sermon, that my father was better dead. 'His heart broken,' I said, 'his days ended in poverty. Why? Because of integrity. Because he would not sell out to the modern world with its paltry perversions and cheap mockeries of values. Printers are different from other men. They carry the miracle of the word to generations yet unborn. Printers have chapels, don't they? Prizefighters and publicans and milkmen can be bought and sold and have their beds disfigured by the mark of the beast. And also –' To Selwyn I said, 'What's your trade?'

'Wheeltapper's arker,' he said promptly, 'afore relwez wuz naturalised. Nah ah work as chif tea-man an swipperoop in Norton and Repworth's. An not too bad of a job an all when yer consider wot yer can mek on side. Lak soapballs fer apprentices. Lak sellin firm's pencils. Lak firm's toilet-rolls, best quality an all, three doozen a wik at a tanner itch.' He was beginning to count things off on his fingers. I came in loudly with:

'A printer has a responsibility to the community at large. And so a printer's wife has a responsibility to the printer. That's logical, isn't it? Right.' Winter the printer had his mouth open as wide as Selwyn's; Ted was leaning on the bar, intent on my flapping lips, not listening, his nose rabbit-twitching; Cecil breathed out rum in steady blasts, trying to catch his breath in his nostrils. 'So,' I said, 'we'll have no adultery among printers. Right? One for the road. One more all round. Finish the bottle.' A shoe rapped on the floor above.

'Coming up now, me duck,' called Ted. 'Just finishing.' He poured out for all except Cedric. Glass in hand, he said firmly to Winter, 'Don't stand it. Don't ave none of er nonsense, or is either. I've seen better men than im in a bucket of lights.' Winter began to cry. This seemed quite natural. I said, 'You're coming back with me. You can sleep in my father's bed. He wouldn't mind. He was a printer too, God rest his soul.' My slaying of him was accepted without comment. As we drank Cedric said:

'A toastmaster, that's what I really wanted to be. You get good money at that. Best hotel and all expenses.' He announced in a thin refined voice: 'Ladies and gentlemen, your president wishes to take wine with the ladies.' The shoe rapped again above, more urgently. 'Right,' said Ted. 'On yer way now, me ducks. I've always wanted to know what was in that bottle.'

'We still don't know,' I said.

'Well, it doesn't matter now, me duck, cause it's empty.' He upturned it, and a few final drops wept quietly on to the counter. Ted shushed us to the door of the public-bar, into the yard. There was a distant cats' concert; with a thrashing screw the half-moon sailed the turbulent sea-sky. Cedric said:

'I'll take these two home in my car. We live at the other end of town, see.' He prolonged the vowel of 'car' as if to impress with an impression of the length of the vehicle itself. I feigned proper surprise at his having a car. Selwyn said:

'Cedric were wetter when Jook er Edinboorer come.' The

28

slack 'cello C-string boomed through the suburban night.

'Yes,' simpered Cedric. 'At the mayoral banquet. I stood right behind His Highness's chair.' Selwyn was staring at the moon as though the moon had whistled his attention. which, considering Selwyn's peculiar gifts, it might well have done. He said:

'Ah can see pipple oop thur. An ah sin pipple wot lives at back of it. Grinny-blue air they as. In drims ah sin em.' This was enough. I could see Cecil getting ready to ask about the sexual habits of negresses, so I walked Winter off rapidly, my arm in his, and left Cedric looking for his ignition-key in the old coach-entrance. I shouted good-night but nobody answered. I could not see a car parked anywhere: perhaps some gang of delinquents had stolen it. Winter began talking rapidly. 'Really, there's no need for this at all, really. I'm quite capable of looking after myself.'

'You'll sleep in my father's bed,' I said. 'You can't spend the night walking the streets.'

'But you can't put me with your father. It's not right. Besides, I don't want to sleep with your father.'

I stopped walking for an instant and realised that my father was still alive, but with a curious eerie Lazarus sort of feeling. 'Yes,' I said. 'I slipped up there. You can sleep in the front room. Or I'll sleep in the front room or watch the television or something, and you can sleep in my bed. Or wait. Why shouldn't we get your key for you?'

Winter giggled and said, 'There's no television at this hour. I can see you've been away for a long time.'

'Your key. Why not your key? We'll wake the bitch up and ask her for it.'

'Don't call my wife a bitch.' Winter was conventionally hot about it, but not very convincing.

'All right, she's not a bitch. But she's an adulteress.' I

took a sudden fancy to the word. 'An adulteress, that's what she is. A bloody adulteress. A woman taken in adultery. Let's go and take her in adultery. And him too. And you can cast the first stone.'

We were out of the near-rural pocket now, had turned the corner and were on Clutterbuck Avenue. I had my arm in Winter's again and he tolerated this Ugly Duchess familiarity as he had tolerated my un-Christian shouting about adultery. I was only the returned Oriental eccentric, drunk at that, a temporary pocket in the suburban flow, like the pub and the village we had just left.

'They're along here somewhere, are they?' I said. There was nobody but us in the street. Only a cat knocked over a milk-bottle and, as the church clock struck a quarter of something, a dog sang dismally.

'I'm not saying,' said Winter, with a kind of sullen coyness.

'Where's your house?' I asked. 'Along here somewhere?'

'Along here somewhere,' he had to admit, mumbling.

'We can get in,' I said, 'and you can make us a cup of cocoa or something. I can work wonders with a bit of wire.' I looked at the houses as we went along. 'They're all the same,' I said. 'I don't suppose it would matter which one you went in, really. I suppose they're all the same inside. Pot ducks flying up the wall. And the telly.' A certain tremor in his arm, an imperceptible speeding-up, as though his feet were trying to get in step with his heart, spoke an unmistakable admission that the house we were now approaching was the house where Winter's wife and the other woman's husband lay in adulterous warmth together, the cosy winter complement to summer's mixed doubles. I stopped. He tried to free his arm. 'This is where they are, isn't it?' I said.

'You're not to do anything,' he warned. 'I'm warning

you,' he warned. He fought his arm loose. I cried to the night in terrible joy:

'Adulteress. Adulterer.'

'Oh, shut up, shut up. I'll send for the police.'

'Throw that key down,' I called. 'Bloody sinners.'

'Stop it, stop it,' wept Winter. 'I'll phone up the police, I will, I will.' And, indeed, he made as if to run to the telephone box at the end of the avenue. I grabbed his arm and shouted:

'Come down, both of you, and face it like a man.' I had the impression of rustlings and sleep-slack voices asking what was going on out there. A light flashed on, but not in this house. 'Adulterous beasts,' I called. There was another light, and then another, making a full common chord of suburban light. Winter fought himself loose again. I turned on him now. 'Be a bloody man,' I said. 'Fight for what is lawfully yours.' But now a man in pyjamas and boots was coming down crazy paving. 'You,' he said, and I could tell he had no teeth in, 'bugger off. We don't want your sort round here.'

'There's too much adultery going on,' I said. 'And I don't think we've been introduced.'

'I'll introduce my big toe to your arse,' said the man. 'Now bugger off. Some people have to work if you haven't.'

'Adulterer,' I said, though with less Old Testament fire than before. I said the word almost conversationally, as the man was now close to me. He had clumsily, his boots being unlaced, clomped over the tiny front-gate of his house. I had lost my bearings now. I couldn't tell which house was which.

'And what if I am?' said the man. 'It's a free country, isn't it? Now get out before I get nasty.'

At that moment a window opened somewhere, a woman's voice called, 'Catch,' and there was a thin tinkle

31

on the pavement. 'That's all we wanted,' I said. 'Good night, sir, and many thinks for your co-operation.'

'You've been smelling the barmaid's apron,' said the man with boots, pyjamas and no teeth. He clomped back clumsily over the gate and up the crazy paving to his front door. A woman's voice, a voice that sounded as if it were in curlers, said, 'What is it, Charlie?'

'Get back to bed. Some bloody drunk or other.' The door slammed weakly, a slap of jerry-builder's plywood. I was on the pavement, the too clean, rain-washed, wind-dried pavement you could eat your dinner off, looking for the key. The lamp across the road showed it, lying a foot from the gutter. 'There you are,' I said to the wretched Winter, 'I've asserted your rights for you.' I handed the key over with a drunk's courtesy. He didn't take it, didn't even look at it.'

'That's not my key,' he said.

'You haven't even looked at it, man.'

'It can't be,' said Winter. 'This isn't his house. You wouldn't listen, would you? You knew best, didn't you?' He was in a real passion, the devil showing through the printer. 'This is somebody's else's house.'

'Christ,' I said in awe. 'Does the cap fit everywhere round here?' I fell over the nearest gate, stumbled up the path and put the key under the door-mat. Somebody would find it some time and give it to somebody. When I came down the path again Winter had gone. There was nowhere for him to go to, but he had gone. 'This bloody country, with people coming and going through trap-doors. Too many bloody cellars,' I thought drunkenly. Then, having set my course by the moon, I went home in a fine forked-lightning pattern.

3

Oh noisy bells be dumb. I awoke tired, without crapula, but with a strong sense of guilt. I remembered very little of what I'd said or done under the Cyrillic influence, and it was only by favour of certain synoptical gospellers that I was able eventually to piece things together. Especially informative, a week later, was the toothless man in boots and pyjamas: he emerged slowly out of a toothed, shoed and suited paraffin merchant who spoke to me in a bar in town and gave me a fairly circumstantial account of my nocturne on Clutterbuck Avenue. Without rancour; indeed, with a definite relish. Charlie Dawes his name was, and he agreed with me about there being too much adulteration in the world:

'Stands to reason, the way I see it, the war made us forget what things is *really* like, and so they get away with watered milk and that, and even cough medicine is weaker than what it was. And tinned salmon. Do you ever see *real* tinned salmon nowadays, and sausages like what we had pre-war?'

However, on this dry and windy Sunday, I was convinced that I had done some great hurt to some lady or other, and I was frightened of leaving the house. Only when, for a late breakfast, I shuffled out some Frostflakes on to a soup-plate, the wind whipping under the kitchen door like a snake, did the name Winter come. And then fornication sang out from the *News of the World* as I sat, biting my

33

nails, before the electric fire, slumped in my father's arm-chair. My father, good and innocent man, was out playing a windy game of golf. At twelve-thirty he and his friends would go to the Royal George, Charlbury, for the nine-teenth hole, and then he would be dropped at my sister's place where he and I were invited, this and every Sunday, for lunch. Carless, I woke up suddenly to my need to be off without delay and shiver at a corner half a mile off, waiting for one of the rare Sunday buses that went to The Priest and the Pig (where there was no priest or pig or pub of that name), whence I must walk another half-mile to the commuters' village. All this for some of my sister's bad cooking, my brother-in-law's zombie smile, and their ancient hairy dog that farted under people's chairs. But also, of course, to maintain the fiction of family solidarity (though Beryl was indifferent to my father and loathed me, and my father and I severally reciprocated) because this mystique had become important to my father since my mother's death. So I had a quick shave, put a tie on, and, with my overcoat-collar up round my ears, set off through the gritty liverish wind to the bus-stop, hoping to God I'd meet nobody on the way.

Stamping around, waiting, I cursed England aloud, hands dug deep into pockets, dancing to the wind that knocked in vain at the Sunday shops. Cigarette-packets, football fixtures, bus-tickets sailed by in dust — ghosts of Saturday. A woman with a puce face and a blancmange-coloured prayer-book was waiting also for The Priest and Pig, and she looked puce disapproval at me. Twenty minutes late, the bus yawned in from town, near-empty, and it swallowed us in a gape of Sunday ennui. So we sun-dayed along, rattling and creaking in Sunday hollowness, I upstairs, tearing my elevenpenny ticket while I read the prospectus of Winter Commercial Classes stuck on the

34

window. It began to worry me to feel that I could never possibly settle in England now, not after Tokyo nude-shows and sliced green chillies, brown children sluicing at the road-pump, the air-conditioned hum in bedrooms big as ballrooms, negligible income-tax, curry tiffins, being the big man in the big car, the bars of all the airports of Africa and the East. Was I right to feel guilty? Who was I to talk about the irresponsibility of modern England? I watched the grey villages limp by, the wind tearing at torn posters of long-done events. What I needed, of course, was a drink.

I got my drink at the cold pub halfway between the bus terminus and my sister's house. I had to push through a capped crowd at the bar, men who were animated in their talk about old Arthur. I felt very much the stranger, resented even by the landlord, when I ordered a double whisky and disclosed, to a cold hush, fivers in my wallet. Unfortunately, the whisky woke up the Cyrillic liquor and made my speech slur when I asked for cigarettes and my hand all finger-and-thumbs clumsiness when I picked up my change. I felt I was being watched narrowly. I had to have another whisky to show that I really could take my liquor (how stupid we all are about feared impugnings of our virility), and when I went out I tried to push the door instead of pulling it. 'Pull it, mate,' said someone, and I had to obey. I nearly tripped over a footscraper and, the door closed, had the impression of loud laughter. The vile blunt-razor-blade wind blew hard from my sister's house. I felt ashamed and furious. In the East there was politeness, doors opened the right way, there were no footscrapers.

In my sister's house there was also very loud laughter. I heard it as I knocked. But this came from the audience of a radio show, and it spread depression like jam over the hard tack of my fury. My father opened the door, wind-beaten from golf, the wind of a cough making glow the coal of a cigarette in his mouth, a Sunday paper in his hand. Seeing it was me, he coughed, nodded, and went back to read the sports results. There was a smell of old dog in the hall, an earthy rebuke at least to the blurry misty pictures of dream-dogs on the walls. The honest black telephone shone coyly from behind flowery curtains – Beryl's home-made booth for long comfy talkie-talkies with women friends, if she had any. I noticed a poker-work poem of slack form and uplifting content: 'In a world of froth and bubble two things stand like stone: kindness in another's trouble, courage in your own.' Beryl's unimpaired high-school humour was indicated by a framed macaronic paradigm: 'Je me larf, tu te grin, il se giggle; nous nous crackons, vous vous splittez, ils se bustent.' Beryl herself could be heard singing in the kitchen at the end of the hall – an emasculated version of 'Greensleeves' – and the fumes of heavy greens gushed out under the noise of the masher. I took my coat off and heard the upstairs lavatory flush and then its door click. Down the stairs, fastening his fly, came Henry Morgan, Beryl's husband. 'Yo ho ho,' I said. 'How's the pirate king?' He never liked this. 'Everett's in there,' he said. As an afterthought, he gave me a pale smile.

'Who's Everett?'

'He works on the local rag. Used to be a big name, I believe. Beryl's doing the village news now, you know. Two-pence a line.'

'That should be a great help to the family finances.'

'Not really, you know. But it's rather an honour, we feel. Come in and meet Everett. He's very anxious to meet *you*.' We went into the living-room and were met by the full blast of dog. I didn't feel like sneering at the décor: the room was warm, and warmth is never in bad taste. But this man Everett protected the fire, as if someone would steal it, roasting his bottom while he leafed through one of Morgan's books. He could have leafed through the whole lot in an hour. Everett looked up with a kind of mad eagerness. He was a scrap of a man in a brown hairy sports-coat whose pockets, from their rattling, seemed to be filled with old ball-points. He was fifty-odd, five hanks of hair like an empty bar of music pasted across his baldness, with army spectacles over very pale eyes, eyes that suggested somehow Georgian lyrics. And then the name clicked, because somebody in the town had talked about Everett as having written a poem he'd had to learn at school, and Everett's was a name you'd find in the Georgian anthologies, a very minor name, it is true, but still representing a more honest tradition of art than the radio show that Henry now switched off. Everett and I were introduced. My father sat deep in the fireside armchair, deep with frowning eyes in the sports page, while his free fingers dabbled absently in the hair of the stinking old dog, as in the water of a canal.

'One of the merchant princes,' giggled Everett. His voice suggested damped piano notes – *una corda*, I think the direction is. 'High on a throne of Ormus or of Ind or where the gorgeous East with richest hand showers on her kings barbaric pearl and gold.' He gabbled the lines as if he had no feeling for words and then giggled, looking at Henry for applause. He'd garbled the first two, too, I noticed with pity, but I only smiled and said, 'That's Book Two, isn't it? I did that for Matric.'

'Oh,' said Everett, 'but you should have heard Harold on *Paradise Lost*. In the old Poetry Bookshop days, that is. I suppose that's one thing one would miss out in your outlandish places – the kindred spirits united by a love of the arts, I mean, reading verse together, keeping, however feebly, the torch alight. Culture, I mean. Though, of course, here in this town –' He smiled sadly. 'Little enough, little enough. Though one does one's best. One writes, in the tradition, but always aware of the need to modify the tradition. Pound, Ezra, you know, Pound said: "So few drink at my fountain." Beauty,' said Everett, his glasses turned to the window. The eyes were lost, and I suddenly saw Selwyn of the previous night and began to remember a little. Something to do with eggs and auras, or something. Somebody in the outside W.C. The dog looked up through its hairy yashmak and farted. 'I thank thee for that word,' I said. Everett said:

'Perhaps a little item for the *Hermes*. Views of a returned exile on a changed England. Or some outlandish tales of the East, perhaps. We must get together, quietly.'

'You won't forget, will you?' said Henry Morgan. 'Something about my Creative Writing Exhibition, a paragraph or so?'

'What's that?' I asked, showing an interest.

'Oh,' said Henry, 'we get the best results that way. They just express themselves as they like. On the analogy of drawing. I mean, you don't worry a child about perspective and proportion and so on. You just let him draw. Well, also, you should just let him write. And the results we've been getting, really –'

Beryl came in, aproned, doubtless pleased with her Creative Cooking. You don't worry about a hot oven or seasoning or cleaning the cabbage properly, you just express yourself as you wish. Beryl always looked pleased about something. She had the right sort of face for looking pleased: fat cheeks for smiling and many teeth. It was hard for me to say whether she was good-looking or not. I think she probably was, but she always impressed me with a sense of unwholesomeness – as of soiled underwear and stockings kept up with string and hair too infrequently washed. She said to me, 'Well, broth.' This, in childhod, had been a genuine apocope of 'brother', but she had soon learned to give it a 'spelling pronunciation,' so that it suggested cold soup taken in the greasy dawn of a bordello. 'Well, Barrel,' I said. Soon, I hoped, this perversion of her name would be entirely appropriate. 'It's ready,' she said. 'Come on in, everybody.' This was a signal for my father to light a fresh cigarette, cough with vigour, and then lumber upstairs to the bathroom. 'Oh, dad,' said Beryl in reproach, 'the soup's on the table.' 'The soup's on the table,' repeated Everett. 'Dear Harold could have made something of that. Let me see—' He drank light from the window reminding me more and more of Selwyn, and improvised, with many halts and giggles:

'The soup is on the table, and the fish
Waits in the kitchen. You shall have your wish—
The wind outside, the fire's gold heart burnt hollow,
A pudding servant-girl, pudding to follow.'

'There's Creative Writing for you,' I said to Henry, nudging him hard, a trick I'd learned from Selwyn. Beryl looked admiration at Everett with shining woman's eyes that said, 'Silly boy, wasting his cleverness on poetry. That's why he's come down in the world: poetry. Oh, men, men, men.' My father, the lavatory's flush behind him like a fanfare, came heavily down the stairs coughing. We went in to lunch.

The meal was pretentious—a kind of beetroot soup with greasy *croûtons;* pork underdone with loud vulgar cabbage, potato croquettes, tinned peas in tiny jam-tart cases, watery gooseberry sauce; trifle made with a resinous wine, so jammy that all my teeth lit up at once—a ghastly discord on two organ manuals. The old dog went from chair to chair, contending with the cabbage and my father's coughs, while Everett talked about poetry and the *Collected Poems: 1920-54* that Tannenbaum and Macdonald were prepared to publish if only Everett were prepared to contribute a few hundred pounds to indemnify them against a certain financial loss. 'Ah,' I thought. 'It's me he's after.' Annoyed, I gave slice after slice of my pork to the old dog. Beryl said:

'That's wasteful, broth. Have you any idea what loin of pork costs nowadays? We're not all made of money, you know.' There we were, right in the middle of it. I said nothing. I put my half-finished main course on the floor, and the dog, all hair and tongue, lapped up the croquettes and cabbage and gravy but ignored the tartlets with peas in them. Beryl went very red and said, 'You never could behave at table, could you?' I smiled, put elbows on table and jowls on fists and said, 'What's for afters?' Everett looked up from his plate with joy. 'A poem,' he announced. I'll say that for him: there was nothing of the lamp about his work, nothing of artifice – it all came bouncing naturally out of other people's speech rhythms. Between mouthfuls of trifle and evident stabs of toothache he composed the following:

' "What's for afters?" You never could behave –
Elbows on table, eating far too fast.
You're eaten now, elbowed into the grave,
And "What's for afters?" That you know at last.'

Then he talked about the great days of patronage, and how Dr Johnson could confidently ask Warren Hastings to play Maecenas to an East India clerk who'd translated some poems from the Portuguese. He was getting closer to me now, but I could admire the delicacy of his angling.

Suddenly, without warning, without relevance to anything that anybody had said, my father broke silence and began a long genuinely absorbing discourse on contemporary faces—Goudy Bold, Temple Script, Matura, Holla and Prisma. Then he went on obscurely about ten-point Fournier and seven-point Ionic, and Everett had to keep saying, 'Yes, yes, I see that, I quite see that, most interesting.' My father brought out a pencil and was preparing to illustrate the differences between Centaur and Plantin on his napkin, when my brother-in-law chipped in with:

'What's all this about you getting Winterbottom drunk last night?' I looked vague because I was vague. 'Yes,' said Henry, 'I heard about it at church this morning.'

'What church? Where?'

'Our church, here. Lusk the organist was at your church for communion, then he drove up here for matins at eleven. He said that Winterbottom was asleep in the church-porch. And the chap who rings the bell said something about you being at it last night.'

'Gill Sans,' continued my father, then coughed and coughed.

'What chap who rings the bell?'

'Little mad chap with glasses. He sees people rise from their graves, he says.'

'Henry,' said Beryl with pride, 'read the lesson this morning.'

'I can't remember very well,' I said. 'West Coast memory. You get it in the East, you know. But how do you know Winter the printer?'

'School magazine,' said Henry. 'Nice little fellow. He said there was something wrong with his watch and that's why he'd got to church too early.' Everett began to quote something lugubrious from A. E. Housman. Beryl said:

'We'll have our coffee in the other room.' We rose, and

Everett said, 'A perfect pentameter. Not many rhymes, though. Womb, tomb. Pity.'

I didn't want any more poetry, and indigestion was growing like a scorch on newspaper that draws the fire. 'What kind of work do you do here?' I asked Everett.

'On the *Hermes*? Oh, the literary page, odd feature articles, you know. How are the mighty fallen. It's a far cry from the old days of *Blast* and the *Adelphi* and the verse sheet I used to edit. I must show you some of my things some time. But wait – I said we'd get something in about you, didn't I? The returned exile and how he sees philistine England. Of course,' he suddenly said with loud conviction to Henry, 'that's Alice's husband, Alice at the club.'

'Yes, that's right,' said Henry. 'Winter, she says, but we all know it's Winterbottom.'

'You may not believe this,' said Everett to me, 'but we actually have a club in this puritanical town.'

'A club?' I said. 'A place where you can actually drink when the pubs are closed?'

'Yes,' said Everett. 'The police didn't like the idea at all, but even they could see the point of having somewhere where visiting business-men can be taken in the afternoon. It's absurd, a rich industrial town like this, and nowhere you can take anybody for a decent lunch and a drink afterwards. Ridiculous having to go to the Leofric in Coventry. Anyway, there's a good Indian restaurant here now, that's something, and we've got the Hippogriff.'

'The what?'

'The Hippogriff. In Bootle Street. What I had in mind was you and I meeting there and then we could have a little talk. To-morrow, why not? Say four o'clock. And I could put you up for membership, if you think it's worth your while. How much longer will you be staying here?'

'It's worth my while,' I said. 'Thanks.' And then I suddenly remembered that I'd done great harm to Mrs Winter and that, if she was going to be there, I'd better not go. I said, 'What's Mrs Winter got to do with it?'

'Alice? Oh, she's behind the bar. A publican's daughter, actually. She does the afternoons, somebody else comes on at six.' Beryl came in with coffee and Everett, taking his cup, quoted:

'Coffee, be fragrant. Porridge on my plate,
Give me new vigour to fulfil my fate.'

Realising that this was not altogether appropriate, he giggled and said, 'Excellent lunch. An excellent, excellent lunch.'

'Well, I'm glad somebody thinks so,' said Beryl, looking at me.

'The dog thought so, too,' I said nastily. The dog now slept, occasionally farting very gently. My father slept too, clutching a crumpled banner headline: TIED WIFE TO BATHROOM GEYSER ALLEGED. I said to Everett:

'What was her maiden name? Mrs Winter, I mean.'

He stirred his coffee excessively. 'Let me see. It was a nice old pub, the Three Tuns. It caters exclusively for Americans now – Chemical Warfare noncoms. The landlord was Tom Hoare,' Everett giggled.

Hoare to Winterbottom, I thought. She hadn't made too bad an exchange.

4

I woke up on Monday morning feeling good and innocent and remarkably healthy. Beryl's cooking had given me indigestion – a hot coal behind the sternum, obscene radiations of heat through the whole of my pluck, acid squirted into my mouth periodically like the automatic flush of a urinal – and I'd purged it with exercise, walking half way home or near. Not that I'd deliberately chosen this. Henry Morgan had offered to run my father back in his sports car, able to hold three at a pinch, and Beryl had said she'd accompany them for a 'bit of a blow'. This was typical of Beryl: if they'd had a saloon, with plenty of room for four, she would have been content to stay by the fire with some ghastly woman's magazine or the Panglossian drug of the *Reader's Digest*.

I felt good because I'd exercised not only my liver but also my patience. I'd let Beryl snap at me without answering back; I'd refused to be drawn into a bitchy wrangle about money. I'd even offered to help with the washing-up, but Beryl had seemed to think this another proof of my fundamental insincerity, another symptom of the personal nastiness that was accumulating along with my money. I felt good also because it was Monday and I was again reminded of my release from English puritanism: that palpable theology – Sunday the uneasy Eden, Monday the fall – meant nothing to my stomach and nerves. Sunday's nightmare lay far behind – the village lying in a torpor of beef and pudding in the bird-deserted afternoon which was also the grease on plates, the unmade beds; the evensong bell, the light switched on to shock, with a sort of Monday earnestness, squalor out of what in the tea-tray dusk loked like holiday abandon. I'd had a pleasant dream about my university days—the one year in which I'd studied English, failing in the first-year examinations and losing my scholarship—and my friends McCarthy and Black, with whom I'd got drunk every Friday night on half-a-crown each, reciting Anglo-Saxon poetry to the whores. I woke happy to soft Monday rain, remembering without sadness that both McCarthy and Black were long dead—at Crete the one, at sea the other—and all my own life since the war was buckshee life, and that nothing had to be worried about, really. My father was coughing in his bed. I went to the lavatory and voided my body sweetly, then I went downstairs to make tea. While the kettle was boiling, the morning paper thrust itself, like the angry world, into the house, and I read the big bad headlines like the salutation of a love-letter. I took tea up to my father, came down to drink my own before the electric fire and to read the strip-cartoons intently. They are myth: the news is merely news.

My father always cooked his own breakfast. He came down, looking somehow very old and broken in brace-dangling trousers and a collarless shirt. But he fried himself an egg and a rasher, singing between coughs, and sat down to a plate swimming in bacon-fat, peppering it from the pepper-carton. Then the letters came—the particular outside world after the general one—and there was one for me, from my firm's head office. Pepper, for some reason, always seemed to allay my father's coughs, and it was with heavy breathing and lip-smackings that he read the news from his sister in Redruth. My firm wanted me to come

up to London on Wednesday – nothing very serious, but
Chalmers in Beirut had just retired and Holloway in Zanzibar was very ill, and there might have to be a redistribu-
tion of senior managers. I felt a light-headed relief that
I was to go to London, not in search of wanton pleasure,
but on business: my emancipation from English puritanism was really not so complete.

I boiled myself two eggs and was just going to eat them
when the telephone rang. It was for me; it was Everett.

'Denham,' he said. 'Good morning, Denham. It's a filthy
morning, isn't it? Look, I may be quite late. I have to meet
a train, you see, my daughter, she's just left her husband
again, oh, it's a long story. Anyway, be there, won't you?
I'll bring her along. I saw Manning last night, he runs the
place, and he says he'll be glad to give you a temporary
membership card. Anything I can do for you any time,
my dear fellow, as long as you're here with us, I'll be glad
to do. Think nothing of it.' *I* was evidently to do plenty
for him. Behind Everett's voice was the heartening noise
of typewriters, the big, busy world. I said:

> 'It was most kind of you to ring me up.
> But now my egg's congealing in its cup,
> And on its plate another –'

I wanted to say that the second egg was hardening like
the earth waiting for man to come to it, but I couldn't find
the words or the rhymes quickly enough. Everett giggled,
embarrassed, as though poetry was all right for Sunday
but not for Monday morning, except, of course, as a com-
modity to sell. He said he'd see me, then he rang off.

I went into town by bus that morning, leaving my father
to do something obscure but useful in his potting-shed.
The rain eased off, but the streets were greasily wet, rain-
bowed with oil. I went to the bank for more five-pound

46

notes, stood like a pauper in the public library reading the *Christian Science Monitor*, then went for the first drinks of the day to a dive-bar popular with merchants. Hungarian refugees waited on at the tables and a West Indian negro collected dirty glasses – we were all exiles together. I had a sudden longing, like a pain, for the hot smelly East, and remembered that Everett had said something about an Indian restaurant. I asked the barman, a hot-haired Irishman, and he asked one of the business-men (who, I saw now, was a Pakistani) and then was able to tell me that the Calicut Restaurant was on Egg Street, by the Poultry Market. I went there and ate insipid dahl, tough chicken, greasy pappadams, and rice that had congealed to a pudding. The décor was depressing – brown oily wallpaper, a calendar with a Bengali pin-up (buff, deliriously plump, about thirty-eight) – and it was evident that the few Indian students were eating the special curry prepared for the staff. The manager was from Pondicherry: he called me '*monsieur*' and was not impressed by my complaints. At least one of the waiters was from Jamaica. I went out angry and, at a pub where the landlady sniffed in curlers, drank brandy till closing-time. My morning mood had vanished completely. When the door closed, the afternoon gaped wide: that mouth had to be stopped with something. Of course, the club. The Griffin or Hippodrome or Hippocras something. Angrily half-tipsy, all I could think of to inveigh against was adultery. Then I was damped by a sense of wrong done to an adulteress, remembered who it was, and had a good afternoon laugh in the grey sour-faced street about whores and winterbottoms. After that, I felt good and humble that I had been so nice to Beryl, and was determined to be chivalrous to all women in future, whatever their faults. I felt a maudlin mood coming on, so I walked to the main street of big shops, where lights were already appearing, and in a mood of sensual abandon bought Passing Clouds and Three Castles at a tobacconist's whose manager was dressed as for a smart wedding. Above the street-lamps the great dying northern winter sky boomed like an organ. I went into a milk-bar for a cup of tea. I sat at the comfortless chrome counter with my mug and was soon given a nudge in the side.

'Aaaah,' said Selwyn. 'Niver thot as ow yer'd be seein me in ere, mister.' He had a swilling glass of some thin custard-coloured beverage; his eyes were blindfolded by the strip-lighting caught in his goggles; his idiot mouth was open. He wore a kind of convict-costume of denim; he seemed both triumphant and guilty. 'Ah know wot yer thinkin,' he said. 'Yer think am teckin tahm off. Boot am not. Ah delivered Mister Goodge's parcel to Enry Street.' He did a kind of restrained dance with static soundless laughter, his custard dancing gravely with him. Then he said, 'Yer've no room ter talk, mister. Ah sin yer Satdy naht.' He laughed like a distant ship's hooter or an empty beer bottle that is blown like a flute. 'Yer wuz well away. Aaah,' he told the milk-bar, 'he wuz.'

'Let me stand you another nice glass of custard,' I said. 'What did I do wrong?'

'Coostard? This int coostard. This is —' He read it off loudly from the placard. '— Gawlden Glawry Milk Shek. Ted's missis pled ell wi Ted,' he continued, 'an Cecil were not too well, an Cedric's motor were id fahve strits off an e ad ell of a job fahndin it. Boot ah wus all raht, mister. Ah roong bell nex mornin. Aaaaah,' he nudged me in triumph.

'And me?'

'Yer went rahnd strits playin ell, mister.' He blew the empty bottle again, five sharp blasts. 'Boot nawbody tole yer dad.' The anaemic counter-girl with the off-white chef's cap, the tired early-edition-reading shoppers, all gave me

a tribute of faint interest. I was sick to death of the irresponsibility thrust on me by suburban England (Ted
Arden? Selwyn? The liquor with St Cyril's script?) I was
supposed to be adult, reliable, a respected senior servant of
a reputable export firm. I got up from the counter-stool,
determined to go to London right away. As I went out,
Selwyn called, 'Yer dint finish yer tea.' Then he told the
others: 'E dint finish is tea.' I knew where the railway station was, London Road; I would telephone or wire my
father ('Decided better go to-day. Back very soon.') As I
walked towards travel, that illusion of liberation, I
strangely felt myself walking back into childhood. It was
the cosy dimness of a newsagent's shop that did it, children's comics in the doorway, so like the one I'd loitered
around on the winter journey home from the elementary
school; the sharp smoky city dusk pinging on my skin like
a tuning-fork. In my head would be the last lesson of the
day — the tattered anthology under municipal gaslight,
some poem about the lamplighter, the cat mewing round
the tea-table, the bell of the muffin-man, nursery shadows,
the poor man's allotments, time you old gipsy-man, cargoes
– some easy and modern innocent poem by a man like
Drinkwater, Davies, Hodgson, Everett. Obviously my mind
had been preparing itself for the entry of Everett, as the
orchestra prepares for the entry of the second subject.
Everett almost trotted to catch me up, panting. 'No,' he
panted. 'You got it wrong, really. *You* were to meet me in
the Hippogriff. *I* have to go to the station. I *thought* perhaps I'd phoned you too early –'

'Your daughter,' I said. A girl he'd written poems to,
dreaming of her future beauty, celebrating her heartbreak-
ing innocence, coltish legs under the plaid skirt, straight
flax hair, a woman who'd left her husband again. 'How
old would you be now?' I asked.

'Fifty-seven.'

'That would be about it,' I said. 'You all seemed so old when I was at school. And Harold Munro?'

'Harold? Harold's dead. He died in 1932.' We were entering the station yard: time you old gipsy-man in the big white clock-face. 'We're early,' said Everett. 'She won't be in till five.'

'And the next London train?'

'Eight-ten, I think. Surely you weren't thinking of leaving us so soon?'

'Oh, well.' We were among holiday posters from last summer. 'I have business there. To-morrow will do, I suppose.' Everett bought a platform ticket. I hadn't a penny, so he bought one for me too.

'We might as well have a cup of tea,' he said, and we noisily marched over the hollow boards of the glass-covered bridge, down the stairs to Platform Four. We entered the filthy Gothic tea-room and Everett ordered. The serving-woman served us with tired disdain; she treated her customers like a dull and endless film that could only, with order and money, make a very rare stereoscopic contact with her real though duller world. Everett took me to a table and began to talk sadly but eagerly.

'My daughter Imogen,' he said. 'She made a very unfortunate marriage really, I'm afraid. But I honestly thought that things were going better lately, because she's not been back home for well over a year. Not, in fact, since I moved from Birmingham to here. I honestly don't know what can be done.' In raising his arm to take a deliberate swig of tea he gently agitated the ball-point pens in his side-pocket. I said:

'Have you other daughters?' I asked because I was pretty sure that Everett, in choosing other names, would not look further than Cordelia, Perdita, Miranda, Marina. But

Everett shook his head, saying:

'My only child.'

'And is your wife still living?' He shook his head again but this time meant something different. He said:

'I shouldn't be surprised if she is. I should imagine she must be a very hard woman to kill.'

'Oh.' I liked this poetic honesty.

'What can I say to Imogen, really? She knows all about her mother. She knows she was always shooting off with a suitcase, back, strangely enough, to her father, whose wife had done precisely the same thing, shooting off finally with more than just a suitcase.'

'You mean?'

'Everything. The whole lot. Even the lampshades.'

'I see. This all goes back a long way.'

He said, 'There are very few poems about marriage, when you come to think of it. It doesn't seem to be a natural subject for poetry, not like love and fornication and wine. That means that marriage isn't a natural state.' He stirred his tea again, as though desperately dredging for sweetness somewhere, anywhere. 'Paternity, however, is a different thing altogether.'

'I should imagine so.'

'You've never experienced it?' he asked innocently. 'You've begotten no coloured children in your sojourns in outlandish parts?'

'Possibly. I don't know. But that's not real paternity, is it?'

'Oh, no.' He drained his tea. 'She'll want a real drink as soon as she arrives,' he said, 'just like her mother. But we can take her to the club, of course.'

'How old is she?'

'Imogen? Oh, twenty-eight, thirty, something like that.' He seemed to lose interest in the subject of his daughter, glooming at a yellow card of ancient railway regulations on the wall. But when the harbingers of the coming train were audible – porters trundling, a scrambled gabble from the station announcer, frantic blowing on hot tea – he became eager again and was out swiftly on to the platform. I followed him. The train slid in. I saw the driver look down disdainful from his cosy hell, sharing – like soldier and auxiliary – a mystique with the tea-room woman. Passengers, disillusioned with arrival, got out greyly amid grey steam; passengers, hungry for the illusion of getting somewhere, jostled their way on. A girl ran up to Everett and cried, 'Daddy!' Poet and poet's daughter hugged each other. So this was Imogen. I think it's relevant here to quote the verses Everett had written about her when she was seven, though I only read them myself for the first time long after this first meeting:

'You take my heart with such unformed grace,
    One, at times, with the heartbreak earth
And its children, fur or bone – fawn, mouse,
    Palpitating duckling, stumbling calf.
    In touching you, silk, silver, I touch half
Of the whole dreadful mystery of birth.

I dread you faring forward into the world,
    Carrying your beauty like an innocent gift
Among the grown beasts. I am appalled
    At the scratching of hungry fingers at the door,
    Already. Two handfuls of years, no more,
And what of this heartbreak changeling will be left?'

I was introduced, admired the strong face in the lamplight, the untidy tawny hair, the neat pliant body. She smiled at me boldly and said, 'God, I'd give anything for

52

a drink. And they don't open for *hours*, do they?' to her father.

'Oh, I think we can manage something for you,' said her father, grinning. 'Can't we, Denham?'

'*You* can,' I said. She put her arm in Everett's, and they began to walk briskly to the stairs, Everett with one of her cases. I, without being asked or thanked, picked up the other. She seemed to take all men for granted. To hell with her. Then I remembered that I was, in future, going to be chivalrous to women, whatever their faults. When we'd climbed the stairs and were going through the ticket-barrier, I could see her beauty more clearly. Everett had not been let down: poet's daughters have no right to be ugly, any more than poetesses have a right to be pretty. We got a taxi, and, while we travelled to Bootle Street, Imogen spoke vigorously to her father about the life she had left behind in Birkenhead; angrily about her husband, who appeared to be something in a shipping agency; without restraint about the nature of their sexual life together. The taxi-driver, uninsulated by glass, cocked a left ear with interest. 'But what *precisely* is wrong?' asked Everett.

'I just can't stand him, that's all,' said Imogen. She spoke very sharp Standard English, like a repertory actress. 'I suppose I never could stand him, really.'

'Well,' said Everett, 'you'd better get a divorce. But you don't seem to have any real grounds, do you? After all, this isn't America, you know.'

'I've given him grounds,' said Imogen in that sharp frost-clear voice, 'plenty. But he won't take any notice. He says he loves me.' This last shot cleanly out of the open taxi-window as we stopped at traffic-lights. A man crossing the street heard it and clicked his tongue hard on his alveolum, flicking his cocked head at the same time. 'You,' called Imogen, 'mind your own bloody business. Mannerless sod.'

There was an atmosphere in the taxi of brief embarrassed coughs as we shot forward with the change to green. We turned into a side street, one of whose glass walls was all grand pianos washed in cold white light, and then into another, pulling up outside an Espresso coffee-bar. 'Oh, God, no,' said Imogen. 'I'm not going to have any of that dish-wash.'

'You'd be amazed,' I said, 'what it does to teen-agers. Far more potent than beer.'

She looked at me, pulled a face, and said, 'I'm no teen-ager.' Then, while the taxi-driver pulled her luggage from the boot, she caught sight of what I'd already seen—a kind of hell-mouth next to the coffee-bar, red light pointing down to a cellar, the legend HIPPOGRIFF CLUB: MEMBERS ONLY. Everett paid off the taxi and said, with small pride:

'I suggested that name, you know. I'm one of the founder-members. Let's go down.' It was left to me to carry Imogen's suitcases. Following the two of them clumsily down the narrow cellar-steps, I felt as though we were all going for a brief holiday in hell, Everett as Virgil leading the way. He rapped at the door at the stair-foot; a face looked through a glass hole, nodded, and we were let in.

Manning was bald, affable, in a smart suit, too clean-shaven, a cigarette grafted on to his lower lip. The club was what you would expect—concealed strip-lighting; wall-paper with a pattern of boulevard café-tables and long loaves; cushioned wall-seats in shadow; a now silent juke-box. At the bar a very big American business-man was being fed Martinis by two smaller local business-men; behind the bar was Mrs Winterbottom, very smart, gay, coquettish. She smiled over at Everett and myself (it was evident that she didn't remember me at all) and accorded Imogen a glance impossible to analyse—the glance of an attractive woman seeing another she didn't know, trying to place her. In the shadows I noticed a West Indian with a guitar. As Everett went to order drinks the West Indian struck chords with a plectrum and began to sing some naïve song of the Caribbean. 'Give us *Home on the Range*,' called the American business-man, but the sad little song continued. I could see more clearly into the shadows now: a youngish couple sat eating each other between bemused sips of gin-and-tonic; a gaunt man with glasses on a labourer's face, wearing a raincoat, read an evening paper intently, though it was a mystery how he could see small print in that amorous dimness. Imogen and I sat down on the wall-settle nearest the bar, and Everett brought our drinks. He and I, in late afternoon thirstiness, were having brown ale, she sipped with relief a double pink gin. 'Ah,' she said. 'That's better.' I handed round my Three Castles.

'Mr Denham,' said Everett, 'is home from the East. I invited him here so that we could have a talk and he could give me the impressions of a returned exile. You know, how things have changed in England since he last came home. For the *Hermes*,' he added.

'Oh,' said Imogen. 'Do you want me to go and sit somewhere else?'

'No, no,' I said, 'really. There's no desperate hurry, you know. Anyway,' I said, 'there's no point in calling an interview private if it's going to be made public later, is there?'

'No,' she said vaguely, 'I suppose not.' Then she smiled very brightly and said, 'But you don't know Daddy like I do. He didn't bring you here for an interview. He brought you here to talk about his poems, didn't you, Daddy?'

'I think, Imogen,' said Everett, 'you better *had* go and sit somewhere else. I'll introduce you to Alice and you can talk to her.'

'Don't get me wrong,' said Imogen to me. 'Daddy's not after anything for himself. He won't make a penny out of

55

his book of poetry, will you, Daddy? It's his duty,' she said, 'to literature.' She pronounced every syllable separately, clearly, like a parody of an old-fashioned elocutionist – 'lit-er-a-ture.' So Cedric the barman, as toastmaster, might have pronounced the word. 'And,' said Imogen, 'you might as well help. You look well-off to me. You'll only throw your money away on drink and women.' She seemed to despise everything – literature, love, even money.

'What do you mean?' I said. 'How do I look well-off?'

'You're a bachelor,' she said. 'No wife would let you come out with your tie tied like that. But that's a very good suit you've got on. You've been professionally manicured. You're bored to death. You've got an expensive cigarette-holder and the best lighter money can buy. You've got a full packet of Passing Cloud as well as these Three Castles. You're home from the East.' She seemed to get suddenly angry. 'Damn it all, the least you can do is to spend a couple of hundred quid on my father. It's the job of the rich to help the poor men of genius, isn't it?'

The American business-man lolled on his stool, grinning. 'That's right,' he said. 'You tell 'em.' One of the other men laughed. Imogen said, very hotly:

'You keep your bloody nose out of it. Nobody asked you to interfere.'

'I think,' said Everett, 'that will do. I think you've said quite enough, Imogen. Mr Denham is my guest. You've embarrassed him and you've embarrassed me.'

'I'm not a child,' said Imogen. 'I'll say what I like.' Then she pouted. 'Oh, all right, sorry.' She looked up at the American, smiled with great sweetness, and said, 'Sorry, Tex.' And then, to me or to her father, 'Let's have another drink.'

'Can I?' I asked. 'How about this temporary membership?'

'He can, can't he, Fred?' Everett asked Manning, who had been hovering near us, uneasy. Manning nodded, said, 'I'll fetch a form.' I went to the bar and addressed that appetising full Nordic beauty I was now entitled to call Alice. 'And one for yourself,' I said. Seeing her in this little world of shining glass and throaty men's chaffing, remembering she was a publican's daughter, I invented quick flashbacks of her life—the pretty little girl made pert by the male drinkers, brought into the saloon bar to be admired in a new frock; the good meals of publican's stew in the back parlour, a robust young woman breathing in the heartiness of malt; the later admiration, always surrounded by men who, after two pints, soon lost their shyness; spoilt, self-aware, always on show, used to having her own way. She gave herself a Scotch, smiled at me and said 'Cheers'. I carried the drinks to the table, hearing the American say, 'I'm not in oil, I'm in epoxy resins.'

'Poxy what?' said Imogen.

'Poxy nothing. Epoxy resins. They stick together. You take a windstream surface on a jet aircraft. You can't use rivets, can you?'

'I don't see why not,' said Imogen.

'You can't because of turbulence round rivet heads. You see that?'

'No,' said Imogen. 'But,' she said to her father and me, 'I *will* leave you boys together. I'll go and sit with Tex and Tex shall tell me all about poxy turbulence or whatever it is.' She picked up her drink and went to the bar. The business-man standing by the American bowed tipsily deep to Imogen, gesturing her, like a barber, to a stool. The West Indian singer finished his glass of stout and began a rather dull calypso about Caribbean politics. With me a very little folk-art goes a long way. I said so to Everett, and Everett said:

'I was really terribly embarrassed by that, you know, and you must have been, too.'

'Think nothing of it,' I said. 'I'd rather talk about that than talk about my reactions to coming home again. After all, I've only been away for two years.'

'Yes,' said Everett, relaxing and at the same time sitting up straight, 'I don't suppose things change all that quickly, do they?'

'No,' I said. 'The sinful go on making money and the righteous go on needing it. Only the ranks of the sinners grow. How much do you want, anyway?'

'I can't say it's really an investment,' he said. 'You'll get nothing out of it except a certain, shall I say, spiritual satisfaction. Three hundred pounds should do it.'

'You mean you want me to throw three hundred pounds away?'

'Oh,' said Everett, 'we're concerned with values, aren't we? And, whether my poetry's good or bad, there's the question of principle, isn't there? In this day and age, when even the dustman's son goes to the university, surely it's sinful and wrong that we should still have mute inglorious Miltons. Not,' he added, smirking and then giggling, 'that I'm a Milton, or anything like it.'

'Nor mute, nor inglorious,' I said. 'People know your name. I suppose some of your things will survive in anthologies. Things survive because they're needed.' I drank some brown ale. 'Would anybody need your Collected Poems?'

'Yes,' said Everett, somewhat breathlessly. 'The single poem, the anthology piece, means so little. It's the total corpus that counts, the picture of the entire poetic personality. That *must* be shown to the world, mine, I mean. I've waited long enough. Perhaps I haven't so much time left.'

Imogen could be heard saying to one of the local business-men, 'All right, if you don't like it, bugger off, then.'

'I'll have to think about it,' I said. 'I'm not all that rich, you know. I can't just throw away three hundred pounds.'

'You won't be throwing it away.'

'Won't I?' I suddenly felt rather angry; Imogen's temper seemed to be infectious. I thought: "After all, what bit of money I've made has been made among mosquitoes and sand-flies, snakes in the bedrom, long monotonous damp heat, boredom, exasperation with native clerks. Who are these sweet stay-at-homes, sweet well-contents, to try and suck it out of me and feel aggrieved if they can't have it?" 'I'll be spending it,' I said, 'on Everett's honour and glory, Everett's not-so-slim volume—"a geuine poetical talent," ' I improvised, ' "in the tradition. A lack of originality compensated for by scrupulous craftsmanship. The themes, though often conventional —" '

'All right,' he said, 'if you won't, you won't.'

'I didn't say that. I said I'd have to think about it.' Imogen could be heard saying to the American, 'Well, nobody asked you to come over here, did they? If you don't like the bloody food, why don't you –' Manning had already put a threepenny piece into the juke-box; it now sang out very loudly, too much bass shaking the glasses. I mouthed; Imogen mouthed; Everett sat in peeved silence.

'Just tell her that, will ya?' said the American businessman, roaring to Everett above the juke-box; 'that's right, just tell her that.' Everett seemed not to hear. The three business-men took their overcoats from a small alcove where there was also a telephone, they and Manning going through a regretful mime, mouths opening and closing in noiseless vigour. Imogen and Alice were deep in talk with each other, heads together, a mouth occasionally put to an ear, nodding, nodding, smiling, frowning, eyes to eyes, oblivious to the juke-box. The business-men left: no hard feelings, but they had to go anyway. I saw from my watch that it was already after six: the pubs would be open. The evening? Drinks, dinner, drinks, television, cinema. Oh, God, the boredom. Let me change the scene, let me get to London. In London? Drinks, lunch, drinks, dinner —

The record came to an end, catching Imogen and Alice unawares in animated chatter: 'No, my dear, he *thought* of himself that way, but really hadn't a bloody clue.' 'Yes, yes, I know.' 'I mean, just to give you one example —' They felt the enormous silence and giggled together. They were both very handsome women, blonde head and tawny head together, looking towards us, good teeth shining. 'Thank God you've shut that bloody noise off,' said Imogen. Manning grinned: he couldn't really take offence. Everett sat in gloom, his brown ale flat. 'We'll meet again,' I said, 'when I get back from London. I'll let you know.' He nodded in gloom. Manning opened the door to a treble knock. A young woman, with, I thought, little allure, smiling across at Alice. Alice's relief. Should I take them out to dinner, I wondered — Alice, Imogen, Everett himself? Then I thought no, to hell with the lot of them. Taking my coat from the alcove, I saw the youngish couple still making a meal of each other, a dark, silent meal, the prole with glasses reading, though God knew how, his paper. The West Indian guitarist smiled at me and proffered an empty cloth cap — 'To show leetle apprisieshun of the music, sah? Thank you very match, sah.' I left the club, slowly surfaced to the shining street. Rain had fallen again.

5

'Sorry we weren't able to tell you about it when you reported back,' said Rice. 'How long have you been back now – a month?'

'About that,' I said. Rice nodded, arms akimbo, feet astride in front of the flagged wall-map, every inch the Export Manager. He said:

'I realise you might have made arrangements, you know, to go over to Biarritz or get lost in Sicily or something. But I don't have to remind you that leave's a privilege, not a right.'

'Just like the Army,' I said.

'Oh, no,' said Rice, beginning to walk up and down like a lecturer. 'You know better than that, J.W.' Four strides took him from Kamchatka to Vancouver. A turn and a stride-and-a-half brought him to the Canary Islands. 'We're a family. There's nothing autocratic about *our* organisation.' He'd been Export Manager about eighteen months. 'Anyway,' he said, 'Chalmers let us down rather badly. We couldn't stop him retiring, but he'd as good as promised to hang on for another year. And Holloway, it seems, is in a very bad way.'

'What's his trouble?'

'Heart. We always said he couldn't continue to carry all that weight in a place like Zanzibar. Not indefinitely.' Rice didn't carry much weight: grey and soldierly would just about do for him. He had, however, a very fine collection of modern Chinese ceramics.

'So what do you propose to do?'

'We don't propose to move you from your present spot.' He stroked Japan like a little tame mouse. 'We're all very pleased, you know that, J.W.' I bowed from my chair. 'We're moving Taylor from Colombo to Zanzibar. Beirut's another matter, but I think we've got a solution there. Colombo – that's where you come in. You were there before, J.W. We're sending a young fellow to Colombo, but we want you to go with him. A chap by the name of Wicker. He doesn't know anything about managing a staff of Tamils and Singhalese, but he's a very good fellow, we think, and if he's shown the ropes for a month or so we're pretty sure he can do the job. Anyway, we'd like a report on him.'

'When do you want me to go?'

'Next week. You'll miss the worst of the winter.' He did a theatrical shiver, his back to Africa. 'You know I'd give anything to be out on the beat again. It's dull being here, you know. Necessary, but dull.'

'Oh, yes. Where do I stay in Colombo? I take it this chap Wicker gets the flat.'

'You can stay up the hill. Mount Lavina. You'll like that. Wicker must live above the shop right from the word go.'

'So I spend Christmas in Colombo. All right.' I stood up. and Scandinavia and Rice's soldierly hawk-face looked down on me. Rice said:

'Oughtn't we to go to a chop-house together? Although, no more chops for me. No meat, no alcohol. If you could bear to watch me eating a vegetarian lunch –'

'So you've become a Hindu at last? But I'm not really surprised. You were always very fond of the Hindus, if I remember rightly.'

Rice knew what I was alluding to – a liaison in Kuala Lumpur, many years before – so he said stiffly, 'I've settled down. It's my stomach that's caught up with me. The doctors reckon they can cure it. Rigid diet and so on.' He forgot immediately about his invitation and shook hands with me. 'We'll send you the air-tickets. Open date return.' He grinned greyly, standing to attention with the whole world, like his battalion, behind him. 'Thank you, J.W.' He let me open the door myself. I passed along the great counter, smiling vaguely at the many clerks, a bigger man than they, and I went out on to Leadenhall Street.

Much of this story is a record of what I found happening when I got back – back from abroad to England, back from London to my father's suburb – so you won't be greatly interested in what I did on my few days in London. I was staying in a small hotel just off Russell Square, a place kept by an Italian widow who was normally waiting up for me when I got back at night, ready for a chat over two glasses of cognac, copies of *Il Giorno* spread over the main table of the lounge-breakfast-room. She was very nearly the only woman I spoke to in London during these few days. I shall mention another woman later, but only because of a peculiar trick she played on me, a trick I'd never met before. The greater part of the time I spent, when I talked at all, talking to men. I liked to take luncheon in some pub or other, sitting on a high stool at the snack-counter, barons of beef, hams, salads and dishes of pickle spread before me, the server in his tall white cap carving with skill. Other male eaters would be wedged against me, champing over newspapers, and there were a peculiar animal content in being among warm silent men, raising glasses in smacking silent toasts to themselves, the automatic 'ah' after the draught, the forkful of red beef and mustard pickle. Sitting with my gin or whisky afterwards I would often manage to get into conversation with some lonely man or other – usually an exile like myself – and the talk would be about the world, air-routes and shipping-lines, drinking-places thousands of miles away. Then I felt happy, felt I had come home, because home to people like me is not a place but all places, all places except the one we happen to be in at the moment.

In the afternoon I would drink in one or other of the two clubs of which I was a member (one was primarily for chess-players, the other for decayed and most loquacious theatricals) or go to see a film. In the evening I would dine – slowly and sumptuously – at Rule's in Maiden Lane. The night before I returned to my father's house, there to pack for Colombo, I walked along the Strand in a content that was almost spiritual (I had eaten blue trout, a pork cutlet with cauliflower in a white sauce, Camembert; had drunk gin-and-Italian, Châteauneuf du Pape, brandy; was smoking an unwonted cigar). The air was mild for winter. Walking slowly, I was accosted and was very willing. Everything to-night seemed holy – the vulgar hotels, the commercial skysigns, the occasional bland belches that came up with my cigar-smoke. My accoster was fair like an angel and seemed no more than twenty-five. She named the hotel and we walked there, her arm in mine. I booked a room for the night – with private bath, she insisted – and we were taken up in the lift to the third floor. When we were alone in the bedroom she made no move to take off her beaver lamb coat (a coat, appropriately, rather like Mrs Winterbottom's). She now seemed shy, furtive.

'A drink?' I said.

'No, thanks,' she said. Her accent was self-taught refined. 'I must,' she said, 'see if the bathroom's all right.' She went off to it, still in her fur coat. I presumed she wanted to see if there was a *bidet* or something. She came back almost at once, smiling, without her coat. 'It'll be five pounds,' she said.

'Is it now usual to pay before?' I asked. 'I ask only for information. I've been away for some time and one gets out of touch.'

'We've got to protect ourselves,' she said. 'There've been some very bad cases – men just walking off, you know, just like that. And what can we poor devils do?'

'Don't I look the sort of man that can be trusted?'

'I don't know. But I'd rather you paid me now, if you don't mind.' I gave her one of my five-pound notes. She put it into her hand-bag carefully, then carefully sat on my knee and kissed my left cheek. Well-fed and liquored, I responded with ardour. She wriggled away and said, 'You get undressed, get into bed. I'll go into the bathroom.'

'But you've only just been there.'

'I know. But I've got to – you know,' she said. She went into the bathroom again, taking her hand-bag, and I heard the bathroom-door click locked. I undressed, got into the bed and waited. I waited a long time. I got out of bed and walked, naked, to the bathroom-door. I called, 'Are you there?' I didn't know her name. There was no answer. I rattled the door-handle. There was no response. I put on my trousers and jacket and went out on to the corridor. There was nobody about. But I knew now what had happened. The bathroom led into another bedroom, empty. She'd gone through, quietly out and off, and was now presumably a whole taxi-ride away. I should have felt a fool but I couldn't help grinning: after all, I'd learnt something, I'd know better another time. But there was never another time, not like that, not for me anyway.

I dressed, took the lift down, and gave my key to the reception-clerk. I said:

'I asked for a room with a bath. The room you gave me has no bath. Is this the way you do business?' The clerk looked at the key and said:

'Number 306 has a bath, sir. You must be mistaken.'

'Don't tell me I'm mistaken. Go up and see for yourself. My wife went off disgusted, refused to sleep in a room without a bath, said it was all my fault. You see the trouble you've caused. I shall never come here again.' And I went off in reasonable good humour for a drink before closing-time. I found a bar where a man of venerable appearance played, with liturgical gravity, Richard Rodgers on a Hammond organ, and there drank a glass or so with a Merchant Navy man whose home was Liverpool. He told me about his pal who were a lad who used to fight with his head, but the other bugger had fish-hooks stuck inside his coat. You should have seen the poor sod afterwards, fish-hooks in his eyelids terrible, terrible. Then I went back to my hotel, where the Italian widow was waiting up for me, two glasses ready for cognac. She laid down her reading-glasses on the crumpled copy of *Il Giorno* and we discussed the state of the world and the shamelessness of to-day's young women. I decided, during this conversation, that I would charge the five pounds to expenses in connection with proposed journey to Ceylon. I said *buona notte*, went to bed and slept innocently.

The next day was Saturday and the train I caught to the Midlands was crowded. Arsenal was playing away. The air was very clear and tasted curiously of fried mushrooms. I bought myself mushrooms at the greengrocer's by the bus-stop where I got off to walk to my father's house, and also a pound of fillet steak. These I cooked as a late lunch with mashed potatoes. My father had gone for a coughing walk, so I sat alone in the front room drugging myself with television till I nearly cried. My father coughed himself in at dusk and we had cheese and celery for tea. During the meal the *Evening Hermes* arrived and, while I was washing up, my father read it by the fire. He called into the kitchen:

'There's something in here about you, lad.'

'Where? What does it say?' I came into the dining-room wiping my hands. He handed me the paper. On the 'Saturday Page' I read as follows:

'TRAVELLER FROM AN ANTIQUE LAND

'One of the most eligible of the more mature bachelors at present living on the fringe of the city is Mr J. W. Denham, who has come to take up temporary residence among us on his return from Japan. That it is still possible for a man of initiative to make money in the East is the firm opinion of balding, plump Mr Denham who adds, however, "Not if you take a wife with you." Mr Denham has scathing things to say about Englishwomen and their lack of domestic virtues. He particularly selects their cooking as a target, but considers also that they are far inferior to the slant-eyed beauties of the Orient in the all-important matter of fidelity to their menfolk. Mr Denham is considered an authority on the women of Japan who, he says, are lovely, demure and submissive.

'Mr Denham believes that money is for putting in the bank. When asked his opinion on the revival of private patronage of the arts he replied that he thought that this was throwing money away. On his own admission he has little time for anything except money, dalliance, and the "imbibing of liquors of all kinds".'

Nous nous crackons, vous vous splittez, ils se bustent. This was my dear sister Beryl with some of her local news. I liked the 'more mature' touch and the conventional *Time*-Homeric epithets. Evidently the catty Everett had helped with 'additional material', as it is called in the radio programmes. The whole thing was nasty, but there was nothing actionable. To-night I would not go out. I would sulk over the fire with a book. My father said:

67

'It's a bit scathing, isn't it?' He coughed, looked closely again at the *feuilleton*, and said, 'Very bad bit of transposition there. Typical bit of local printing.' Then he went in to the front room to check his pools coupon with the televised football results. I tried to settle down with Anthony Trollope, but the siren voice of the modern world kept calling me, luring me to submit to the blue hypnotic eye and the absence of the need for thought or sodality. After the football results and my father's disappointed coughing came loud orchestral preludings, cheers and raised voices. I put Anthony Trollope away and went in to be drugged.

And so it was that we returned to the previous Saturday, another instalment of American police brutality, the epilogue of the officer in the trilby exhorting my father and me to help the State Troopers to wipe out the traffic in child prostitution, a toffee ballet, marching cigarettes, a song about instant coffee, the gloriously imbecilic woman announcer with her 'Right now we're going over –' She went over like a swivel-mirror when I turned her off, scared as I was by the drug of the screen, of the gas-fire, the voices that began to whisper in my spinning head. And so the walk up Clutterbuck Avenue to the Black Swan or Mucky Duck, a Flayer's ace.

I sat with my father's cronies and drank whisky – no more nonsense about good old English beer – and heard my father say:

'My lad's going to spend Christmas in Ceylon.' Old and middle-aged faces of envy and suspicion turned on me, and the traveller in medical supplies said:

'Some people are lucky, that's all I can say.' Ted Arden, behind this man's back, had just received the present of a plump dressed goose. Selwyn leered round from the public bar. The smoke-room was crammed. There was loud male jubilation about Arsenal's defeat, the women giggled over Babycham. Cedric minced about like a dancer with his tray that rang merrily through the smoky air. Ted Arden brought up a case of light ale from the cellar and was given, by a scholarly-looking man I had not seen before, a single perfect green orchid in tissue-paper. The ladies, in sororities, made excursions to the toilet. The men went out to pump ship. The warning of 'time' hung hungrily like a hawk. And then they came in.

There was Mrs Winterbottom, with beaver lamb coat, there was her regular escort, Jack Brownlow. There was Mrs Brownlow, cuddlesome and low-browed, with the scooped passionate Charlie Whittier. There was Winter the printer and there was Everett's daughter, the swearing fairy-child, lovely and tawny, and Winter's eyes on her as on a very good film. One of Everett's poems had found a printer; the printer, the bearer of the word to men, had succumbed to the game.

'Disgusting,' I couldn't help saying. 'Disgusting.' One of my father's cronies heard me and said:

'You're right, it *is* disgusting, bloody disgusting. But what does the Government do about it? People who should know better mortgaging their whole bloody lives on the never-never. Seen inside some of their houses? Television sets, electric blankets (and I wouldn't have one of those on my bed, I can tell you), toasters, electric mixers and polishers and God knows what. No sense of responsibility, somehow. And all on the never-never.'

Ah, well, if they wanted their adultery, what did it matter to me? I hadn't much room to talk, anyway, with my five-pound prostitutes who did a bunk and the Japanese girls who cost far less and didn't do a bunk and whatever I was likely to pick up in Colombo. But I had a feeling at the back of my mind that I wasn't really sinning against anything and that these people were, that this harmless week-end game was playing with fire and that more than one person would get badly burnt before long. Like the man with the electric blanket, bought on the never-never, that my father's crony insisted, at great length, on telling me all about.

6

So, after a few more days spent with my father and in the
town bars (in one of which I met the dressed and dentured
Charlie Dawes) and one dinner out with the Ardens, I flew
into summer with young Wicker. A bachelor flat was waiting for him in Colombo, shining complete from cook-boy
down to Benedictine glasses. A lucky young man, but I
could see that he had a lot to learn: shy of the brown-
skinned smiling people, he felt a need to bluster and parody
the old-time nigger-whipper. He didn't mean any harm:
being white felt like a disease or having no clothes on.
Somebody like myself seemed definitely needed to show
him how to behave. And the Chief Clerk, a Tamil who
used his age and seniority in the Company to balance
deficiencies which were not hard to uncover (irregularities
in the use of the petty cash, careless filing) tried to intimi-
date him. So I spent a month in which, though I recorded
few man-hours, I did some delicate tuning and adjusting
and left, I think, a smooth enough machine at the end of
my stay.

I had a high cool room in the Mount Lavinia Hotel, with
a balcony from which I could watch the traffic of ravens
round the great rain tree. These ravens entered by the open
window in the morning and stole the fresh pineapple from
the tea-tray. They also stole, on different occasions, a cuff-
link, a bottle-top, a rupee and a stud. They cawed in
triumph, rudely, but I liked them as much as anybody I'd

so far met on this leave from Japan. These thieves were honest thieves, not like that girl in the London hotel. And they had a vast stable community, so that their squabblings sounded like a choir; with so much thieving to be done they could never have found time for adultery or TV.

Colombo was the only night-stop between London and Singapore, and the hotel was a caravanserai for crumpled civil service families, junior planters and commercials – all the non-tourists who travelled tourist-class. The world is small for the professional expatriate, and practically every evening I drank with somebody I knew. And also I became acquainted with the nice young men and women who make up the patterns of aircraft crews, arriving in clinical white, the doctors and nurses who preside over the brief illness of travel. And in the downstairs bar one evening I met with a stranger, a sort of racketeer, lonely, sentimental, highly moral. His name, he said, was Len, and he carried something or other from Singapore to London every month. He talked fussily and with a sense of grievance about the difficulty of distribution in London and beyond, the lack of loyalty, the way you couldn't trust anybody nowadays.

'I don't mind talking to you,' he said, 'because I can see you're mixed up in something yourself, but there's so many I see in here that I wouldn't trust no further than I could throw them. Him, for instance.' And he made a fingerpost of his left shoulder. I followed the point to a very harmless State Treasurer of some protectorate or other. 'You can tell just by looking at his face. But you're different, more straight-looking,' said Len. 'I can tell you that the game's hardly worth the candle any more, what with transport and the actual cost of the stuff going up, and some pretty fierce cut-price competition, so that you find yourself getting mixed up with violence, and violence is the last thing in the world I like.' He had the face of an El Greco saint. 'And the treachery of the customers,' he said. 'Especially women.'

'Yes,' I said, 'women.' And I told him about the girl in the hotel. He nodded grimly, saying:

'You get in touch with me when I get back. I've drunk with you and you're my pal, and what they do to a pal of mine they do to me. They only do it once, that's about it. I'd spoil her beauty for her, I can tell you.'

'But you don't believe in violence.'

'No, but violence is a different thing from punishment. You mustn't be too easy on people. It only encourages them to carry on with the same lark. Give them a good sharp punishment, something that'll last. It's only for the good of humanity, when all's said and dcne. And for their own good, too.'

'What kind of punishment?'

'A good beating-up, a couple of teeth out, something that doesn't hurt too much but makes them remember all their lives, that sort of thing. It's a sort of duty, that's about it, the way I see it.'

'You ought to be God,' I said.

'Me? God?' He grimaced up at the ceiling as though God were staying just above it. 'I'd do things different, I can tell you. There's a lot of things God made wrong and that's a fact.' And then this moralist nodded sadly but benignantly, raised his fingers in a kind of blessing, and went to bed. Take-off was at four in the morning.

The month passed, and I met nobody else so fiercely moral. Wicker and I had Christmas dinner together in the hotel, and Wicker cried briefly in the lavatory, whimpered gently on the dining-room balcony that overlooked the sea, to think that this was his first Christmas away from home. (He had been lucky with his National Service.) I patted him like a dog and said, 'There, there, it is our destiny to be exiles.'

'We always had sixpences in the pudding, and I had a half-bottle of claret all to myself.'

'There, there.' The surf whistled and rattled; there was a full Ceylon moon, palms.

'And it's going to be three years – three years.' He sobbed boyishly, healthily. 'I must fix him up,' I thought, 'with some nice girl or other, a Eurasian schoolmistress, perhaps.' And then I thought: 'Why should I?' Anyway, unwritten Company law forbade such fraternisation on a probationary tour. Let him be red-eyed at night: it would make him all the clearer-eyed in the morning.

Christmas went and New Year came, and Wicker again had dinner with me and, with champagne, saw the New Year in. He cried again, though not so intensely as a week before, and said: 'New Year. Tim was the darkest, and he always brought the New Year in with a piece of coal and Nigger. Nigger was our cat.' He cried in a brief strong spurt at Nigger's memory. I patted him like a dog and said, 'There, there, it is our destiny to be exiles.'

'And I always had a half-bottle of Lanson to myself.' To pursue this curious family custom of reserving half-bottles of things for the youngest Wicker would mean, perhaps, altogether to much delving into Adlerian constellations. I said, still patting:

'I know how you must feel about Nigger. I had a cat that was always admiring itself in the garden pond. I called it Conrad, and, do you know, there were very few people who could see why.' He raised puffy eyes. 'A black cat?' he said.

And then Mr Raj came into my life. With fine teeth parted in the song of Anglo-Ceylonese speech, he said:

'It would be better if your young friend did not talk so

74

much about niggers.' He was wearing a superbly cut shark-skin tuxedo. 'You and I,' he said, 'understand these things, but there are very many people here who do not. It would be prudent, I think, not to –' Young Wicker gave him a bleary look, saying:

'It was our Nigger I was talking about, not you lot. You lot can go and get stuffed.'

'Now, Ralph,' I said, 'remember. Remember what I told you.' Oh dear. I was leaving in less than a week and, despite all my instruction, he was not yet ready to be received. But then he said:

'Yes, you can go and get stuffed. What right have you lot to think that you're better than we are? Just because you're black and I'm white. Well, what's wrong with being white? In any case, it's not my fault, is it? I apologise for being white – will that do? Perhaps I'd better jump into the sea.' He made as if to do so: the tide was high;. it was only a matter of leaping over the balustrade. Mr Raj said:

'Come, come.' In the manner of near-tipsy Orientals he tried to embrace one who, he knew, was no longer, in Santayana's phrase, his sweet, boyish master. 'I meant no harm. My name is Raj. I am a B.A., a man of some education. You and I know that so many of these people are what you have just called them. But sometimes they can be turning into very fierce and resentful people.' He nodded over towards a fat buck Tamil and his wife. 'A happy New Year,' he said to me. 'And to you,' he said to Wicker. He was a tall man, with very handsome classical features – Apollo in frozen milk chocolate, though the eyes melted and burned, playing like twin radios broadcasting a romantic concerto. His body seemed not unlike Charlie Whittier's, scooped and passionate, and his hands talked, juggled, took flight, returned. He said:

'It gives me pleasure to know you, Mr Denham. I was looking –'

'How do you know Mr Denham's name?' said Wicker. 'One of the best men in the firm, old J.W. How you get hold of his name?'

'I understand,' said Mr Raj, with smiles and lubricated politeness, 'that he and I are to be fellow-travellers. Yes,' he said to me. 'I saw your name on the list in the airline office, and I wondered if this was the Mr Denham who taught me for a time in Trincomali. His initials I did not remember – to his pupils he was just Mr Denham and greatly loved and feared of them all. And when the waiter pointed you out I knew it was not my old teacher. But –' He prepared with a new smile and a raised finger like a mouse-gnawed *langue de chat* to come to his point. Wicker said:

'And he is a teacher, too, old J.W. Taught me a –' (He wagged his head, trying to pump up the strongest possible aspirate) '– hell of a lot. Good old J.W.' And then, 'Nigger,' and seemed ready to cry once more.

'Nigger's his cat,' I said to Mr Raj.

'Yes, yes, his cat. Well, in the letter-rack I see an air letter addressed to Mr Denham, and what do you think is the address on the back?' I shook my head, in no way offended at a stranger – so long as he was Welsh or Oriental – pawing my mail. 'It is your father's name, as I take it,' said Mr Raj, 'and the town where I am to go to study at the University.' He gazed at me with a wide fanatic smile, waiting for an expression of wonder, gratification, congratulations. 'That,' he said, 'is why I determined that I should travel on the day you are travelling and not the day after or the day after that.' He looked at me again with a white suspended smile and then a spice-gale shook tiny temple-bells of laughter.

'But,' I said, 'you have a degree. And the University year starts in October.'

'I expected you to make just those very objections,' rejoiced Mr Raj. 'And I am a mature student, yes? I am thirty-five, though you will say I do not look it. And my brother is thirty and looks every day of it. He is in London, the hub of the universe, at Gray's Inn. He confesses still to a certain difficulty in penetrating into the folds and recesses of the better English society. But he has always suffered from a certain shyness. Moreover, his face is not what one might term prepossessing. Quite unlike mine,' said Mr Raj, smiling, no man for false modesty. 'I doubt not,' said Mr Raj, 'that with your help I shall soon be *persona grata*.'

'I can't help, you know. I don't really live there. But,' I said, sincerely, 'you won't have any difficulty in making yourself well-known.'

'Yes? Yes. That is gratifying. I am going for post-graduate study on a scholarship,' said Mr Raj. 'I am to write a thesis on Popular Conceptions of Racial Differentiation. I must go about and be talking with the people. I must be welcome in all classes of society, from the highest to the lowest. It is the initial impression that counts. That is why I am so grateful to you, sir, Mr Denham, that you will be helping me to ease my feet into new shoes.'

'But how, what? Adressing a Borough Councillor, using a knife and fork, giving the correct tip to the senior waitress of a tea-shop? For my part –' Mr Raj was standing to smiling attention, prepared to listen. Young Wicker said:

'I'd better go back.' I felt sorry for his blubbered formless face, behind which, like a sinus pain, moved a wretched nostalgia for his brother Tim, Nigger his cat, his very own half-bottle of black-labelled champagne.

'You've got the station-wagon?' I said. Wicker nodded. Mr Raj said:

'Naturally I know how to use a knife and fork.' He smiled brilliantly at Wicker. Wicker blushed, hesitated as if he were committing some solecism of behaviour, as if Mr Raj's statement might or might not be a sort of delicate fishing for an invitation to dine in a white man's house and whatever response one made or did not make would be wrong. So Wicker said:

'A happy New Year.' Mr Raj was delighted. He wrung Wicker's hand like a wet towel, pummelled his shoulder like one washing shirts on a river bank, saying, 'Yes, yes. A very happy New Year. A very, very happy New Year. For you in your new country and for I in mine. And for Mr Denham, the citizen of the world, in whatever place he shall be in the twelve new months which are just beginning. And,' he concluded, to Wicker, with very heavy humour, 'a most happy New Year to Nigger your cat.' He smiled with his nostrils widely splayed, as though he thought that this was how Wicker, the white man, would like him, the dark man, really to look. I very speedily got young Wicker off the premises and into the Company station-wagon, then wandered round, in the warm odorous dark, hoping that Mr Raj would not find me. I listened to the sea and to a couple of collective nightmares from the ravens, then I returned to the hall of the hotel, entering cautiously. By the notices advertising church services, visiting violinists, an amateur madrigal concert, there was, to my relief, no Mr Raj, smiling, ready to pounce. I crept up to my bedroom.

In the morning I went to the airline office and was able to antedate my flight home.

'The day after to-morrow, then,' said the Singhalese clerk. 'There has been a cancellation. But,' he looked up at me with suspicion, 'the cancellation was Mr Raj's cancellation. Mr Raj was my old scholmaster. You were Mr Raj's old schoolmaster. Mr Raj and you were to travel together.'

'He discovered,' I said, 'that I was not the Mr Denham he had previously thought I was.'

'I see.' The clerk looked up at me with reproach. 'The day after to-morrow, then.'

I went to the Company offices and typed out my report on young Wicker and also, gratuitously, an account of how Taylor had left things before going to Zanzibar. Taylor would do as much for me one day. Then I bought belated Christmas presents. For my father, a small Buddha's tooth to hang on his watch-chain; for Beryl, a cheap sari whose colour, I was assured, would run in the wash; for Veronica Arden ear-rings of coral; for Ted Arden a clump of the hellishly strong cheroots popular in Jaffna, one of which I hoped he would give to Cedric. On my last night young Wicker had me in to dine on chicken curry. The exile's tears were out of his system now: he sat at the head of the table, fingering the stem of his wine-glass like a man. We had each a half-bottle of Australian claret. He was grateful for my help, but he would not, if I did not mind, see me off at the airport: he hated seeing people off. And so, next morning, Mr Raj had me all to himself. He said, smiling brilliantly in the sun, the whole terminal behind him like his palace:

'It was such good fortune, Mr Denham, such very good fortune that there was a last-minute cancellation. One of the intending passengers, an Englishman, was drunk in the town and broke his leg. He is now in hospital. But,' he wagged his finger roguishly, 'you should have told me of your change of plan. I did not give you my address, but my address was safely recorded in the airline office. Still, perhaps you were labouring under the press of other preoccupations. I forgive you,' he said generously. There was still hope for me, however – this was an FT flight; perhaps it was a tourist cancellation.

'I take it,' I said, 'that you're travelling tourist.'

'Ah, Mr Denham,' he said, 'I am already up in the world. I travel to my post-graduate studies in style.' There was nothing more I could do: whatever the seating arrangements were, Mr Raj would be equal to modifying them. And so he was. We took off at last, Mr Raj enchanted by everything – the Chief Steward's inaugural lecture, the charm and helpfulness of the stewardess, the quality of the glucose sweet he was given, the prospect of prolonged proximity to my person. From Colombo to Bombay he talked about his unhappy childhood, his father a poor tea-plantation worker but frequently drunk, his saintly mother, the difficulty of equipping his sisters with reasonable dowries, how he and his brother had struggled hard with their studies and achieved, the one – that was to say, himself, R. F. Raj – a university scholarship, the other – P. Raj – a place in a solicitor's office. He spoke of the beauties of the Colombo Plan, of the post-war opening-up of the great world to humble men like himself. Then we had lunch, and he praised every course, stabbing into the food vertically with his right-handed fork. After lunch he saw that I was sleepy, so he read every article in *Punch* anxiously, as though he expected me to examine him *viva voce* when I awoke. Feigning sleep, I watched him, horribly fascinated. We landed at Bombay in blinding rain and, drinking tea loudly in the refreshment-room, Mr Raj gave me a comprehensive account of this city-island – history, population, administration, flora, fauna, ethnographical distribution. And so on to Karachi, where we had a long wait. Fortunately, I met one I knew, and I drank with him, in desperate exclusiveness, at the bar, seeing, from the tail of my left eye, Mr Raj giving a long lecture to a tired Englishwoman and her two fractious children, laughing frequently. Back on the aircraft we had dinner, which Mr Raj praised. Then, as we approached the desert-towns of the Middle East, lights were dimmed and people tried to sleep, stretched in their slumberettes. But this was the time for Mr Raj to talk of his abundant sexual experience, as though there were something erotically exciting in the fact of people lying down, the black night all round the purring aircraft. Mr Raj spared me no details, sounding the whole gamut from twelve-year-old Tamil girls to Parsee matrons of fifty. He had read the great Sanskrit manuals, he said, and had con-scientiously worked, like five-finger exercises in all the major and minor keys, through the prescribed techniques. Then he asked me about my sex-life. What I could tell him seemed inadequate and shabby. 'But,' said Mr Raj, 'you have had experience outside my field. You have been with European women, and I have not. That,' he said, as we sped west, 'is something for me to look forward to.'

'I know nothing about *English* women,' I said, 'nothing at all.' And, as Mr Raj lay back complacently, I felt a queer apprehension which I quickly shook off—the height, the pressurised cabin, I thought. Mercifully, Mr Raj slept till the first of the successive dawns that the perpetual putting-back of time imposed on us. Coffee and Mr Raj in barbed-wire Damascus, beer and Mr Raj in cedared Lebanon. Mr Raj on economics, the internal combustion engine, Tagore, the Upanishads, ice cream, the legs of the stewardess, the state of his bowels, the best place for a hair-cut in Colombo, the correct way of making a curry, his father's jokes, till lunch—which he praised—with Athens beneath us, Mr Raj, approaching Rome, on the glory that was Rome. At the Ciampino airport Mr Raj began, for the first time, to exhib-it signs of shyness. 'This is your world,' he said, 'the world

81

of Europe. See, I am perhaps the only black man here.'
When we got to Düsseldorf, I showed off my little bit of
German. Mr Raj's teeth chattered with the cold; his eyes
looked hunted. And so the final leg to London. 'Do not
leave me,' said Mr Raj, 'it is your duty to stay with me.'
He looked furtively at the white-skinned cool ground-host-
esses, listened like a dog to the rough London talk of the
porters.

'Where are you going?' I asked. 'Have you booked a room
anywhere?'

'I have to report to-morrow morning,' said Mr Raj, 'to Mr
Ratnam. To-night I have made no arrangements.'

'How about your brother?'

'I will be very honest with you, Mr Denham. My brother
and I are no longer on speaking terms. The whole of the
U.K. is perhaps just big enough to hold my brother and
myself.' We were standing outside the airport now, waiting
for our luggage to be loaded on to the bus. Mr Raj was
wearing a very thin overcoat; he shivered. 'Look,' I said,
'I will take you to a hotel. You have English money?'

'I have traveller's cheques.' So we made the long ride to
the airline terminal and I took Mr Raj in a taxi to a large
central hotel full of fur-coated and cigar-smoking Levan-
tines. As we waited for the lift to come down, Mr Raj,
looking hunted still, said: 'We will meet to-morrow? We
will travel up together? Please, Mr Denham, do not
altogether desert me.'

'I've got business to-morrow. I don't quite know when
I'll be through with it. But you'll be all right, Mr Raj.
Your own people will look after you.'

'My own people?' he said reproachfully. 'I am a citizen
of the British Commonwealth. You too are my people.' I
was rebuked. 'What is your address?' he asked. 'Assure me
that I shall have one friend in a big heartless city.' And

then I found, as often happens, especially after many years in the East, that I couldn't remember my father's address. I said:

'There is a public house called the Black Swan or Mucky Duck.' I told him how to get to it. 'I shall be there the day after to-morrow, Saturday. Say seven-thirty. Then, if you want to meet people –' The lift-man, a Hungarian refugee, was waiting with refugee's patience. 'A Flayer's ace,' I added, for some reason.

'Thank, thank you, Mr Denham. You are a real friend.' And he was taken up.

I went to my own hotel where, having been warned by cable (charged to the firm) of my arrival, my Italian widow was waiting up with cognac and *Il Giorno*. Also, with news for me. She said:

'A lady and a gentleman have been here looking for you. A very pretty young lady. The gentleman not so pretty but with very nice eyes.'

'Who? How?' Then I remembered I'd forgotten to buy her a present in Colombo. The sari, of course. She'd never wear it or wash it, wouldn't see how inferior it was. Beryl could do without.

'They said they thought you might be back. They know nobody in London, they say.'

'What name?'

'An impossible name. I could not pronounce it. But the gentleman left a note for you.' She waddled to her sideboard and, from a rattle of old rosaries and a clink of duplicate keys, produced an envelope. I took it with apprehension, somehow cognate with what I had briefly felt on the aircraft, approaching the desert cities, seated next to the reposing and complacent Mr Raj. The note was signed boldly W. Winterbottom, the 'bottom' rather more assertive than the 'Winter'. I read:

'You were quite right about my wife being an adulteress. You cannot go on living all your life like that, so I have come to London to start a new life with Imogen. When we can get our divorces through we will get married. Your father showed me a letter from you with your address in London on it. When you get back from India will you come and see us at the above address? I have no job yet, but I don't think it will be long. Yours sincerely –'

Well. There was I, the middle-aged commercial, smiling fatuously at the ravens of Colombo, belching comfortably over my after-dinner brandy, pottering about in the sun, getting young Wicker settled in, fundamentally bored, and there was a great gestation of love proceeding in the suburbs. A month, not much more than a month. I looked at the address – a very small hotel in West Kensington. They wanted money, of course. I hardened my heart, thinking of the incredible ingenuousness of Winter the printer's system of morality: you reject, with righteous disgust, the game of adultery in the suburbs, only to plunge into the full-dress real thing – double adultery, the world well lost. Then my heart softened: there was, at least, something romantic about this, an attempt at large-scale Arthurian myth. But I also felt cheated, left out of things. It was not fair that so much went on behind my back.

7

I arrived in West Kensington fairly early the following morning – that is, at about half-past nine. I turned off a curious street which still forbade German bands, into a smaller street which probably forbade nothing. The hotel that Winterbottom and his fellow-sinner had chosen was really a sort of superior lodging-house that hooked its finger on to respectability with a name that Beryl might well have thought up – The Trianon. I had to ring and wait. I gazed down the street, at whose corner dead respectability seemed to heave and churn like a miasma. A woman, grey and in grey, just up, yawning and crumby, came at last and I asked for Mr and Mrs Winterbottom. She yawned the direction – first floor, Number Three. I said, trying to be pleasant: 'Why is this hotel called The Trianon?'

'Eh?' she said, waking up. She seemed about to say, 'If you've come here to be funny –' But she gave an answer which might have pleased Earl Russell: 'Because that's its name, I suppose.' She looked after me as I went up the stairs, as at someone with more hidden bombs of subversive speculation. I knocked at Number Three, and there was the noise of a bed being bounced, a whistling of wraps, a rattling of money in trousers being drawn on, the cry, 'Just a minute.' Then Winterbottom's face appeared, bearded. A lot had been going on behind my back. It was a young beard of bristling straw, part of a new persona which was even aggressive about asserting the 'bottom' of the name. 'I knew you'd come sometime,' he said. The room had the awful naked shameless look of lodging-houses – no pictures or even cheap ornaments – and there were open suitcases on the floor. Warmth came niggardly from a gas-fire, more generously from Imogen. She sat up in bed with a wrap around her, tawny, tousled, showing a magnificent throat and white full arms. I wondered whether she would tell me to bugger off, but she smiled and said, 'Hallo'.

'This,' I said, 'comes as a great shock. This I never expected.' There was only the bed to sit on, so I sat on it. Winterbottom half-lay on it, nearer the pillow, and started to stroke Imogen's right arm. She smiled.

'She failed,' said Winterbottom dramatically. 'She never had any real conception of what love is, that's her trouble. Nor,' he added, 'did I.' He stroked more vigorously.

'I see. And how long has this ménage been operating?'

'We had to get away,' said this new Winterbottom of London. 'We've been here a week. We're going to make a life together.' Printers are not necessarily more literary than other men; I expected all the clichés from Winterbottom and I got them. 'Only the two of us matter,' he said. 'We've given up everything for each other.' It was now Imogen's turn to speak. She said:

'Don't talk so bloody wet, Billy. We're trying it, that's all. We're giving it a try-out,' she said to me. 'He needs looking after, poor devil.'

'No,' said Winterbottom. 'We love each other. I never knew what real love was,' he repeated.

'And where do I come in?' I asked.

'I forgot to bring my winter overcoat,' said Winterbottom. 'And tell her that I've no hard feelings really, but I can't send her any money. And don't tell her where we are.'

86

'And what's she expected to do about all this?'

'She'll be all right. Now she can marry that blasted ice-cream butcher of hers.'

'But I always thought that wasn't really the idea,' I said. 'I thought the idea was just to swop partners at week-ends. An innocent suburban game, like tennis.'

'Well, it's gone past a game,' said Winterbottom. Imogen took from under the pillow a square of nut-milk chocolate. She gave half to Winterbottom, and they both looked at me solemnly, munching their breakfast. 'I hope she realises now where that sort of game can lead people,' munched Winterbottom.

'It seems to have led you to falling in love,' I said. Winterbottom was confused. I thought of that odd theology which praises Adam's sin because it produced such a Redeemer. Winterbottom would not be equal to that double-think.

'I'd say it was all a hell of a mess,' I went on. 'What are you going to *do*? I mean, is anybody going to do anything about divorce, for example?'

'He'll give it me now, the bastard,' said Imogen. I remembered what she had told her father and myself and the taxi-driver on the evening of her arrival and said:

'He acquiesced before, didn't he? Or perhaps I shouldn't say that.'

'You can say what the bloody hell you like,' said Imogen. 'Billy here takes me as he finds me. I'm in London now. I'm going to see a bit of life.'

'We both are, dearest,' said Winterbottom. 'Together.' She smiled with great sweetness and kissed his yet un-clothed neck. His shirt needed washing, I noticed.

'How long has it been?' I said. 'A month. A little over a month. People can't make up their minds as quickly as all that.'

'Oh, yes, they can,' said Winterbottom fiercely. 'It's the

87

only kind of love. You meet somebody and you know that's it. And Imogen felt just the same.'

'He needs looking after,' said Imogen, putting a bare arm round him. 'The way that bitch treated him.'

'Oh, she was all right,' said Winterbottom. 'It was just that she didn't seem to understand about marriage. But I'm going to ask her for a divorce. And then Imogen and I will be married.'

'Yes,' said Imogen. 'But we'll have to see, won't we? And, in the meantime, what do we do for money?' She smiled so blatantly at me when she said that that I had to smile back. They munched their sickly breakfast in and on bed, and I was struck by the social gap their accents represented. Their voices seemed for an instant to freeze and be held as for a photograph in the cold air above the bed – Imogen's not patrician but stage, with a stratum of goodish girl's school beneath, Winterbottom's plebeian, pinched, with the impure diphthongs of all industrial towns, bloodless. They were a queer pair. I could see what he could see in Imogen, but not what she could see in him. I still could not believe that a Wagnerian gale, with eight harps and four tubas, had shaken the suburb and blown down the aerials: one needs a love-potion of great potency to accomplish that in a month. But I saw that Imogen's glances at Winterbottom were, though affectionate, healthily calculating, smiling, mocking, tolerant: she looked at him much as she'd looked at her father. She was not entranced by any new big magic. He was probably nicer to her than any man had been for some time; he might conceivably be a comfort to have in bed. He was, I noticed, clean-looking and not badly made. But I had a feeling that, in this running away to London with Winterbottom, it was the curiously sensual allure of the town (so grey and ascetic a town) that had excited her far more than her partner in double adultery:

she had run away to London with someone who was, accidentally, Winterbottom.

'Are there any other messages you want me to take back?' I asked.

'Tell Daddy not to worry, I always land on my feet,' said Imogen. 'Tell him that I just had to do something and that Billy here's very nice, really.'

'Right,' I said, getting up off the bed, 'I'll give him that message when I give him his three hundred quid.'

Winterbottom looked startled, as if he'd never heard of so much money before. He was not quite well enough brought up to conceal his curiosity. 'Oh,' Imogen said, 'that's for Daddy's book of poetry. Mr. What's-his-name here's going to back it.'

'An investment, is that it?' asked Winterbottom. Imogen laughed. 'No, he's just sort of throwing it away,' she said, 'for the glory of lit-er-a-ture. We might as well be honest with you,' she said to me, 'and tell you that *we* could do with that money more than Daddy. His poetry's waited long enough. We are, except for my fifteen quid in the Post Office and the little bit that Billy got from flogging Alice's TV set when she wasn't there, quite, quite broke.' On the last phrase the repertory actress came out – ironic, with a roll of the r.

'It wasn't all Alice's,' said Winterbottom. 'It was half mine.'

'That's not the point,' said Imogen. 'You tell Mr What's-his-name what you had in mind.'

'Well,' said Winterbottom. 'It's an old hand-press, you see. A chap's got it in a cellar. It's only for small jobs, of course, but that's all I've been used to. I met the chap in a pub – where was the pub, Imogen?'

'Somewhere,' she said, 'not too far from here.' They were both very vague about London. 'But that's immaterial.'

'There's a chance of a small shop,' said Winterbottom, 'with a couple of rooms downstairs. A basement flat, they call it. What I thought was, if I could get a bit of a start –' He was embarrassed, pulling at the hairs on his chin as viciously as if they were hairs in his nose. I sat down again, to listen.

'You want to print things,' I said. 'What sort of things?'

'Oh, the sort of thing I can do. Our firm wasn't much of a firm. It was more like a shop, really. We did programmes and the parish magazines and club membership cards. I never told them I was going,' he said gloomily. 'I never gave notice or said a word or anything. Perhaps I ought to write to them.'

'You're a sort of John Bull Printing Outfit printer,' I said, not without scorn. And he was growing a beard, as though getting ready to become William Morris. 'You want me to lend you the money to make a start, is that it?'

'You'd soon get it back,' said Winterbottom doubtfully.

'Why lend?' said the bold Imogen. 'You were going to *give* it to my father.'

'I still am,' I said. 'I think.' And then I said, 'You're asking me to finance your ménage. Your father's need is an honest one, perhaps even an honourable one. But you two have run away, breaking up two marriages. Now you want to pretend that you're starting something that's going to be stable, that's going to last for ever and ever. And you know it won't. And you want me to finance you.'

'It *will* last for ever and ever,' said Winterbottom passionately.

'We don't know,' said Imogen. 'Nobody ever knows. But as for the bit about finance, the answer's yes. Daddy's got a job, Billy here hasn't. If you've got money to give away, for God's sake give it where it's needed most.'

I became very moral and said, 'You want me to finance

something that's immoral.'

'Oh, you and your bloody immoral,' said Imogen. 'You sound just like Eric.' The peculiar venom with which she articulated the name showed me that it was her husband's.

I was stubborn, though God knows what right I had to be stubborn. 'You're breaking up two marriages. Go back, for God's sake. Give them both another chance. I mean, everybody makes mistakes. But you can't just break up marriage like that. If you let it happen once, you'll let it happen again. Go back. Give it another try.'

'I didn't break it up,' said Winterbottom, with his new London ferocity. 'She broke it up. You said she was an adulteress. I'd never really thought of that word before. She smashed everything to bits. Everything. And she still expected me to believe her when she talked about *love*.' He wanted now, I could see, to sneer out the word again with a bitter laugh, but, I could see, he felt that would defile the word and the new experience it represented. As I expected, he took Imogen's wrist in a firm grip.

'You could have smacked her on the arse,' I said, 'if you want plain speaking. You could have locked her in the bedroom or the lavatory or somewhere. You could have stopped her little games.'

'They didn't have locks,' mumbled Winterbottom, the literalist to the end. Imogen laughed. 'And,' he said, 'I'll thank you not to use that word in front of –' He cast round, bewildered, for a non-pejorative term that would indicate Imogen's status.

'Your mistress is what you mean,' I said. 'Arse,' I repeated loudly. Imogen thought this a great joke. 'Oh, all right,' said Winterbottom. 'You can all laugh at me.'

'I'm not laughing,' I said. 'I'm serious. But I'm not going to help.'

Imogen was surprisingly cool about it. 'You think, then,'

she said, 'that it's better for people to live in hell just because, once upon a time, they thought it was going to be heaven. What I mean is, you expect sober people to abide by promises they made when they were drunk. You think marriage is more important than happiness.'

'People shouldn't get drunk,' I said. Then she tore into me:

'Oh, what bloody right have you got to talk about marriage and happiness and all the bloody rest of it? You smug single sod, sitting in the sun with your bloody money.' The air was filled with brief spray. I brushed an *s* off my cheek. 'Don't start giving me your pious bloody aphorisms about the sanctity of marriage and keeping things stable and the bloody rest of it, while you're away fornicating with Chinks and Japs and what-not. You ought to have tried marriage, that's what I say, before you decided to set yourself up as a bloody marriage guidance expert. You ought to have tried living with bloody Eric for a few years, gone what I've gone through.' She saw my very slight grin and said, 'Oh, you know what I mean.' And then, very viciously, 'Yes, you might have made a lovely pair, the two of you, sitting before the fire and blah-blah-blahing about the sanctity of this and the bloody inviolability of the other, marriage is a sacrament and all the rest of the High Church bloody twaddle.' There was no doubt about it, she was an extremely desirable woman, flushed, tawny, becoming more naked as the violent words shook the wrap off her shoulders. The room now felt really warm. I looked at my watch and said:

'I think perhaps we ought to go out and have a couple of drinks somewhere, and then we could go somewhere else and have lunch.' Quick as a flash, Imogen said:

'We don't need your bloody charity.' But I was ready for that and joined in with her, with just her intonation, on the second word. She had to laugh, but Winterbottom looked very uncomfortable. 'It's this beard,' he said, stroking its thinness. 'I don't think it's really ready yet, you know, not for going out anywhere.'

'Shave it off,' I said. 'You can start again when you come home.' I looked round at what they had to call home. Was I condemning them to this? Of course not, stupid.

He looked at me seriously. 'But it's such a waste,' he said. 'I've had it for nearly a fortnight already.' In other words, he'd started it before his adulterous elopement, growing it as a new organ of courage.

'It's pretty,' said Imogen, kissing it. 'They'll just love it, Billy-boy, you wait and see.' She rolled out of bed, her nightdress stuck into her rump.

'If,' I said, 'you're going to get dressed, I'd better go and wait somewhere, hadn't I?'

'There's the breakfast-room,' said Winterbottom, 'but they don't serve breakfast any more. Still, that's what it's called.'

'Don't be bloody wet,' said Imogen. 'He knows what women look like.'

'I wasn't thinking of your modesty,' I said. 'I was thinking of – er, Mr Winterbottom's.'

'Well-named,' said Imogen, crouching, facing me, by the gasfire. 'As you'd know, if you'd slept with him. God, it's bloody perishing this morning. Whatever made you come back from India or wherever it was?'

'I'd done what I had to do. It was Ceylon.' And then, 'If you've been here a week, you must have come just about Christmas.'

'Boxing Day,' said Winterbottom proudly. 'She was the best Christmas box I've ever had.' Then I felt a sort of mixture of pity and admiration for them, thinking of their journey to a cold empty city while others gorged, warm, on cold turkey and bubble-and-squeak, tickets for the pantomime on the mantelpiece. But they wouldn't get a penny out of me.

Imogen, in a wrap, dashed, burring with cold, out of the room to, presumably, the bathroom. Winterbottom and I were alone. He stood manly in front of the gasfire, putting on his collar and tie, and said :

'I still think we did the right thing. Life shouldn't be all pretending.'

'You can set that up,' I said, 'as your first printing job, and send a copy to my sister Beryl.'

'You *will* help?' he said, hopelessly. 'I'm sure I can make a go of it. I don't really need much. A couple of hundred.'

'But you don't really know me. It's not as though I'm a close friend you've known all your life. I'm a complete stranger, somebody just passing through. I mean, you've no claim on me.'

'Oh, that,' said Winterbottom, trying to fix his stud. 'Oh, no, it's not a question of *claiming* anything.' The gas-fire sank, sang urgently its hoarse swansong, exploded out. 'Oh, damn,' said Winterbottom, 'it just *eats* money. I don't know how we shall manage.' He found a shilling, fed it in, and relit the re-born fumes. Fire danced merrily but coldly again. 'But as an investment,' he continued. 'Or as a loan.'

'I'll think about it,' I said weakly. 'But it's the morality of the whole thing.'

'Don't say that,' he whispered in fright. 'She'll be in again in a minute.' But she was in right away, glowing, yet looking cold as only a woman can look cold. 'Bloody freezing,' she trembled, holding herself as if there were a small flame at her navel. She began, in a business-like manner, to put on the strapped and elasticated garments with which a woman sneers delicately at gravity. Winterbottom had to fasten things at her back and she yelled 'Jesus Christ' at his frozen butter fingers. Stockinged, smartly suited in green, high-heeled, she feather-finished, kissed her moving lipstick, lengthened her eyebrows, fought her hair with a comb, swearing, and then was ready. Winterbottom had a tie and a jacket on now, but said hopelessly:

'Oh, dear. I've forgotten to wash.'

'You look clean enough,' I said, wanting my first drink of the day.

'Oh, Billy, you bloody little nuisance. Go and rub yourself with my flannel. Dirty little devil,' she said, as he went out.

'Well,' I said.

'Well,' she said, checking her handbag.

'What exactly is going on?'

'He needs someone to look after him, you can see that,' she said, 'so don't start asking damn silly questions. What *is* your name, by the way?'

I gravely took out a business card and gave it to her. She grimaced over it, rocking her head sideways as though it was music and she was mockingly trying to show that she couldn't read music. 'Your real name, I mean,' she said.

'They all call me J.W. There is one man in Tokyo who calls me Percy, but, like Lucia in the opera when they call her Mimi, I don't know why.'

'Clever little sod, aren't you?'

'Enough,' I said. She put the card in her handbag. Winterbottom, his hands and face flannelled clean, came in in time for us to go out immediately. It was I who remembered to turn off the gas-fire. We walked to the tube-station and waited for a train to Piccadilly. Whatever I did I was doing wrong, like Archbishop Morton's victims. If I'd called a taxi I would have been a show-off, mocking poverty which I wouldn't help; to wait for a tube was a stamping, shivering, hand-blowing advertisement of my meanness. But we got to erotic Piccadilly after a journey

95

like a sleep, with Imogen and Winterbottom suspiciously checking the stops with the map that was set, like sweet geometrical reason, among the advertisements at strap-hanger's eye-level. Mouths slightly open, eyes raised, they seemed two innocent bumpkins up for the day. Occasionally they would look at each other and giggle. I, slouched opposite in my overcoat, felt sour and unloved: they would not get a penny out of me. A drink and a meal, however, they would get. I took them to a large new drinking palace which was no pub, a place with its own grim perpetual daylight. We had to climb to a hall of hushed carpet, full of pink and scientific comfortless chairs. Imogen pulled off her gloves with pleasure, saying, 'Ah! It's warm,' in her clear repertory voice, and every man looked at her. We sat at a table and, from behind the bar, a Juno of forty, a blonde in black at the peak of her large beauty, came for our order. She and Imogen took in each other in a quick animal glance. The woman said, 'And what will it be, gentlemen?' I smelt burning and said, 'We'll all have a nice dry sherry, shall we?'

'No,' said Imogen. 'I'll have a large gin and Italian. Large,' she repeated.

'Large,' nodded the woman. 'And Tio Pepe?' she suggested.

'Tio Pepe.'

The woman went off too slowly, huge, shapely, dignified, and must have heard Imogen say: '*Large* is just about it, isn't it?' And this tawny poet's daughter laughed.

'Now,' said Winterbottom, 'please, Imogen, don't start anything. I mean, nobody's doing you any harm.'

'Manners,' said Imogen briskly. 'Nobody has manners any more. I didn't like the way that bitch looked at me, and I didn't like the way she said "Gentlemen", and I didn't like the way she said "Large".'

'All right,' I said quickly. 'Let's anticipate, shall we? Your gin and Italian will be too warm, and there won't be a twist of lemon in it, and it will taste remarkably weak. Right? This is obviously that sort of place. Complain now, to me, and let's get it over. After all, I brought you in here.'

Imogen pouted and said, 'Oh, you're too bloody clever to live, aren't you?' But, when the drinks came, she giggled to find that my prophecy had been only too accurate. She sipped and, while the Juno woman gave me change, said with great charm, 'This is really excellent, you know. First class.' The woman looked puzzled, and I whipped her off rapidly with a large tip. 'Thank you, sir,' she said, more puzzled. The smell of burning receded.

This Imogen was, I foresaw, going to cause Winterbottom a lot of distress. She was already like a pain to him — other men's eyes on her, wondering what she would do next, the intolerable sweetness of her clothed and inaccessible body. And now she said:

'Where are we going to eat?'

I was ready for that one, but only just. I had thought of the Café Royal, but Imogen had warned me off with visions of plates thrown at waiters. And there was the question of Winterbottom's beard. I said:

'There's a charming little place near here where they have chickens in the window turning all day long on electric spits. They'll send out for a bottle of stout for you and they don't mind if you gnaw the bones. And they serve chipped potatoes.'

Imogen looked at me with suspicion and said, 'I don't like stout.'

'Well, beer then, or Beaujolais, or whatever you want.'

'I don't quite get that,' said Winterbottom, 'about stout and bones. I mean, I don't see the connection.'

'Oh, Billy,' said Imogen, 'don't talk so bloody wet.' The

97

ears and eyes of the male drinkers were drawn again to that clear stage voice and its possessor. 'Let's go now,' said Imogen. 'I can still taste bloody chocolate.'

Winterbottom was born to more embarrassment than seemed his fair share. As we walked down a narrow street full of fruit-barrows, a couple of teen-age girls in tight trousers and pony-tails rushed on him in delight, armed with autograph-albums. 'Johnny Crawshaw!' they called, and two other, smaller, girls appeared from behind a barrow. One screamed, 'Johnny!' and the other ogled and simpered, 'Oh, sign my book, Mr Crawshaw.' They had mistaken him for a very nondescript skiffle-group leader much seen on commercial television. When Winterbottom denied that he was Johnny Crawshaw and told them that his name was Winterbottom, the girls were first derisive, then angry. They called 'Winterbottom!' after him down the street and made rude remarks about his beard. Imogen laughed gaily and said, 'Oh, Billy, you are a bloody fool.'

But soon we were sitting down to a half-chicken each with hot golden potatoes. Imogen having said that she didn't like stout, ordered stout, and Winterbottom and I had a bottle of Bass each. Hot fat glowed in Winterbottom's beard. He ate with rare concentration. 'This,' said Imogen, 'is a bit of all bloody right.' We had pancakes afterwards, and Winterbottom suddenly looked distressed. He said:

'Oh, dear, I'll have to go.'

'Where to?'

'The lavatory. Oh, dear, it's just suddenly come over me.' He twisted and fidgeted and looked round. Imogen called to the waiter:

'Hey, where's the gents?'

'The ladies, madam?'

'The gents.'

'We haven't got either,' said the waiter with deep satisfaction. 'You'll have to go to the tube-station.'

'You hear that, Billy?'

'Oh, dear.' And he was off in his beard and raincoat. Imogen laughed and said, 'Poor little Billy. He's terribly bloody sweet.'

'Is he?' I asked. 'I mean, is this really the real thing?'

'Oh,' said Imogen. She put down her pancake-fork to say seriously, 'Yes. Billy's all right. He needs somebody to look after him. He doesn't pretend he's the big strong man and knows it all. He doesn't pretend to be much good in bed, but he is, you know.' The waiter, chewing a match, hovered, interested. 'You bugger off,' said Imogen, casually. 'Bloody nosy parker.' And to me she said, having chewed up her last bit of pancake, 'He reminds me a bit of Daddy. I shall look after him.'

'Will you marry him?'

'I don't see why not. It wouldn't be too bad.' She drank off her stout and wiped her frothed lips. Then she said:

'How long are you here for?'

'Where? Here in London?'

'Here in England. Before you go back to your Javanese or Japanese girl friends or whatever they are.'

'I haven't got any.'

'Ha ha ha,' said Imogen. 'How long?'

'Well, I was a month on the voyage and a month at home and a month in Ceylon and I'm going back by sea. Another month. Why do you ask?'

'How would you like me to be your girl friend?'

'Say that again. I didn't quite——'

'You heard,' said the calm strong voice. 'I'll be your girl friend as long as you're in London. A flat rate. Say, two hundred pounds, payable in advance. That's fair, I think.'

'But, good God, I mean, you've only just run away with another woman's husband. Damn it all, where does Winter-

99

bottom fit into all this?'

'Sex,' said Imogen. 'You make too much bloody fuss about sex. You think sex is the same as love.'

'I certainly don't. I never have done.'

'If I'm your girl friend it doesn't mean I love you and not poor little Billy. I just give you sex. But,' she qualified, 'not too much of that. I'm somebody you can take around. That would be nice for you.'

'No,' I said. 'Thank you very much. I'm highly honoured and all the rest of it, but no.'

Imogen began calmly to make up her face. 'That was a nice bit of chicken,' she said. And then, 'All right, I shan't make you another offer. You've had it now. But you'll be to blame if I start doing anything worse.'

'I accept no blame for anything. You ought to spend a nice quiet evening sorting out your own moral position,' I said. 'You can leave me out of it.'

'All right,' she said. 'But you might at least give us some money. Just to get poor bloody Billy started.' She made an O of her mouth and lipsticked it. I sighed. She finished her operations, smacked her lips complacently at her compact-mirror, and snapped the compact shut. Then she turned to me, as if to give me all her attention. The waiter brought the bill.

'I'll give you fifty pounds,' I said.

'A hundred.'

'Seventy-five,' I said. I brought out my cheque-book in its nice gold-stamped leather case. I brought out my heavy business-man's fountain-pen. The waiter came back and said, 'Sorry, sir. Payment strictly cash, sir, if you don't mind.'

'You,' said Imogen, 'keep your bloody big nose out of it. The cheque's for me, not for you.'

'Sorry, I'm sure,' said the waiter, adding heavily.

'madam.' He went off huffily. Imogen sighed a woman's satisfied sigh as she folded the cheque and put it away in her bag. Then Winterbottom returned, looking paler and thinner. 'I hope you were long enough about it,' said Imogen.

'It was the lock on the door. I couldn't get it to open. A man had to come along and open it from the outside.'

'Oh,' laughed Imogen, 'poor little Billy.' Those seemed, at the time, to be definitely his epithets.

8

Chugging to the Midlands next day, seated opposite the one inevitable *Times*-reading clergyman who is reserved to sit opposite every rail traveller in whatever otherwise empty first-class compartment and who is, for all we know, quite possibly God, I watched the sad sordid little story unwind on the telegraph wires. It was all I had to occupy my mind after the bumpy lunch, being ashamed to read the low-class magazines I had bought in the presence of a *Times*-reading clergyman. I had dismissed, or been dismissed by, Winterbottom and Imogen after the previous day's golden chicken and pancakes: fed and beered and stouted, they had showed signs (footy-footy, held hands, bold eyes, vacuously smiling lips) of now asking nothing more than each other in bed. I, feeder and cheque-giver, went off like a sour Pandarus, having handed Imogen a couple of pounds as ready money against the opening of the banks next morning. They had told me nothing more of the outer history of their love, but I saw it all so clearly. Alice had drawn Winterbottom into the game with no difficulty, sensing at once in Imogen the qualities that he would fall for, having earlier fallen for them in herself. Publican and poet had bred the same sort of lavish-limbed, loud-laughed, full-bodied women, wearing confidence like a perfume. But she should have recognised that Winterbottom was a man for sonatas rather than sextets and that, anyway, the sextet is too big a combination for this light-hearted week-end music.

So, soon, the sonata was played in one room and the quartet in another. And then, one day, the sonata-players thought they were good enough to be professional, packed their music and the one portable instrument, and made off for the big world. It had to happen that way.

The train advanced through the drugged afterlunch towards the true afternoon of closed pubs and station bars. The clergyman opposite me, a very big man in his sixties, suddenly laughed quite loudly at something in *The Times*, something apparently so good that to read anything more in those long-nosed columns would, apparently, be anti-climatic, for he put the paper, which rustled like a skirt, on the seat beside him. I smiled wanly at him, shifting my bottom on my hidden magazines. He nodded vaguely and, having read close print with his naked eyes, now put on spectacles and yawned at the landscape. The three sudden pawnbroker O's of glasses and open mouth gave him a slight look of Selwyn, so I spoke. I said:

'What, sir, is your view of morality in the world today?' It seemed a fair sort of professional question. The clergyman looked first contemptuous and then charitable and said, to the floor and my cigarette-ends:

'My view of morality is, inevitably, the orthodox Christian view. You say, "In the world". Is there, then, such a thing as morality out of the world? You add, "Today." Can, then, good and evil change with the times?' He had an intimidating sort of refined West Country voice. 'A nonsensical question,' he said, and coughed with loud satisfaction, smiling on the moving drab acres as if they were his own, turning to me then with the pendant 'If you don't mind my saying so.'

'Not at all, not at all,' I said. 'After all, that's one of your jobs – rebuking people.' And now, without shame, I was able to take one of my low bookstall magazines from under my bottom. On its cover was a young woman in opera stockings and black underwear, kneeling, smiling stupidly up to heaven with proffered bosom, an acceptable sacrifice. I started to read an article about flick-knives. The clergyman coughed, leaned forward, and said, 'Morality. You may have expected –' I looked up, patient sweet attention, from the flick-knives. '– expected me to say that there is more immorality today than ever before, because, of course, there are more people in the world than ever before. But I cannot say that. There must, of course, be more evil acts, but evil is not a matter of arithmetic, after all. It is a spiritual entity beyond mensuration.'

'So,' I said, 'there isn't more evil now than there was when Cain and Abel were strapping lads?'

'No. Well, in a sense no. It just had to be realised, that's all. Made flesh. In the medium of time.'

'*Had* to be? Why had to be?'

'My dear sir –' He leaned closer. Soon we were in the middle of a blazing theological argument in which he quoted Aquinas and Augustine and Origen at me, as well as Peter Abelard and Juliana of Norwich and *The Cloud of Unknowing*. He knew it all, by God, but it didn't help to put Winterbottom and Imogen more firmly in the moral picture. I saw clearly, as the train eased itself into my station, that they hadn't sinned against anything except stability. Why, then, should I feel so self-righteously outraged? The clergyman, was was travelling on to the North, said merely a curt 'Good afternoon' and took up his skirt-rustling *Times* again as I got out with my two bags and my magazines. When the train pulled out he would, I knew, vanish, slowly but firmly, into ether and, by operation of some time-warp or space-warp or something, be waiting to face some other traveller somewhere in another first-class compartment otherwise empty.

One of my bags was strongly taken from me and a known voice said, 'Mr Denham, you are here at last. I have awaited all trains today and am at last rewarded.' It was Mr Raj of Colombo, smiling teeth set in smooth milk chocolate which was dusted with a blue mould of cold. 'Not,' he said, 'that my time was wasted. I have asked many waiting travellers questions concerning racial relations and made copious notes of their replies.'

'Oh,' I said. 'I thought we'd arranged –'

'Yes, yes,' said Mr Raj, now wearing, I noticed, a smart and warm overcoat of a kind of cinnamon colour. 'Tonight. I remembered. I have already done reconnaissance of the place mentioned at the lift doors in London hotel and made myself known as your friend to the master of the place and his lady, and, moreover, been received with kind welcome. I have also visited that esteemed old man your father who, at first, believed I was selling carpets.' Mr Raj laughed. 'I enlightened him on that point and recommended a good medicine for his cough which, I fear, is troublesome. So, you see, young Mr Denham, I have not been idle.' I looked sharply at him, with an old colonial trader's suspicion of insolence, but he had tapped the 'young' just hard enough to render it harmless. I stood now on the cold platform, the train preparing to pull out, holding one bag and my magazines while Mr Raj smiled and smiled, swinging the other bag gently, and I just did not know what to do. The station bar was closed, the winter afternoon gaped in an iron rictus, and there was Mr Raj, keeper of the keys of whatever door I wished to open. I said:

'All right. We'll go and have a drink at the Hippogriff.'

'I am very much yours to command, Mr Denham. Let me carry your other bag, sir, or at least your bundle of reading matters.' He felt himself free enough with me to parody the old-time native bearer. The train was ready to move north, nether steam bunching up like effects in a Faust-play, the pistons working up quickly to the vinegar strokes. We walked past the Station Master and the Telegraph Office and the Restaurant, stations of the Cross, and up the stairs and across the bridge and out to walls of posters and a taxi which Mr Raj hailed with slim hand and smiling teeth. I told the driver where to go, and Mr Raj said:

'One thing mars my felicity, Mr Denham, in this great and flourishing provincial city, and that is my difficulty in obtaining lodgings commensurate with position. I have been sent to low streets where West Indian negroes brawl and carouse in common lodgings, and that is not seemly. Your friends, the master and lady of the public house, I asked to accommodate me, but that they regretfully could not. Your father also I requested, but he stated that the other bedroom is reserved for your frequent homecomings. But, Mr Denham, I have not the slightest objection to sharing with you, and then, when you are away, I am able to keep the bed warm.' Warmly he smiled. I tried to smile back, aware of teeth all tartar near the gums, tobacco-stained below, and said:

'We will find you something really commensurate with your position.' Then Mr Raj sat up royally in his seat, his nose flared with pride, smiling from side to side at the pavements of shoppers. Soon we came to the Hippogriff, and Mr Raj was out fussily with my luggage like a paid companion, bargaining with the driver to my shame, calling him rascal and robber. The driver said, 'I don't like being called names like that by a black man. You ought to be made to stay in your own country, that you ought.' I gave the driver five shillings and winked at him, but he didn't see the wink. Mr Raj said, as the cab moved off, 'You see difficulties here which must be analysed with scholarly precision. Racial prejudice seems to be rife among the taxi-driving classes.' I bade Mr Raj, still talking, follow me down into the hell-mouth of the Hippogriff Club. The face of Manning, who ran it, appeared at the glass hole in the door, nodded, grimaced on noticing my talking companion, then disappeared with the click of the opening lock. We went in. Rosy dimness, the juke-box, a couple dancing with arms round, respectively, neck and waist. Alice Winterbottom, née Hoare, behind the bar; seated at it, the one in gloom, the other near tears, the poet Everett and the Caribbean calypso-singer. 'Very pleasant,' smiled Mr Raj, 'very typically English.'

'The question is,' wailed the West Indian, 'where are we to go, man? My wife and I are British subjects. My child is also a British subject. Is it then considered right that British subjects should sleep in the streets?' But both Alice and Everett had recognised me and both spoke at once, sharply, as if I were to blame for something. Urbanely I introduced Mr Raj. Everett said, wearily:

'Yes, yes, Mr Raj is already well-known at the *Hermes* offices.' Alice said:

'You've seen them, haven't you? You've just come from London. Your father gave him your address. Where are they? What's going on?' She had lost no weight, no sleep. Her eyes were clear, her hair lustrous, her fine full body clothed in something smart and demure. Here, apparently, was one person whom Mr Raj had not yet met: he admired her with bold eyes, flared nose, all his many teeth. 'A very epitome,' he said, 'of the beauty of the English female.' The compliment was ignored. 'Come on,' said Alice, 'tell us what's going on.'

'I was asked to go round and see them,' I said. 'He wants his winter overcoat.'

'Is that all?'

'He said there aren't to be any hard feelings and that he can't send any money.'

'He can,' said Alice bitterly, 'keep his blasted money.'

'He didn't seem to have any,' I said. 'I had to give them some. He wants to start up a little business. At the moment they're living in what one might call extreme squalor. I took them out for a meal.'

'I do not think,' said the admiring Mr Raj, 'that I have yet had the honour of real introduction.'

'Where are they living?' asked Everett. 'I can't allow it, I just can't. After all, she is my daughter.' He drank some brown ale. I remembered that I was thirsty. Courteously I asked Mr Raj what he would like. 'Whatever you yourself are going to have, Mr Denham.' Alice sharply uncapped two brown ales and poured, saying. 'He can keep her, that's what he can do. And she can keep him.'

'I think she probably will, you know,' I said. And Alice said, nether lip over nether teeth, 'Little bitch.'

'Come, now,' said Everett, 'I'm not having that. Who started all this anyway?' Alice turned on him, sightlessly putting a brown before Mr Raj, Mr Raj saying, 'Thank you a thousand times, beautiful lady.' Alice said:

'Couldn't we all have a bit of fun without everybody getting all serious about it?' The juke-box record gave a loud jazz Amen and hissed out. 'All we wanted,' said Alice, too loudly for this sudden shock of silence, 'was a bit of fun.'

'All right,' said Manning, emerging from the cloak-room which was also his office, putting his hand on the shoulder of his West Indian singer, 'give us a bit of a song, boy.'

'How can I sing when I am homeless?' said the West Indian. 'Could you sing if you had no home?' Mr Raj nodded gravely, his eyes smiling. He said:

'I myself have been directed to common West Indian

lodgings. I think it is, perhaps, better to be on the streets than call such a place a home.'

'Are you now,' said the singer irrelevantly, 'speaking as a British subject?' He had his guitar clasped firmly round its neck. 'You do not look to me like a British subject.'

'I am of the British Commonwealth and I am a B.A. and I am here to do important research on race relations,' said Mr Raj with dignity.

'You *must* give me their address,' said Everett to me. 'I demand it. I dread to think what will happen to her, poor little girl, penniless in London.'

'I gave them seventy-seven pounds,' I said. Everett looked at me, doubtful, thinking of the Collected Poems. The West Indian, now heeding his master, sat on a chair and began to sing:

> 'It was love, love, love and love alone
> Made King Edward give up his throne.'

'What,' I asked Alice, 'are you going to do?'

'Do?' She stared at me with malevolence, wiping a glass. 'I'm going to get a divorce, that's what I'm going to do. And then when he crawls back to me it'll be too late.'

'He says he's in love,' I said.

'Love,' she sneered. And the brown voice over the guitar echoed:

> 'It was love, love, love and love alone
> Made King Edward give up his throne.'

'And till the divorce comes through?'

But she didn't answer. Two men had come in, overcoats open showing prosperous waistcoats, one with an old-time watch-chain. They ha-ha'd rosily in the rosy gloom and she gave them a welcoming barmaid's smile. Mr Raj, who had been talking with animation to a gloomy nodding Everett, turned to these newcomers with glee. 'I have not,' he said, 'yet had the pleasure of meeting you.' He announced his name, his provenance, his qualifications and his present project and eagerly said, 'It would be of inestimable assistance to give me full views on problems of racial relationships.'

'Look here,' said one of the men, 'we've only come in for a couple of quick ones before opening-time. We didn't come in for nothing serious, did we, Robert?'

'That's right, we didn't.' This man squirted soda into double whiskies.

'You have no desire to talk about important problems which may affect felicity and even ultimate existence of the civilised globe?'

'Not now,' said the man who was not Robert. 'Some other time.'

> 'It was love, love, love, and love alone
> Made King Edward give up his throne.'

'You are admitting, then, to frivolity of attitude to important global problems?'

'Anything you like,' said not-Robert. But he added, 'You certainly speak English good for a native. Where did you get all them jaw-breakers?'

'All right,' said Manning, coming over and frowning at me. He put his hand on Mr Raj's sleeve and said, 'People come here to have a good time, that's all. To have a bit of fun. That's the English way, you know.'

'Yes,' said Mr Raj, nodding. 'I see, I see. 'The Caribbean song came to an end:

> 'It was love, love, love, and love alone
> Made King Edward give up his throne.'

Manning went over to the juke-box and fed it sixpences. 'I see,' said Mr Raj. 'The English are wise in their generation. We must still learn from them.' Mr Raj took off his overcoat, displaying a well-cut lounge-suit of grey herring-bone, looking lean, handsome and distinguished. Music with a slow steady beat to which one's gut vibrated in sympathy, triplets on the piano, then an epicene voice breaking its vowels in the glottis—to this the amorous couple, returned from a dark corner, danced. Mr Raj watched with benevolent Asian eyes. Unfortunately, Alice chose this moment to leave the bar to go, presumably, to the ladies'. Mr Raj, afire and ashine, advanced on her with wide arms. 'Do me, most beautiful lady, the inestimable honour of a dance.' Alice retreated. 'Go on, love,' said not-Robert. 'Hands across the sea. Stop him talking for a bit.' And then Mr Raj, quivering with his first white woman in his arms, was on the tiny floor, dancing well.

I spoke to Everett. 'She's got her own life to live,' I said, 'and I'm quite sure that Winterbottom will look after her.'

'I have,' said Everett, who, I noticed, had been maintaining a steady intake of brown ale, 'certain premonitions of harm. Poets have the prophetic gift. The poet is also the *vates*.' He hiccoughed. I felt sorry for him and said:

'We must discuss your Collected Poems again some time.'

'Never,' he said violently, 'never. I don't want your patronage.' And he hiccoughed again.

'No,' I said, 'sorry, I was forgetting. Your little *feuilleton* in the *Hermes*, yours and my sister Beryl's, recording in the files for all time my crude nabob's philistinism. All right, forget it.' I looked round, buttoning my overcoat, seeing Mr Raj occupied and happy. Now was my chance to steal away. 'No, no, I didn't mean that,' said Everett feebly. My two bags were near the door. I foolishly began to tiptoe towards them, forgetting that carpet and music deadened my footfalls anyway, that Mr Raj, twirling gracefully and ecstatically, could see me quite clearly anyway and was not likely to let me out of his sight, and that, even if he did, he would have no difficulty in finding me again. And, in full confidence, he now called over the music:

'You will now go to see your father, Mr Denham, and prepare for the evening. We shall meet again later and continue to have bitter fun.' And then, as I opened the door, the West Indian came up to me and said:

'It is not fair, man, what this foreign man is doing. He is trying to get Mrs Alice to give *him* the spare room in her house and not myself and my wife and child, who are all *real* British subjects. Please speak to her, sir, and tell her which is the real deserving case. And please, sir, show apprisieshun of the music.' He held out a cloth cap. 'Thank you very match.'

'Yes, yes,' I said, 'yes, yes, certainly,' as I laboured up the stairs with my bags. My magazines had disappeared somewhere, but never mind. In the winter dark, ringing with football editions, I limped along to the bus-stop, this being no town for cruising taxis. The bus was full and, in order to keep an eye on my bags under the stairs, I had to sit in the lower saloon. There I could not smoke and a child called Elspeth tried to crawl all over me. 'Stop that, Elspeth,' the mother kept saying.

9

My father had aged more than my month's absence. He gave, before and on opening the front door, a symphonic cough of welcome, pathetic as the report of ill-usage one's cat will make when one returns to it after a holiday. And, like the cat one has trusted the neighbours to feed, he was thinner. Yet how far could I, who had my own way to make, regard myself as responsible for him? I bit off my guilt with the Buddha's tooth for his watch-chain, and he coughed and coughed over it. He swigged something from a sticky black bottle, breathed painfully, then more freely, then—after I had turned from getting Ted's present and Veronica's out—performed his bad film continuity trick: a white-hot cigarette-butt protruding like the tip of a cat's tongue.

'Letters for you, lad,' he said, but there was nothing important except grateful thanks from young Wicker in Colombo and a standing invitation to drink a half-bottle of anything with him any time: thanks that, judging from the postmark, had travelled with me and Mr Raj. 'I gather,' I said, 'that you've had a visit from a coloured gentleman.'

'He thinks the world of you, lad,' said my father. 'But I couldn't have him staying here, even though he is a friend of yours. Not really. I'm a bit (cough cough cough) old-fashioned about having blackies in the house.'

'They'll be in all our houses,' I said, 'blackies of all colours, before the century's over. The new world belongs to Asia.'

'All right,' said my father. 'Now then, I bought a few pork sausages for our tea. I thought you'd like those after all that curried rice and so forth.'

'Sausages,' I said. 'Yes.' I grilled them brown and also put cheese and celery on the table. I was home again, high tea by electric light, winter-crisp celery, draughts whistling from the radio football reports, the flop of the football edition of the *Hermes* on the door-mat. But there was a new flavour I could not at first identify; then I remembered – Mr Raj in the suburbs, a breath of turmeric and coriander to season our cold meat. I, who would be free of him soon, would be free only to return to his world, or something like it. I washed up and then joined my father in front of the tonic-water-coloured screen. The brutal man with the hat, our weekly friend, told us of our duty to assist the State Troopers to be violent with High School drug-addicts. He nodded his way out to grim music, and then two girls sang a shampoo-song, a meat-cube banquet was dished and served, a cat purred for a cat-medicine, a small boy ate bread with unnatural relish. The lady announcer smirked in a new dress and said we were going right over, meaning herself. She span out into the dark, my father coughed and coughed, and then we were ready for the Black Swan or Mucky Duck, a Flayer's ace.

'Was it hot there?' asked my father, cold on Clutterbuck Avenue.

'Warm,' I said. 'Not too warm up the hill.' Then I said, 'You ought to go somewhere warm. Just for a holiday. I don't like that cough.'

The cough, thus drawn attention to, cracked out again vigorously. 'I'll be all right,' coughed my father, 'when it's spring.'

'You ought,' I said, 'really to come back with me. The sea voyage would do you good.'

'No,' my father said frankly. 'It's time you got married, and I don't like living with in-laws. And if you don't get married,' he said, brutally frankly, 'what should I feel like getting mixed up with geisha girls or whatever you have about the place?'

'Who told you about geisha girls?'

'Oh, I guessed about it. And this Indian friend of yours was on about superior potency. He seems to think the world about you in lots of ways.'

'Oh,' I said. Mr Raj had been purely Orientally and fancifully complimentary ('so great a man, his *lingam* as long and thick as a tree, the father of whole villages') but this, I must tell him, would not do in a Midland suburb. We had arrived at the Black Swan, and we entered a great close singing summer of noise and thirst and light, the Saturday jam-pack that breathed, over the sweat and discomfort, the exciting promise of venery afterwards. But not for me. My father's cronies had saved a seat for him, but not for me. I joined the queue of present-givers at the bar, standing behind a wedge of Lancashire cheese, a Fairisle pullover, home-bottled plums and a musical tankard ('Bloody marvellous, that is,' said Ted, holding to his ear the drowned tiny tune.) Blushing at their inadequacy, I handed over my Jaffna cheroots and coral ear-rings. 'She'll love them, me duck,' said Ted. 'She won't get nothing like them round ere. She'll be dying to wear them, bloody marvellous she'll look, and what's this ere? Cigars. You couldn't ave given me nothing better,' he said sincerely. 'I love a good cigar. Ere, just ave a look at these, Arnold.' I blushed further with pleasure and felt more and more mean, hiding in a glass of light ale. And then along came Mr Raj.

'I apologise,' he said, 'for being late. But, in a sense, I am not late.' He smiled against a background of bar-drinkers, holding up for my inspection a pint glass of mild beer. 'I have,' he said, 'been in other room, learning intricacies of local game. You must stand many feet from round numbered board and hurl pointed weapons at highest possible numbers.' A small man, hunchbacked and with glasses, listened open-mouthed and serious to this, his beerglass suspended. 'An educational game,' said Mr Raj. 'I have also been obtaining opinions of the working classes on this over-riding matter of racial relations. I am never idle,' he told with flared nose-wings and cheesy smile the parade of bottles behind the bar. 'Much useful work can be done in the hours devoted by others to pleasure. But now,' said Mr Raj, 'I am ready for harmless pleasure with you, Mr Denham. Let us, ha ha, begin our evening of bitter fun together.' He spoke better than he knew. Kindly our bar-neighbours watched Mr Raj down his pint of British workman's beer without too much trouble: he smiled round at the end of it, nodding modestly. I bought him a small whisky as a reward and, remembering, asked how his search for lodgings was progressing. Mr Raj said:

'Pardon me, Mr Denham, but it is not, strictly speaking, *I* who am properly engaged now on such a search. You said distinctly in that rude man's taxi that *we* would now be engaged on it, taking "we" to mean perhaps yourself and the rest of the interested community. But,' he said, watering his whisky well, 'I have already made enquiries of this lady I met this afternoon, the lady with whom I was dancing, and I have hopes that she shall eventually give me room in her house, her husband, so she tells me, having left her and the house itself hers, it being a wedding present from her father and mother who are prosperous publicans.' Mr Raj held a quick smiling pose for a photograph to be captioned 'Tireless Ceylonese Research Worker'. After the imagined flash he drank watered whisky thirstily. 'The principle of a person whose skin is not white making such a request was already earlier established, the negro from the West Indies having almost begged on hands and knees for such favour. Though,' looking round in amiable challenge, 'what, after all, *is* colour?' Nobody could answer this, too philosophical a question for Saturday night. 'It is, in a sense, a duty,' said Mr Raj. 'I am here, a member of the British Commonwealth, engaged on important research, and it is unseemly that I live in, as at present, infamously expensive hotel room. Negroes are, I told her, a lowly race, and this one merely sings songs to a stringed instrument. It was not seemly for him to make such requests. Moreover,' said Mr Raj, 'is there not here an opportunity, useful for a post-graduate student of race relationships, to learn more precisely of the general attitudes of white women to men of different colour? Though what,' looking round in amiable challenge, 'after all –' He remembered just in time that he had asked that question already, then he smiled at me, no speck of disingenuousness in his brown Colombo eyes.

'It can't be done,' I said. 'It just can't be done. Think it over carefully and you'll see why it can't be done.'

'Oh, yes,' nodded wise Mr Raj, 'oh, yes. It can and will be done.' Then he bought me whisky and himself mild beer, enquiring carefully about the price of each separate item, asking politely but firmly why he was charged more for beer in this room than in the other. Ted, playing all his percussion instruments – bottles, glasses, till and pumps – said:

'We charge more in this room than in the public bar, me duck.'

'That I have already pointed out. I merely ask why.'

'Because this is the best room and we charge best room prices.'

'But that is a bigger room and has also musical instrument and game with arrows.'

'That's the way it is, me duck.' Cedric, hovering near with swilling tray, gave a tiny waiter's sneer. Mr Raj said to me:

'There are many social inequalities. Those men in the other room are really your untouchables. All these undemocratic things will have to change.' And he nodded almost grimly. Maplike patches of beer-damp on the counter showed me China spilling over into India and India into Europe. I shivered and discovered that I had a cold coming.

Mr Raj talked on – about the admirable amenities of the town, the beauty of its women and the peculiar sumptousness of legs seen through nylon, the quality of coffee in an espresso bar he had visited, a film he had seen, some peculiarly-clothed long-haired youths he had addressed politely but who had rebuffed him. And then there was the sense of closing-time aproaching and then the mixed doubles came in.

I had not really expected them. I had supposed vaguely that, since Winterbottom and Imogen had broken the rules of the game, the game would no longer be played. But here they were – Jack Brownlow's wife and the slice of melon, full of seed, that was Charlie Whittier; Jack Brownlow himself and Alice in her beaver lamb. I wondered why they looked different – coarser somehow, somehow unsavoury – and then realised that I was not watching their performance through Saturday night haze from a distant chair; I was actually on the stage with them, I could see pores staring through make-up, leg-hairs flattened by nylon, a shaving cut on Charlie Whittier. And then, inevitably, Mr Raj had to thrust in his brown but handsome nose, greeting Alice Winterbottom with two brown hands clasped over her white one that was warm from its doffed glove. Mr Raj's eye were whisky-and-beer-bright as he gave gallant greeting. He said:

'Most beautiful English lady, I am here as I said I would be. Let me, first, offer thanks for the delightful bitter fun of this afternoon, That, I assure you, was new experience for me, of bodily and spiritual import. Second, let me again make, in all sincerity, renewed requests to share your abode. I come from Ceylon with the highest credentials.' Mr Raj spoke in a drink-flush of eloquence. He pressed and pressed Alice Winterbottom's hand in the rhythm of a cat dilating its claws. Alice evidently didn't know whether to giggle or be angry. Charlie Whittier and Jack Brownlow's wife looked on with goldfish mouths. But Jack Brownlow was not pleased. He said to Alice, 'Do you know this bloke?'

'He came in,' said Alice, 'into the Club. With Mr What's-his-name here.'

'Is this bloke a friend of yours?' Jack Brownlow asked me. Mr Raj meanwhile smiled with wide wings at everybody, his long brown hands caging still, like a bird, the smaller warm white one. I said :

'Yes, he's my friend.' The claws of my infant cold had started scratching my soft palate. Mr Raj nodded and nodded, beaming, saying :

'Mr Denham is my very, very good friend.' He dropped Alice's hand and tried to seize mine. He challenged the room to challenge this declaration of friendship, looking round proudly, and saw, through smoke and a momentary gap between packed and chattering bodies, my father coughing soundlessly. 'Both Mr Denhams, the senior and the junior, the young and the old.'

'Well,' said Jack Brownlow, 'tell him to leave this lady alone.'

I didn't like Jack Brownlow's voice. 'He speaks very good English,' I said, and then sneezed. 'As you may have noticed,' I said, blinking. 'Tell him yourself.'

'You,' said Jack Brownlow, 'leave this lady alone.'

'I have not yet had,' said smiling Mr Raj, 'the pleasure of introduction. My name is Raj. I am here from Ceylon to conduct research in your university. If you will tell me your name I shall be happy to make your acquaintance.'

'Never you mind my name, and I don't care about yours. Leave this lady alone.'

'Why?' asked Mr Raj, dedicated seeker.

'Because I tell you to.'

'That is not very adequate reason.'

'I know your lot. I've been in India, helped to save your lot from the Japs.' I did quick sums in my head—Brownlow's probable age, the years the war was over: Brownlow was lying. 'Leave her alone.'

'I am Ceylonese, not Indian.' The evening had reached its maximum centrifugal phase—pairs or, at most, trios talking hard, the women absorbed in obstetrics, the men in football and cars—and no heads turned or voices quietened to attend to snarling Brownlow or smiling Raj. Alice said:

'Oh, stop it, Jack. Buy us a drink, time's getting on.' I sneezed.

'Drink with me,' said Mr Raj. 'Everybody drink with me.'

'I wouldn't drink with a Wog,' said Jack Brownlow, 'not if it was the best champagne.'

Mr Raj said cheerfully, 'I think the term you used then was intended as term of opprobrium. It was much used in Ceylon and in India by the lesser and more vulgar sort of white men.'

'Go on, get away,' said Jack Brownlow, turning to order drinks.

'Drink with me,' smiled Mr Raj at Alice. 'It will be a pleasure to buy you drink after the pleasure you, gracious lady, accorded me this afternoon.'

'Now stop it,' said Alice, friendly. 'You'll only get yourself into trouble. He's a bit of a boxer, you know.' Mr Raj surveyed with interest the back of Jack Brownlow. Alice motioned me with doorward eyes, head and mouth to get Mr Raj away. But Mr Raj said, 'I too, who am Bachelor of Arts, have studied arts of self-defence. But to-night we are having bitter fun and wish neither for harsh words nor fisticuffs.'

Jack Brownlow, turning from the bar to hand round full glasses, saw smiling Mr Raj, swaying slightly over Alice, and believed he saw what he, one-time imperial master, had read and heard confusedly about – namely, insolence from a member of a subject race. He said, 'I'm telling you for the last time – leave her alone.'

'Again, respectfully,' said Mr Raj, 'I must ask for your reasons.'

'I've told you already – because I say so.'

'Oh, for God's sake, stop it,' said Alice, 'both of you.'

'But,' said Mr Raj, 'there is the question of your authority. You are not the husband of this lady, her husband having gone away and left her, nor, I think, are you her brother. You are not old enough for her father nor for her uncle, and you are too old for her nephew or her son. So I ask for your authority. Perhaps, of course, you aspire to be her lover. In which case I grant you some slight authority. But perhaps I too might have temerity of the same aspiration, and then *I* ask *you* to leave the lady alone.' The terms carried no nuances for Mr Raj: this speech was more insulting in its effect than in its intention. Jack Brownlow said, 'Why you –' and seemed to make a move towards Mr Raj.

I had again the impression of cut film. Seconds seemed to have been missed out somewhere, for there was Jack Brownlow on the floor, on the bar a glass that rolled in an arc across its spilt contents solemnly counting him out, drip by drip, on to his head. Mr Raj seemed to have done nothing except execute a forward feather-step. Cool and smiling he looked down at the floored Brownlow, saying, quick-witted and loud, 'Poor fellow, perhaps it was the air that did it. The air in here is very thick.' I don't think anyone outside the five conscious of us took it for other than a faint. Seeing the body, everyone except Mrs Brownlow and Alice seemed pleased, their evening – just before the bell – crowned with somebody else's misfortune, their own superior capacity making the men guffaw, male inability to take it making the women tut-tut. Ted, not so pleased, handed over a glass of water. Mrs Brownlow, inexplicably, turned on Alice: 'I thought you were looking after him. You can't be trusted, you see. Lost one husband, after somebody else's, and it's me who'll have to take him home.' Mr Raj nodded and smiled at everybody, giving the official hand-out: 'It was the heat, yes, yes. Very close in this, which they call the best room. It was the heat and the bad air.'

'Let's hear less about the bad air,' said peeved Cedric, loyal to his pub. 'You and your Black Hole of Calcutta.'

'Calcutta,' said pedagogic Mr Raj, 'is not in Ceylon. It is in Northern India, former East India Company trading post, now great and prosperous city and no black hole.'

Alice Winterbottom, for some reason, answered Mrs Brownlow's vilification with a fit of the giggles. I suppose my growing cold prevented me from seeing the fun, bitter fun, of the situation. Nobody seemed willing to take Jack Brownlow out into the cold air, not because of any lack of altruism, but because it was nearly closing-time and it was necessary to snatch a last drink. 'Leave him there,' said somebody fat and authoritative. 'It's dangerous to move 'em when they've chucked a dummy. Let him come round in his own time.' So the overflow of last orders dripped on to Jack Brownlow and on to Mrs Brownlow who, kneeling by her husband, said, 'Speak to me, Jack. Speak to me, love.' Charlie Whittier looked scooped and thwarted; Alice Winterbottom continued to giggle, but one could see now that the giggles would modulate through laughter to weeping and possible cries of 'Oh, Billy, Billy, why did you leave me?' Selwyn peered round from the public bar, offering open mouth and flashing glasses in interest. And then the bell clanged. Mr Raj said to Alice: 'Do not be afraid. You will not have to go home alone. It will be an inestimable and completely platonic pleasure to escort you hence.' Then came Alice's laughter.

Ted shouted, 'Come on, all of yer, on yer way now, the police car's round the corner, there's a new sergeant on duty and e's a real bastard, oh, come on, me ducks, aven't yer got no omes to go to?' Jack Brownlow was now borne on many shoulders, like Hamlet in the film, and Mrs Brownlow wept after, like a widow. Ted whispered to me, his breath redolent of little arves, 'You stay be'ind, me duck, and we'll try them cigars.' And then he kissed and hugged everyone out, and we all went to the door to see Jack Brownlow laid in the biggest car available, all except Alice and Mr Raj. And now Alice began to weep, decently, quietly, as I returned, and Mr Raj considered putting comforting arms about her but, smiling, thought better of it. As I had expected, Alice now sobbed for her lost husband. Mr Raj and I looked at each other, our arms flapping at our sides like empty sleeves. 'Oh, Billy, Billy,' sobbed Alice. While we two stood, doing nothing, both Mr Raj and I shy of touching an Englishwoman, Cedric burst in from the gents and became fussy and capable. 'Oh, you two,' he said. 'She's upset, can't you see that?' And he was on to Alice, saying, 'Come on, my dear, don't take on so. My car's just down the street.' And he fussed her, weeping, out, throwing at Mr Raj the words 'Bad air, indeed'.

'Well, Mr Denham,' said Mr Raj, 'contact at last is, meta-phorically if not literally, established. Now you will be going home to your father who seems, already, to have gone. And I go to my hotel room, there to pass a lonely night amid railway noises. But you will walk with me to my bus.'

'I've got to stay,' I said, now wretchedly aware that my cold had settled in. 'I've got to see Ted Arden. About business,' I added. Actually I wanted to drink rum, rapidly, that being my own particular cold-cure, though, like all cold-cures, quite inefficacious.

Cedric ran fussing back. 'She's forgotten her hand-bag,' he said. 'I *do* think somebody round here might help a little.' He went off to the back-door again, swinging the bag. 'Tell Ted I'll be back in five minutes,' he said. Mr Raj said, smiling, witty:

'And black hole to you too.' Cedric ignored this but banged the door sharply. Mr Raj said, 'So I go home alone. Now, Mr Denham, what are our arrangements for tomorrow? What time do we meet, and where?'

'Tomorrow,' I snuffled, 'I shall be in bed. I have a heavy cold coming. And,' I said, watching Mr Raj ready to become a nurse emptying bed-pans, 'don't, whatever you do, come near me. If you catch my cold you'll really suffer.'

'For you, Mr Denham, I am prepared to suffer.' I groaned. Mr Raj stood stiff, heroic, a chocolate soldier. I said:

'An English cold can be fatal to anyone coming from the tropics.' So Mr Raj suffered me to see him to the door, where Ted was loving and kissing off the last of the voluble. After many expressions of good-will, eternal amity like the palm to flourish, thanks for a pleasant evening, anticipatory thanks for many more to come, hopes for a happy future, Mr Raj went off, a formidable upright figure in his new overcoat, hatless, a tropical man walking into the black winter night. Ted said, 'Queer bugger that is. It Jack Brownlow, quick as a flash, right in the goolies.'

'You saw that?'

'E ad it coming to im, me duck. I didn't let on when e did it so quick like. E did it real gentleman like. But e'd better not do it again. Not in *my* pub.'

As we performed the usual chores—Selwyn, Cecil and myself, Ted being in the cellar with dipsticks, Veronica nowhere to be seen—Cecil, in wasp-sweater, growled some obscene song of the early nineteenth century, a song about sailors begetting little bastards in the Rowlandson ports of England and then going back to climbing the rigging and being keel-hauled. Then Selwyn stopped wiping, looked into space with his three face-holes, and said, 'Ah can see im, mister. Ah can see is car coomin rahnd corner nah. Nah car stops an e gets aht on it. Nah e blaws is naws wi big ankichief. Naw e cooms in back-weeeh.' And, indeed, Cedric entered, stuffing a handkerchief into his trouser-pocket, saying, 'She'll be all right now. A bit upset, but she'll get over it.' And he tut-tutted at the glasses I had wiped and began to wipe them all over again. Meanwhile my cold sent out more shy fingers and began to tickle my bronchii. I sneezed again, miserably.

Soon we were all drinking rum, breathing sweetly on each other, and smoking Jaffna cheroots. Ted said, 'And a very nice little smoke too, me duck.' Cecil and Selwyn smoked theirs impassively, Cedric rabbited his nose at his and then stubbed it out. I kept on with mine, coughing and coughing. I mimed that I was afraid I might be disturbing – that is to say, if Veronica were——

'She's away, me duck. Gone off to er mother's Er mother suffers that bad from er stomach. Like coals of fire, she says, every time she tries to eat onions. Loves onions, she does.

125

Ere,' said Ted, animated. 'I'll bring 'em down for you to see, seeing as the wife's away.'

'Regurgitated onions,' I thought, 'preserved. No, no.'

'You're a reading man,' said Ted, 'and a shooting man. I'll bring down me dad's books and me own guns.' He was off, and then could be heard thumping up the stairs, then bumping boxes about above. Selwyn turned on me the gun of his open mouth, his blind bright glasses, saying, 'You, mister. You bin aht er coontry.'

'Ceylon,' I admitted.

'Aaaar' said Selwyn, dancing a slow backward dance, his rum dancing, gleaming, in his hand. 'In drims ah sin them furrin paaarts. Chinks an indoos an all. In drims ah've spocken to 'em. Strenge words ah've spock. An nah ah can see woon black man from them paaarts, bein bitten oop.'

'What do you mean?' I asked. 'Who's being bitten up?'

'They're on to im,' said Selwyn, with sibyl's eyes. 'Lads bittin im oop fer bein from them furrin paaarts. Aaaar, ah can see.' I would have demanded more of this vision if Ted hadn't at that moment appeared, hugging a box under each arm. 'Ere we are, me duck,' he said. 'Me guns.' And then, as new rum was poured, I was encouraged to handle and admire a whole history of armaments — highwaymen's pistols, a blunderbuss, a rifle from the Crimean War, heavy service revolvers, a slim hand-bag model for a lady killer, a Mauser. Soon, fascinated, we were all clicking and levelling, and in Selwyn's eyes walked, slowly, in grim procession, all that these weapons had killed.

'Why,' I asked, 'why do you keep them?'

'A obby, me duck. I love guns. Ammunition I've got, too. And to defend the ouse, of course,' said Ted vaguely. Then I looked at Ted's father's books, mildewed, unread in this century, garnered from street barrows. Among the titles were:

A Tooth-comb for the Hair of the Ungodly
Sermons of the Rev T. J. Purlwell, D.D., *Vol XI*
Martyrs of the Great Rebellion
John Manwell, or The Story of an Eager Heart
Transactions of the Corresponding Societies
Maude's Hebrew Primer, Vol I
Eureka: Thoughts on Agnosticism
Work for the Night is Coming
The Anatomy of Systematic Doubt:
    Talks to Working Men's Clubs
Lady Brendan's Indiscretion
Educational Voyages Round the Ionian Islands
The Boyhood of Shakespeare's Heroes
Gems from Carlyle

There were others which I can't now remember, and my memory may have played tricks with some of the above titles, but I looked through these scarred and mottled books with a dull fascination, sniffling sadly to the dry peppery gun-clicks, and was about to open a thin quarto volume that looked older than any of these when there came an urgent rattling at the latch of the public-bar yard-door. 'Sup up them drinks,' said Ted, 'just in case.' We swallowed our rum then waited, innocent among the cocked weapons. 'Oo is it?' called Ted, moving towards the door. A known voice called in reply:

'Mr Denham! I must see Mr Denham!'

'Somebody wants you,' said Ted, unnecessarily. 'Oo knows you're ere?'

'Mr Raj,' I said. 'Let him in. He's harmless enough.'

'We don't want no more kicks in the goolies,' said Ted, but he opened the door and there was Mr Raj, near dropping, blood on his overcoat, the marks of violence on his face. He made a good sagging film entrance and collapsed on a chair. Selwyn said, impassive:

'It were im ah sin. Im as was bein bitten oop bah Teddy Boys.' He pronounced the last as though it were a man's name. Cecil said:

'His blood's the same colour as what yours or mine is.' Nobody seemed prepared to help: everybody, even Ted, gazed on Mr Raj as though he were a television programme. I poured rum into my glass and took it over and fed it into the head that rolled like an overturned glass on a bar-counter. He didn't seem badly hurt – exhausted more than anything: what seemed bruises were mostly dirt, some of the blood just couldn't – from the position of the smears on his overcoat – be his own. Mr Raj had been fighting hard, but he'd probably won. I asked what had happened.

'More of that drink, please, Mr Denham.' He was given more. Mr Raj drank quite deeply and said, 'I will smoke if I may, Mr Denham.' I gave him a cigarette and he puffed it unhandily. 'Perhaps,' said Ted, 'e'd like one of them cigars.'

'I,' said Mr Raj, always the soul of politeness, 'apologise for untimely intrusion. There are people here to whom I have not yet been introduced, but they will forgive me if I omit customary courtesy. Some young men in strange dress attacked me because they said I was not British subject. I told them I was a member of the British Commonwealth, but they said that they had not heard of that.' Mr Raj drank more, of rum and then of smoke, and said, 'So then they said they would hurt me because I was of wrong colour.'

'Bit you oop,' nodded Selwyn.

'How many were there?' I asked.

'There were five, Mr Denham, with very thin ties and very thick shoes. Three are now lying on the pavement of a street that leads from here to the main road of buses, and the other two ran away. They ran away shouting I was coward and dirty fighter.'

'You gave it 'em in the goolies, did you?' asked Ted.

'Yes.' Mr Raj smiled at the homely soldier's word. 'But I am very sad about this evening. I have to knock down four men all told. It is not for this I have come to U.K. I have come to study Popular Conceptions of Racial Differentiation. I have no strong desire to hurt people, believe me. And all I ask Mr Denham now is permission to accompany him home, his good old father by now being surely in bed and not available for noisy knocking up, my desire being to brush clothes and make general readjustments. I cannot enter my hotel like this or they will come to wrong conclusions.' He had perked up a good deal with the rum, sat up, smiling a smile now much qualified.

'You can do all that ere if you want to, me duck.' But now Mr Raj saw that Cedric had a gun in his hand and was absently cocking it. With great agility but a look of utter weariness on his face, Mr Raj rose, jumped the space between the chair and the bar, dove at Cedric and, in a flash, had wrenched the gun from him. It was the dainty hand-bag automatic, a lady's killer. 'I have had enough for one evening,' said Mr Raj. 'That I have struck down, in complete justice, white men to the tune of four is no reason why I should be summarily executed.' Mr Raj was certainly very good value. 'Have you no law here? Perhaps you have exported it all,' he said.

I was very tired, and now my sinuses ached. 'Come on,' I said to Mr Raj. 'Come back with me. Then I'll set you on your way.'

'I demand explanation,' said Mr Raj. 'I demand that the police be summoned. I am not to be shot down like a dog by a bar-boy.'

'What did you call me then?' asked Cedric.

'Look ere,' said Ted. 'Nobody meant no harm. All these

guns is mine. They're all unloaded. We was just aving a look at 'em. That's all.'

'Did he call me then what I think he called me?' asked Cedric. Nobody took any notice. Cecil said, surprisingly:

'My Mother Bore Me In The Southern Wild And I Am Black But Oh My Soul Is White.' He added, 'Learned that at school. Old Jim Morton, who's dead now, he made us learn it. Every week we had to learn off a different piece. Well, that piece is about everybody being the same underneath. Sisters under the skin, as another piece says, but that was a piece we never learned. Now, what call did them lads have to have a go at him here? He's the same as what they are.'

'I,' said Mr Raj, with proud nostrils but eyes dulling in fatigue, 'refuse to be associated with them.'

'That's what I mean,' said Cecil. 'We're all the same, there's no two ways about it. And if I wanted to go to bed with a blackie, where would the harm be?'

'In drims,' nodded Selwyn dreamily, 'ah sin em.'

'All right,' said Ted with startling sudden briskness, 'everybody out. Tomorrow at twelve sharp everybody welcome, regardless of religion, colour or creed. But now not. Everybody to bed. And I,' he said, leering as at something scabrous, 'am sleeping on me own tonight.'

Outside, Cedric said good-night without cordiality, Selwyn occultly, Cecil philosophically, and Mr Raj returned it with tired courtliness. He had had a busy day. Then he and I began to walk, arm in arm, towards my father's house, under cold northern stars that milled like fire-ants, in a night so coldly tense that one felt one could almost pluck it like a violin string. As we walked this open deck of the world, alien fleets flashing messages, I felt my cold already better: the two jets of sharp night in my nostrils seemed to snip at the tangle of cold-germs like scissors. Mr

Raj the voluble said nothing, did not even give me the name of an odd constellation.

I unlocked the front door of my father's house. My father coughed in his sleep in greeting. 'Shhh,' I warned, as Mr Raj stumbled in. 'That good old man,' mumbled Mr Raj, 'your father.' I led Mr Raj to the sitting-dining-room, switching on its light. Mr Raj blinked as the light leapt and held the pitiable little cube for living in its claws: my father's R.A.'s on the walls – outmoded, discredited; his doffed shoes by the fireplace; the fire out; the brass letter-rack stuffed with letters; the ashtrays stuffed with butts; the newspapers of a week in an untidy pile on a dining-chair. I dragged the electric fire from its corner, set it in the hearth and switched on both bars. Then I looked at Mr Raj. There were a few scratches, a bruise or two, dirt, blood. 'Sit down,' I said. He sat down in my father's arm-chair. 'Now,' I said, 'I'll bring things down from the bath-room. If we go up there we'll only wake my father. Hydrogen peroxide is good.'

'Whatever you say, Mr Denham.'

'I shan't be a second.'

'As many seconds as you like, Mr Denham.'

But I was rather more than a second. My bowels woke up at the sound of running water and barked for attention. Fingers were scratching the back of my eyes and the back of my throat: I had to gargle. When I got downstairs with towel and peroxide, ready to fetch hot water from the kitchen, I found Mr Raj asleep, snoring thinly, Asiatically. I couldn't send him back to his hotel now. I dabbed at the cuts and the bruises, thinking that he couldn't very well be left to sleep downstairs, either: my early-rising father would be puzzled, Mr Raj embarrassed. I jabbed Mr Raj on what was evidently a sore place, for he came up fighting. 'Come on.' I soothed, with bunged-up nasals, 'bed, bed.'

'Eh? Eh? Eh?' Only his pilot-light was burning. It was enough, however, for him to see his way upstairs, stumbling twice only. My father coughed and coughed, then turned over loudly and began to snore healthily, Englishly. I got Mr Raj, still in his overcoat, on to one half of the double-bed in my room. I took off his shoes. His feet were long, straight, well-socked. He would be all right in the morning. I wouldn't, however. I fetched warm pyjamas from the airing-cupboard in the bathroom, undressed shivering, put on battle-dress for what, I estimated, would be about a week's battle. I got under the blankets, shivering and shivering. My father called out his robust snores, Mr Raj answered with his thin ones. And here were Asia and Europe sharing one bed — one in, one on. I clicked the bed-switch and then one black blanket covered us both. Sleeping with a blackie. In drims ah sin em.

10

'So,' said my father, 'he reckons that's what he'll have to do. And he'll certainly make more money out of it than out of schoolmastering.' He was sitting on the edge of my rumpled bed, just back, by bus, from lunch with Beryl.

'And is Beryl happy about it?' I asked. My head was clearer. I'd sweated a good deal on whisky and aspirin.

'Oh, she says she's always liked Tunbridge Wells.' The brilliant day of fire and ice was declining. I had been aware of it intermittently since morning, the sun, like a kitten, pawing me out of my dozes. 'Though I can't see (cough cough) Henry as a tobacconist (cough) somehow.'

'How many seizures has he had?' I asked. I referred to Henry Morgan's father who, it appeared, had fallen in a stroke while serving twenty Gold Flake.

'About the tenth or twelfth, this is,' said my father. ' "Caesars" he always calls them. Rather an ignorant old man, a bit of a bore always going on about his Caesars. There's a book about twelve Caesars, I seem to remember.'

'Suetonius.'

'Yes. I knew it was something fatty. A limited edition, in Fell type italic for some reason.'

'Will it take them long to sell the house?' Now, I thought, my father was really going to be on his own.

'I shouldn't think so. It's becoming a popular sort of village with car salesmen and suchlike. I don't know why.'

'And what will you do?'

'What will I do? I'll be all right. I'm used to being on my own.' He coughed very thoroughly, as if, somehow, to prove this statement. 'I've never had to call on Beryl for anything. As for my Sunday dinner — well, I can always fry myself something special, something a bit different from the other days of the week. I can have a rice pudding afterwards,' he added.

'But you *might* have to call on somebody. I don't like that cough. And I'll be in Tokyo.'

'Now, lad,' he said briskly, 'if you're going to be on about that business again, I'm telling you once and for all that I'm not going to spend my decining days in any foreign parts, not for you nor anyone. I've lived in England all my life, except for North Wales which (cough cough) is England for all practical purposes, except for the people. I've lived in England, and I'll die in England.'

A fine sunset speech. The light slowly dimmed down on the cyclorama behind him. In my left hand I crumpled the courteous note that Mr Raj, quiet early riser, had pinned to his pillow. 'So as not to disturb you, Mr Denham, nor that worthy old man your father . . . both sleeping sleep of just . . . today I will collate my notes and, like British lion, lick wounds gained not without honour . . . tomorrow I will come with curry ingredients to make large Ceylonese curry, good for colds and sick chests . . . cannot forget or sufficiently repay your most hospitable kindness . . .'

'You know,' I said, 'perhaps I'm not being as realistic as I should be. It's very likely that I'll die before you do.'

'You're a fine healthy man,' said my father. 'Although you're fatter than you should be. I've coughed most of my fat away. But you'll die late, like all our family.'

'I wasn't thinking of dying in bed,' I said. 'I travel a lot. There are plenty of air crashes. You remember that plane

I missed, the one I should have caught in Bombay? I was lucky there, you'll remember.'

'You always were lucky.'

'I don't know. Anyway, every time I leave home there's always a possibility that it's for the last time.'

'Now, look here, lad, it's the cold you've got that's depressing you. It's most likely a touch of flu.'

'So I've got a right to ask a small favour before I go.'

'What sort of favour?' My father thrust out his lower lip, suspicious. Great splashes of plum and apple adorned the dying sky.

'I want you to take in a lodger.'

'My father rose, appalled. 'Lodger? I don't need any lodgers. I can pay my own way, thank you very much. Lodgers indeed, at my time of life. Now listen, lad. You just turn on your side and have a nice little sleep, try to sweat the cold out of you. And in about an hour I'll heat you up a tin of soup. Tomato soup, very hot, with toast.'

'You can't buy me off with tomato soup,' I said, 'however hot. This is my room, isn't it? That was agreed when you took the house. My room. Well, I want Mr Raj to have my room.'

My father shook his head very sadly. He pretended to think that I was delirious. 'If you mean the Indian gentleman, I've got to say no. Not because he's Indian,' he added quickly. 'I've nothing against his colour, though I'm getting too set in my ways really to start having new ideas about black men. It's the way I was brought up,' he said in apology. 'But I'm not having any lodgers, whether they're black, pink, yellow, or any of the colours on a snooker table. And tomorrow, when you feel a bit better, you'll see it the same way as I do. I'm going downstairs now,' he said. 'Give you a chance to get a bit of sleep. They've got a new thing on the Children's Television now, every Sunday. Something about the twelve apostles or something. Funny,' he mused. 'Twelve apostles, twelve Caesars. And I read somewhere that if we'd been born with twelve fingers instead of ten we'd have had a far better system of arithmetic. I wonder,' he said, 'if I really am getting too old to learn? Anyway, we'll talk about all that tomorrow.' He stumped his way downstairs, coughing into the stair-well. 'Hrrrodgers,' he coughed in contempt. He left me in the approaching dark, which was supposed to act as a sort of sleeping pill.

The next day the cold germs had evacuated my head and started to colonise my chest. My father and I woke about the same time, both coughing, as if the house were filling with poison gas. I heard him drawing his money-chinking trousers on, coughing, while I just lay in bed, coughing. His coughs downstairs seemed louder than usual, less inhibited, as though at last we spoke the same language and he wanted to show that he could speak it better. I got up at about ten-thirty and went downstairs, dressing-gowned, coughing.

Like a great cough from the East, Mr Raj came in by the back door just after eleven, smiling like the sun, a carrier-bag in each hand. 'I greet two coughers,' he said, accurately. 'I hope that one will soon be better. The senior Mr Denham's,' he said, with deadly Eastern realism, 'will perhaps only be better in the grave, which destination however we trust he will be long arriving at. Our young Mr Denham is a different kettle of fish. He has a great deal of life before him.' He smiled, and I had a sudden picture of the book from which Mr Raj had extracted his kettle of fish: made in India, a stolid inaccurate guide to the English of a former generation, compiled by A. A. Surendran, B.A., or Dr P. Gurasamy, very fat, ill-printed, ill-bound, full of examples of letters to lawyers and invitations to afternoon tea. I looked at Mr Raj with a kind of love. He said:

'As promised, we shall eat today Ceylonese curry. Neither of you shall stir. I shall cook all.' My father, above his *Daily Express*, looked at Mr Raj in wonder. 'Yes,' nodded Mr Raj, 'all. Without help. To repay infinite kindness.' He took his carrier-bags into the kitchen, then re-emerged to say, 'Those boys have already recovered. Black eyes I saw, as well as threatening looks, but no more. That was in the town, not far from my hotel.'

'And the other victim?' I asked, coughing.

'Of him,' said Mr Raj, 'I have heard nothing.' Then he went back into the kitchen. My father said:

'What's all this about victims?'

'Mr Raj,' I said, 'is a formidable man. Gentle but formidable. Do you like curry?'

'You know,' said my father, 'I don't think I've ever had it. Wait,' he said. 'In a Lyons place I once had curried beans on toast. That wouldn't be the same thing, would it?'

'No,' I said, 'not at all the same thing.'

My father, somewhat shyly, as though he had suddenly become merely a guest, went upstairs to wash and shave. He came down again to a smell of frying onions and loud chopping noises. 'I've got to go to the bank this morning,' he said, 'to see about some shares. I think really I'd better get myself some lunch in town. I mean, I'm a bit too old really to start anything new. Curry and so forth.'

'That,' I said, 'would be a deadly insult. There are some things you've got to learn, even at your age.' I think that was the nastiest thing I'd ever said to my father. But he merely said, 'Oh'.

'You know what I mean,' I said. 'How would you like that kind of slap in the face if you'd put yourself out for somebody?'

'All right,' he said, 'I'll be back.' And he coughed his

way out. I went into the kitchen, which had been transformed into a cool kind of Ceylon, full of ground turmeric, chillies, cardamoms, loud aromatic frying, busy Mr Raj. 'Can I help?' I asked. Mr Raj almost hurled me out, windmill-threshing, wild-eyed with his 'No, no, no, no. It is I who am to do this, you see, I.' So I crept away and hid behind my father's *Daily Express*, coughing at intervals. I did not smoke one cigarette that morning.

My father, returning in time for the one o'clock news, almost sidled in. Curry had taken possession of the house; he had the shy eyes of an intruder. And then Mr Raj, as one o'clock pipped out from the radio, mine host in an old apron he had found, white teeth and shining nose-volutes, clattered in saucers of sliced chillies, sliced bananas, coconut, cucumber, tomato-rings, hard-boiled eggs, sweet pickle, raw onion, gherkins, to glow on the table still dressed for breakfast. Then he brought in rice and chapattis, and then dishes of fish, both fried and curried, and then fat meaty chunks of mutton in a fat hot red-brown sauce. As in a check-mate move, he slammed down a huge jar of chutney, labelled with a happy dark family eating with their fingers, lettered in Singhalese curlicues. My father looked frightened. The news droned on, but nobody listened. 'Eat,' invited Mr Raj. 'Fall to, one and all. To repay hospitable kindness.'

We fell to. My father spooned in curry and panted. He frequently tried to stagger to the kitchen for fresh glasses of cold water, but Mr Raj said, 'No, no. I will get. This is my privilege, Mr Denhams both.' To my father all this was a new world; he ate with Renaissance child's eyes of wonder. 'I'd no idea,' he gasped. 'Never thought.' He was like a youth having his first sexual experience. The news came to its end and somebody began to talk about antiquities in Northamptonshire. Still we ate, sauce-stained, gasping for air, when we coughed coughing more loosely. 'Incredible,' dying-gasped my father. Mr Raj beamed and beamed, lithe fingers tearing at chapattis. It was a remarkable curry, an orgiastic indulgence and an austere medicine. After the talk came music. Still we ate. We were still eating when the High Church vicar called to take my father for his Monday afternoon nine holes. My gasping father brought him in. He was an iron-grey actor-type, a checked waistcoat under his dog-collar. 'A reverend gentleman,' said Mr Raj. 'Fall to also, sir. There is plenty for all. I can never sufficiently pay my debts for excellent primary missionary education.'

'Well,' said the vicar, 'it certainly looks bloody good.'

'This is Mr er,' said my father, never good at names, 'and this is Mr er. And this is my son.'

'I've had my luncheon,' said the vicar. 'But my housekeeper's cooking gets bloody well worse and worse. By Christ, it does.' And he consented to break a chapatti and, with it, mitten to his mouth a fat dripping mutton-piece. We must have looked strange there, the four of us – the eager Mr Raj, brown, shining in an old apron; my father with morning in his eyes, dripping with brown-red oily sauce; the vicar showing, between mouthfuls, how well he could swear; myself, unshaven, in a sick man's dressing-gown. Meanwhile radio music played, and we seemed to be playing the curry itself, like some rich organ with many stops. The vicar said something with 'sod' in it, and I tried to answer but my voice had almost gone. I said:

'Horr hurry harfar.' The vicar laughed like an actor and said:

'Bloody good thing you haven't got my job, losing your voice. Tonight I have to address the old cows who call themselves the Mothers' Union. I remember, ha ha, at the Theological College, old Bertie Bodkin had to give a sermon on

"I am the light of the world", and we could hardly hear him at the back, so I called out, "Turn the bloody wick up, Bertie.".' He laughed immoderately and Mr Raj said:

'And did this gentleman do what you requested?'

'He was very fond of dipping it,' said the vicar. 'Ha ha.'

At the end of the meal there was little left. 'We'll throw that rice to the birds,' said my father, 'and it's about time that cloth was washed, so the best thing to do is to bundle everything up and just shove it in the sink.' And then he said, 'There's a drop of brandy in the cupboard, so I suggest we have a little glass each and then toast the donor of the feast.' Mr Raj was confused and radiant. 'No, no,' he blushed. 'It was altogether my pleasure. You are not to think of toasting me.'

'You'll toast sooner or later,' twinkled the vicar. 'So will we all, including me, and I'm in the trade. The bloody trade,' he emended.

'There is a lot of blood in Christiantity,' said Mr Raj. 'The blood of the lamb. Why do people have to be washed in the blood of the lamb? Blood is something you wash off, not wash in.'

'Come,' said the vicar, embarrassed now. 'No impiety, if you please. Ah, the blushful Hippocrene,' as he took a glowing thimble of brandy from my father. 'Thank you, Denham.'

'Well,' said my father, 'Monday's not a day when you expect celebrations and banquets and so forth, especially Monday afternoon with the clothes-horse in front of the fire. But our friend here has made, for me anyway, this Monday a very memorable Monday. And I don't think that the vicar will mind our not being able to play golf this afternoon, the light going already. Anyway, our friend here has shown me that I'm not too old to learn. Anyway, I'm grateful to him for doing what he did, and I hope it won't be the last time. So I give you Mr er. What's the name again?' said my father.

'Raj,' said Mr Raj.

'Any relation to the British Raj?' asked the vicar.

'Ister Arge,' I toasted. Mr Raj rose to reply:

'Mr Chairman and gentlemen. There is no need for me to enlarge on theme of inestimable pleasure at myself having humbly given pleasure, however small and unworthy, to old Mr Denham and young Mr Denham, and also, though unexpected, yet still a pleasure, to Mr Bloody here, gentleman in Anglican orders.' You could see from Mr Raj's face that he meant no harm. 'I come here to your beautiful country –' Mr Raj saw through the window bare branches, coil after coil of dirty clouds, washing on neighbour lines, forlorn pecking birds, a distant brace of gasometers. '– your beautiful country, I say,' he said defiantly. 'I come here to study ineffable and imponderable problems of race relationships. So far I have had mixed career. Fights and insults, complete lack of sexual sustenance – most necessary to men in prime of life – and inability to find accommodation commensurate with social position and academic attainments. But I have seen the nylon-stockinged beauty of your women and I have been granted friendship by two men, one senior, one junior, I shall always revere. Let that be a lesson to the world,' nodded Mr Raj. 'It can be done, twain can meet, despite inordinate tensions created wantonly by demagogues in both East and West. Most cordial race relationships can and will and must and shall be established in world of bitter racial strife. And this,' concluded Mr Raj with gravity, 'I give you.' He drank off his brandy and sat down. 'Hear, hear,' said my father. He coughed loosely, with rattling phlegm, his eyes bright. The vicar said:

'So, no golf today.'

'It's getting dark already,' said my father. 'It'll be tea-time soon.'

'My handicap,' said modest Mr Raj, 'is twelve.'

'Is it?' said my father. 'Twelve, eh? Good average, very good average.'

The vicar said that, as he could not play golf, he had better visit the sick, so he went. My father said he would walk as far as the bridge and back again. Mr Raj, alone with me, said:

'That man is not very good specimen of Christian minister. Bloody this and bloody that. Why does he use that word so much, Mr Denham?'

'I don't really know.' I hadn't much voice.

'I think,' said Mr Raj, 'if you are well enough and fit enough, Mr Denham, I shall leave washing of dishes to you. This is no laziness on my part, and, if you so wish, you can leave dishes till tomorrow, when, after meeting with the Professor of Social Studies, I am perfectly ready to come and do this chore myself. Though, if I do that, you will have to clean plates for other meals tonight and tomorrow morning. I have used *all*,' he said with pride. 'But, Mr Denham, I have plans for this afternoon and for this evening. And into those plans you could not, well or ill, alas, be able to be fitted. I am to see Mrs Alice, the unattached lady of the Club and ask her to accompany me to University Film Society showing this evening. It is the only way,' he said, 'the only way. Real contact must be established, Mr Denham, for the sake of furthering my studies and,' he added, being no blushing hypocrite, 'for other sakes as well. The film in question is, strangely enough, a Hindustani film, about twin brothers in love with twin sisters and the resultant mix-up.'

'She may say no,' I said.

'She may, Mr Denham, but she will not say it for ever. No woman says it for ever, as you yourself know, Mr

142

Denham. I can give her,' smiled Mr Raj, 'a very great deal.'

I didn't doubt it. When Mr Raj had taken his flowery leave, I started the washing-up. I still had four saucers, three plates, all the cutlery and a couple of pans to wash when my father returned, not coughing.

'A very nice lad, that is. A very good cook and a very fine speaker, and very good-hearted. He ought to go far. I've learnt a lot today,' said my father, leaning against the kitchen stove. 'Marvellous thing, that curry is. I can see we've got a lot to learn from the East. I suppose, if he came to live here, he'd cook that every day?'

'He's got his studies to attend to, of course. But he might.'

'Wonderful stuff, that is. Do you know, I haven't coughed all afternoon.'

It was entirely up to me whether I flew or sailed back to
Tokyo. A provisional air booking had been made by the
firm right at the beginning of my leave – third week in
February: London Airport Tuesday 17.00; Tokyo Thurs-
day 19.15 – but, with the taste of Colombo in my mouth
and in my pluck a ponderous cold which breathed the
whole damp cabbagy essence of winter England, I decided
to get out as soon as I could. It had not really been much
of a leave. Besides, the sooner I moved out the sooner Mr
Raj could move in. I wanted to help both Mr Raj and my
father: my father would have somebody to look after him;
Mr Raj would not again beg Alice Winterbottom to take
in a lodger. Mr Raj just didn't understand that you couldn't
do that sort of thing in suburban England; I didn't want
Mr Raj to get into trouble. But Mr Raj had an outstanding
astounding capacity for getting into trouble, a genius un-
dreamed of, unthwartable by any number of good intentions.

I rang up Rice in London and asked him to arrange my
sea passage, quickly. By the end of the week I had ticket,
luggage labels, plan of ship marking my first-class Bibby
cabin, polyglot passengers' instructions: I was to embark
at Southampton a week later. The ship was Dutch and
called the *Koekoek*; it called at the usual places, as well
as at some unheard-of and shady-sounding ports in Indonesia, and got me back at the beginning of the last week

in February, which was just about right. Archie Shelley, who was standing in for me in Tokyo, was due to go on leave himself at the beginning of March.

That week of my cold was a week of achievements, but not for coughing television-watching me. 'Curry's what you need,' said my father, nodding at my trumpeting naso-pharynx-emptying, handkerchief-filling evening misery. 'You can't beat curry.' Meanwhile the curry-master mastered a new art — that of getting to know a white woman. He came in to see me on Wednesday morning, a new and holy look in his melting eye. He said:

'It was very much a new experience for the lady, Mr Denham, to mix with the cultured and the enlightened. True, the rawer element of the students threw things at the cinema screen, and three times performance had to be stopped, but I introduced her to Professor A. R. Flaxman, who has Eskimo wife, and to Professor Dulfakir, who was with his English betrothed, a lady many years older than himself, but he is no very prepossessing man, and I think she became convinced that new approach to racial relation-ships was possible. Afterwards she had coffee with me and met post-graduate students of all races, then I took her to her home and again pleaded with her to take me in as pay-ing guest, but she was, though charming, Mr Denham, quite adamant in her refusal.'

I told Mr Raj that it seemed quite definite that my father would have no objection to his taking over my room on my return to Japan. The rent would be in kind: coinage of curry. Mr Raj nearly went down on his knees. 'Where is he?' he cried. 'Where is that good old man your father? He shall have curry for breakfast, if he so desires, and for afternoon tea also. Where is he, that I may embrace him?' I told Mr Raj that my father had gone to see an exhibition of gardening implements at the Town Hall. I also told him

145

that it would not be good for my father, at his age and with his cough, to be caught up in any Oriental gale of gratitude. I would pass on sober thanks from Mr Raj; Mr Raj could start laying in a stock of curry ingredients. Mr Raj said:

'Already, Mr Denham, I begin to feel that I am accepted. I feel, indeed, that I am almost about to be absorbed. But, Mr Denham, I must still preserve, at all costs, scholarly spirit of detachment. My work, Mr Denham, my work must come first.' Mr Raj tried to pump into his eyes the feverish smoke of the intellectual fanatic, but it didn't come off. What was evidently stirring inside Mr Raj was something much more mundane: he stroked and stroked the smooth arm of my father's chair; he fingered a vase; he gazed up shyly at the calendar beauty above the mantel-piece (With the Compliments of Fred Tarr and Son, Radio and TV Specialists, Electrical Repairs and Installations of All Kinds Undertaken). It was then that I should have smelt trouble, but my cold had killed my sense of smell.

On Friday came the second achievement—that of Winterbottom. I received a letter from him with no super-scribed address—in case, he said, it should fall into the wrong hands—asking pathetically for his winter overcoat. He was not doing too badly, all things considered, he said. He'd put down a deposit and bought the second-hand print-ing press, and he'd installed it in the place he'd had in mind, and Imogen had already started bringing in a bit of money, chiefly by working in the evenings. They'd only been in this new place, which was a bit damp but other-wise adequate, two days, and of course he hadn't actually started any real work yet, but I might be interested in the enclosed. And he was mine sincerely. The enclosed was a piece of poor quality orange-coloured paper on which was, not very handily printed, the following:

THE WINTERBOTTOM PRESS
at 19 Gillingham Street, W.14
High Class Printing Letter Heads Visiting
Cards Parish Magazines Menus Leaflets etc
Give Us A Trial You Will Find Our Prices
Highly Competitive

The bloody fool, not wanting his address to fall into the wrong hands but nevertheless wanting his winter overcoat. And here was the address, blazoned in a kind of 1834 fattened Modern type, to be given hopefully to the world by shivering bearded Winterbottom, all fingers and thumbs with his pile of orange leaflets on London's wet defiled streets. Still, I reflected, he and Imogen hadn't been so dilatory about getting something started as I'd thought they would be. I'd expected my gift cheque to afford an excuse for delaying the growing of a backbone — long sloppy mornings with chocolate under the pillow and plenty of shillings for the gas ('We've still got ten pounds; we can easily make that last another week perhaps a fortnight). They must have acted on the very Saturday that I started back for the Midlands. But I didn't like the sound of Imogen's evening work; the sooner Winterbottom got something to print, the better for both of them. Mr Raj could undoubtedly be persuaded into ordering several thousand visiting cards, and perhaps the swearing vicar would like his parish magazine to go to a London printer. And Everett might help his errant daughter by producing rhyme sheets. And Ted Arden could give to his friends copies of *What the Tories Have Done for the Working Man* — a printing job that, surely, would not over-tax Winterbottom's resources. And Selwyn could consider a pamphlet of sibylline prophecies. Really, there was no end to the possibilities of the Winterbottom Press.

As for the overcoat, that was another matter. I would send Winterbottom five pounds to buy a second-hand one: I had surely saved five pounds at least this week by not drinking. I was much too shy to go to Alice Winterbottom's house and risk having the wardrobe thrown at me. Nor, having railed one drunken night at adultery, did I wish to appear on the side of two serious, as opposed to casual, adulterers. I was a respectable business-man with respectable geisha girls awaiting me in the tinkling cherry-blossom land of fabulous Cipango Balls.

By Sunday I felt very much better, but still not well enough to go to Beryl's for a last and perhaps ceremonial lunch — possibly with toasts of great insincerity drunk in alum-solution wine. When Mr Raj offered to make a really large and various curry tiffin — in gratitude of an awe-inspiring order — my father struggled with a strong flow of saliva and hesitated, poor man. But duty prevailed, and he went to Beryl's for the usual bout of dyspepsia. Still, there weren't many more to come: another month would take the Morgans off to Tunbridge Wells, the house, if still unsold, left in the hands of an agent. So, ready to start my packing, I could feel that I was leaving something like stability, however irregularly achieved, behind me. One's head reeled, considering the elements that had produced this stability (curry, adultery, thrombosis, a beard, a mess of old type) but, at that time, I held the strict Machiavellian view of order: I still had not learnt much from the East.

On Monday I sent my cheque to Winterbottom; on Wednesday I had a reply from Imogen — an unexpectedly neat and cowed hand on lined paper, making her violent words seem all the more violent:

'You sod, you (if you want to do anything about that, you can). Typical of you, isn't it, to take the easy way. You wouldn't get hold of poor bloody Billy's overcoat, and the poor little bugger's perished for want of it, and in any case it's got sentimental associations for him because it's the first one he ever bought for himself, but you of course wouldn't appreciate that. And all you do, taking the bloody coward's way out, is to dig your hand — not too deep, i notice, oh no, not on your bloody life — into your fat pockets and send another bit of your measly charity. You don't seem to have the bloody sense to realise that five pounds is a bloody insult. If you want to help, help. If you want to do what you're asked to do, do it. But don't let's have any more of these mean bloody little insults which are neither one thing nor the other. If you want to know, I can make double that amount without any trouble at all, any evening I care to go out. *And* I don't have to do what you think I'm bloody doing, you and your dirty unmarried man's mind with your squashed-nosed Javanese or Japanese or whatever they are, not that I care. I'm getting my own back on them all, see, bubbling over to pay their money when they've had a bit of a leg-show. And it serves them all bloody well right, left there with their tongues hanging out, wondering where it's gone to. And it's not cheating, whatever you think, it serves them all bloody well right. If you want to help, help. But you obviously don't, being what you are. I'll write to Daddy asking him to get poor bloody Billy's overcoat. He's a man, anyway.'

There was no valediction, no signature. I suppose, in a way, Imogen was right, but I couldn't understand the violence. And I debated within my head the ethics of what Imogen was evidently doing. Leave sexual morality out of it and you saw a flagrant cynical tort, a breach of contract. But Winterbottom, who obviously knew what she was doing, would, after saying, 'Take care of yourself, dear,' undoubtedly approve: let all such fornicators be punished. He'd seen his wife give herself to Jack Brownlow regularly

149

every Saturday night, and what had he, Winterbottom, ever got out of it? Not a sausage. Ah, hideous, corrupt, TV-haunted England.

Which now, with relief, I began to leave. I booked my single first-class rail ticket to Southampton at Dean and Dawson's, and the clerk there was, for some reason, disturbed that I didn't want a return. My trunk, labelled with a large red 'D' for hold-stowing, was sent on in advance to the shipping-line's agents in Southampton; my bags were almost packed. On the day before I left there were satisfactory hailstones and winds, and Mr Raj, coming with the vanguard of his luggage and materials for a farewell curry, shivered but was still enthusiastic for England. This curry was like a performance of Beethoven's Ninth Symphony that I'd once heard played on a player and amplifier built by personnel of the Royal Electrical and Mechanical Engineers, especially the last movement with everything screaming and banging 'Joy'. It stunned, it made one fear great art. My father could say nothing after the meal. He sat in his armchair, shrunken rather than inflated, tremblingly lighting his pipe, looking like some aged man of letters, O.M., not to be regarded as imbecilic despite his stutterings and blankness for, after all, one has read the fine works of his maturity. My father was, so to speak, eaten out.

Mr Raj, warming in his long hands the brandy I had bought, made a long speech. It extolled the Denhams, senior and junior; England, past, present and future; the British Commonwealth of Nations; the Colombo Plan; the nameless suburb of which he would, tomorrow, be a resident; the city; the city's university; the red buses of the city; the unripe girls and the mature women; nylon stockings; fair hair. Cosy afternoon dark closed in as the peroration opened out to its final word (what it would be one could only guess: Denham? England? Commonwealth? Race? Beauty? Home? Shakespeare?).

'And so,' said Mr Raj, 'I give you—love. Yes, love.' He smirked in the dusk, above the played-out orchestra of dishes. 'Love that makes the world go round, Love, yes, that is the answer. We need not fear, ever, if only we have in our hearts, if only we give and, in reciprocity, receive, this greatest of all human treasures. Love.' And then, uneasily, we had to drink, mumbling 'Love'.

Mr Raj insisted on washing the dishes himself. No, he said, it was my last full day in England and it should not be defiled by such lowly chores; nor would it be right to wake that good old man my father, now snoring, quite worn out, in a fireside sleep, drugged by fennel and paprika, pimento and turmeric, tarragon, saffron, rubbed basil and bay-leaves. And, when he had finished, Mr Raj seriously asked me to go into the front room with him for a little talk. Seated before the gas-fire, he said:

'I understand, Mr Denham, very fully the nature of responsibilities entrusted to me. I shall protect that good old snoring man, I assure you, with last breath of my body. When you return, I shall present him to you whole and well. In sickness he will be tended my myself and by growing body of Indian medical friends, skilled in medical arts and sciences. He shall be fed, I promise you. His sleep shall be watched over by myself. Fear not, Mr Denham, for I am of no small strength. And, Mr Denham, I have this weapon.' Mr Raj took from his pocket a tiny automatic, pearly-handled, a dainty lady-killer. I said:

'How did you get hold of that? That belongs to Ted Arden.'

'Yes,' said smiling Mr Raj. 'That night, one fortnight ago, when the bar-boy made as if to shoot me. I took it from him and forgot to hand it back to your friend, the landlord. But I have not been asked for it back. He has many guns and will not miss it. And I, Mr Denham, have many enemies. This Mr Brownlow and the young boys with thin ties and thick shoes. And doubtless others. It is difficult for an Asian man here. But, Mr Denham, I will never have cause to use it. Nor have I, as yet, ammunition.' He laughed pleasantly, displaying strong twin ivory fans – everything there in the large red Asian mouth, unbroken lines from incisors to molars. He replaced the gun, innocently proud of it, in his jacket pocket. 'Protection, Mr Denham, for your father and for myself.'

'You'd better give that back,' I said. 'Especially as you haven't got a licence.'

'I am not stealing it, Mr Denham. Only borrowing it. For purposes of intimidation which, I hope, will never be necessary. I shall be out much in the evenings, with, I hope, a lady. A black man walking out with a white lady ought to carry a gun, Mr Denham. There are many stupid people in this town. I can see that my thesis on Popular Notions of Racial Differentiation will be a very large work.'

12

An extremity of the English sky wept bitterly on the massed shipping of Southampton. I boarded the *Koekoek* and found it full of Dutchness, a kind of jolly nightmare parody of England. I entered via C DEK and, by the *Hofmeester's* sodium-lighted office, was met by fair plump men in blue who spoke English so well that, when they returned to Dutch among themselves, one grew afraid as in the presence of Ray Bradbury Martians, clever at quick human disguises. For Dutch, though it looks like a reasonable language, never really sounds like one: it is, as Gulliver implied, the right tongue for talking horses. Anyway, I was led to my *kajuit*, stepping over squatting brown boys, the dregs of the ports of Indonesia, and was given a boy of my own: hunched, one-eyed, grinning in cunning, he gave his name as Tjoetjoe, pronounced Chuchu. The cabin was L-shaped and roomy. '*Boenga*,' said Tjoetjoe, in cunning laughter, pointing to a bouquet on the bunk. Yes, flowers from Mr Raj, narcissi and daffodils from Scilly. And a farewell note in Mr Raj's spider-writing – *bon voyage*, and at every port I would receive a postcard. '*Boenga*,' said Tjoetjoe again, meaning flowers, '*oh, boenga, boenga*.' I gave him a daffodil to wear in his velvet cap, and he went out in wonder. Then I heard a sharp Indonesian quarrel for its possession, quick dog-snarls. A Dutch steward in German-student spectacles came by, dealing slaps, neighing briskly. I closed my cabin-door and unpacked.

It was not a bad ship, though it lacked the glorious eccentricity of certain British vessels I had travelled by. Here was no drunken orchestral leader to yell to the dancers. 'No, you've had your last bleeding waltz, now sod off.' Here were no table-stewards who said, 'You've eaten sweet F.A. You was on the booze last night, wasn't you?' Here was no labyrinth of amorous intrigues among the crew, betrayed on the passenger-decks by lingering smiles and jealous frowns, here were no stokers wearing party-frocks at midnight. Only the rat-life of the Indonesians escaped in scuttlings and screams from the sewer-holes: a reported knifing, boiling water poured over an unpopular deck-steward, odd pre-Islamic rites involving animal sacrifices.

The two bar-stewards, with Martian names of Toon and Maas, were all too efficient, knew every possible drink, and even – horrible – brewed tea and coffee. Never once did I see either of them carried out insensible. Drinking a gimlet before lunch, I thought nostalgically of barmen on other ships of the Eastern run: fat Bill Page, who drank two cases of stout every morning; Dicky Carstairs, who always fell out of the launch at Aden; Bob Something-or-other, who strangled a man in Port Said after brandy and black beer. There was something drilled, over-precise, about these Dutchmen.

The passengers were what you would expect: returning planters and government officers with sun-washed-out wives; shy boys going out to work in banks; bold nursing sisters, the new post-partition people, Bombay-bound, drinking hugely, aware of a dry India awaiting them; a couple who had married on a rich-sounding waterworks appointment out East, making this trip their honeymoon. During my third gimlet the loudspeakers barked that we must fall in on A Deck, and there dining-room seating was arranged with Teutonic precision. I was placed opposite this couple, a wild-haired old monoglot Swede next to me. The couple wanted to giggle and fondle each other, so, over the salty soup, I spoke to the Swede, saying, '*Hur står det till?*' He said he was very well, thank you. He passed me the pepper and I said, '*Tack*'. '*Ingenorsak,*' he answered. Almost the only other Swedish I knew was '*Vad är klockan?*' – a superfluous question, as a large clock from a Fritz Lang film mooned down at everybody from over the swing-doors. The couple blushed and smirked at each other, as at the memory of something that still seemed illicit, two very thin people, as though they had been pared down to pure love. I thought of Charlie Whittier, then of Imogen and Winterbottom, and then of Mr Raj, wondering if he was learning much about race and racialism from Alice. They all seemed very far away, even though we were still in rainy Southampton.

But one could not be far away from Mr Raj for very long. His voice was in my mind as black whooshing dragon-tails lashed us in the Bay of Biscay; I imagined that I heard him comforting – 'Soon, Mr Denham, you will be through to clearer seas and a more tranquil stomach.' After the anvil of France, the square face of Portugal, and I imagined Mr Raj saying. 'Lisbon is the nose of Portugal, Mr Denham. The reputation of the Portuguese smells to heaven in Ceylon. Racial intolerance and forcing of the Christian religion, Mr Denham.' We sailed into the Mediterranean between the sundered lips of Africa and Spain, and mail was picked up at Gibraltar. There was a postcard from Mr Raj – a glossy picture of Shakespeare's birthplace, a question from that tireless enquirer: 'In your view, is a love not involving the lust of the body possible between man and woman? I should welcome your views quickly. Your father eats well.' I posted brief messages with views of the ship, sending my father my love, to Mr Raj the cautious opinion that it all depended, would answer more fully from Port Said.

One day, on the way to Port Said, walking on the promenade deck, I met my Swedish messmate coming the other way. To my joy he asked, '*Vad är klockan?*' I looked at my watch, which said twenty to four, but could only remember the Swedish for a quarter to five. '*Klockan är en kvart i fem*,' I said, and he ran off, whimpering for his tea. For me life was nearly as dull as on leave, but it was getting much warmer. There had been no glimmering of the opening of a shipboard romance, the library was mostly Nevil Sjoet and A. J. Cronin, the bar-stewards thought it insubordinate to converse with their customers, I hate deck games. But at Port Said a photograph of Banbury Cross was waiting, and on the back a telegraphic and urgent Mr Raj: 'Very important question. Must know if love possible without sensual desire accompanying. Please reply at length.' Looking at the dusk skyline of Port Said I saw the de Lesseps statue gone, and I felt a black hostility to the fat ringed Egyptians who stamped passports in the second-class lounge. Ashore in the evening I was picked up by a dragoman, an Egyptian barrel in a chocolate-coloured overcoat. His card said Mohamed Kamal Abul Kheir, but he said, 'Call me Jock.' There was no known language he did not know, and he spoke seven accurate English dialects. Wherever we went there were Big-Brother portraits of the President, and in a window full of photographs of school gymnastics I read: 'Modern Egypt. Never a Dull Moment.' This cheered me a little.

I drank Stella beer and Jock, appropriately, Scotch, in a night club – tarbooshed waiters, American-suited Syrian pimps, moon-coloured hostesses called Pallas and Aphrodite, a decayed French orchestra. Male fellow-passengers materialised around, grown suddenly beef-red and chortling. To cheers and a drum-roll the Greek belly-dancer cheesed in, ochreous, steatopygous, dendrosomatic. With a fixed tyroid smile she shook her flesh to the music and then started to mount tables. I grew fearful: I did not want her to mount mine. 'Paper,' I said to Jock. 'Paper, quick. I've got to write a note to somebody.' *'Kertas!'* – or something like it – shouted Jock to a waiter. A lined notebook came and I began to write to Mr Raj. I wrote in furious concentration, hearing, like a storm, the belly-dancer coming nearer. I wrote:

'You mean Platonic love. I do not really think it is possible between man and woman, unless perhaps there is great disparity in their ages rendering sexual attraction very difficult, or unless perhaps one or other has a beautiful mind and an ugly body.' The dancer was now on the next table but two. 'I take it that you are not asking these questions in the abstract but are actually experiencing what seems to you to be this kind of love. I would say this: beware. Do not become involved too much with anyone. If as I think, the woman in question is –' And now this blasted gasteroterpsichorean was on my table and she chucked me under the chin with a fat bare toe. I looked up, hearing beef-red laughter all round. A mile above me was the heaving fleshy mound of her stomach, a mile further up a pair of plucked armpits: I was caught looking up, in an act of involuntary worship. Then this woman kicked over my half-full glass of Stella beer, soaking the letter to Mr Raj, filling my lap with cold wet. It was all good fun, had to be taken in good part, as the beef-red laughter insisted, as the smiling picture of Nasser demanded. Never a dull moment.

Anyway, no letter to Mr Raj was posted at Port Said. I paid off Jock with many half-crowns and piastres, and he kissed my hands sentimentally. The British, he whispered, would always be his friends. Then I got aboard again, ready for Suez and the Red Sea. At the top of the gangway I met the wild-haired old Swede: he was trying to bring a bracelet-jangling middle-aged Arab prostitute aboard, and the night-watchman, red-bearded, with a surgical boot, said it was not to be. '*Omöjlig*,' I said, meaning it was impossible, and the Swede took this to be a mocking reference to his senility. I left them to it, went to my cabin, slept, and Tjoetjoe brought my morning tea to the ship's crawling through a landscape, which meant we were in the Canal. '*Roempoet*,' said Tjoetjoe, pointing to grass; '*djam*,' he said, as we inched past a public clock. Life to him was all wonder.

In the Red Sea, with its thundering Jehovah hills and its thumped bloody rock tables of the Law, I became better acquainted with Mrs Thorpe, who was one half of the honeymoon couple. The other half was ill in his cabin, having in Port Said eaten something he should not have eaten. The old Swede now merely grunted at me, did not even say '*Tack*' when I passed the vinegar. So Mrs Thorpe and I were drawn together, first at meal-times, later on deck and in the public rooms. Her name, she said, was Linda. Though thin, she was not unseductive: in her flame-coloured evening-dress she wriggled about like a flame. At dinner I said:

'Is he any better?' The ship's officers were in mess jackets; the trio played in the gallery; there was to be a dance after dinner.

'The doctor,' she said, 'thinks he ought to go into the sick-bay for a few days. He vomits all the time, you see. I don't get much sleep.'

'Did you get much sleep before?'

'Oh, yes,' she said. 'Like a log. Oh, I see what you mean.' She giggled. The old Swede read through the menu sourly, up and down, down and up, as though looking for a train.

'You shouldn't say things like that,' she said. If she'd been carrying a fan she would have hit my arm playfully with it. The trio played Rodgers and Hammerstein; Mrs Thorpe ate heartily through every course; outside in the dark the grim rock Bible lands glowered and prophesied. I ordered more wine. The free wood alcohol liqueur that was served after dinner was undrinkable, so, for Mrs Thorpe and myself, I ordered Grand Marnier. We got on very nicely that evening, and during the dance, by the lifeboats (why always by the lifeboats?) I kissed her.

It was mainly this brief spasm of interest in Mrs Thorpe that prevented me from writing another letter, not this time to be beer-soaked by belly-dancers, to Mr Raj and posting it at Aden. Mr Thorpe was still in the sick-bay but recovering fast when we sailed into the Gulf, so Mrs Thorpe and I were to spend a last cosy afternoon together, shopping in the Aden shops, drinking in the Aden bars. Before we disembarked I received letters. My father said he was well, eating like a horse, coughing better, Mr Raj was very good in the house but kept rather late hours. Mr Raj wrote at length and reproachfully. This time there was no glossy frippery of postcard views. He said:

'Not once, Mr Denham, have you replied to my enquiries about love transcending the demands of physical self. First I thought you were too busy to write, but then I recollected that you have ample leisure on a ship. Second, I thought you had difficulty in posting letters, but this I know to be not true. Third, I thought perhaps you were angry at what many white men would consider the presumption of a black man speaking of love for, as will now be surmised, a white woman, but you are in no wise a man of racial prejudice. So I must think, Mr Denham, that you are becoming lazy and are too idle to write to your good friends. For good friend to you and that good old man I consider myself to be. Mr Denham Senior is eating very well. Last Sunday we played golf together, I having borrowed clubs.

'Oh, Mr Denham, I consider my whole life to be changed. Yes, I consider myself to be in love. But thereof it is necessary I have expert confirmation, as, for instance, from yourself. I have no desire to make physical demands. All I ask is to stand and worship. And since that time of the cinema performance at the University I have not been able to give Mrs Alice further treats of that nature, chiefly because she herself has not been willing to accept them. Moreover, she says that people will talk. Let them talk, I would say, for love is not to be considered a secret thing. But all I do is to go to the Hippogriff Club where she now works till closing-time at night, needing the money, though she has obtained her husband's address, indeed it was your own father who gave it, having found it on an advertising circular sent to your good self, and having written asking him to come back to her and not, to use her own words, continue to be bloody foolish. But soon I must pluck up courage and ask her to forget about this worthless man her husband and, when she can obtain freedom after the law's delay, to marry myself. There is ample precedent here, I having seen many men much blacker than I, being negroes and, moreover, of inferior race, walking about with very fair white women and becoming married to them.

'I have had to hit this Mr Brownlow once more, this time in public lavatory for men only in the yard of the Black Swan. He was very ill after this hitting but will not, I surmise, cause further trouble. The weather continues very cold. Please do not be so lazy and write to say whether this is really love.'

I would write, I really would, but first there was the question of obtaining launch tickets and then actually boarding the launch with Mrs Thorpe, and then we got rather drunk in Aden, I solemnly, she gigglingly so. Back on board, she willingly came to my cabin, but it was Tjoetjoe, like a brown conscience, who saved me from the true act of adultery. He had his own key to my cabin, and he entered, bearing my laundered tuxedo, to the sight of Mrs Thorpe and Mr Denham jumping from the bunk in disarray. 'Djigadjig,' said the wondering Tjoetjoe, drawing on the small international vocabulary that, presumably, saw him through shore-leave in Rotterdam, Southampton, and all ports west of Kutaradja. And now, with a groan of the weighed anchor, the ship began to ease out of the roads, the steersman, whom we had met drunk in Aden, steering drunkenly. That night he was, presumably, summoned to *Kajuit* 101 to be tortured, keel-hauling being no longer in fashion.

Mr Thorpe was about next day, fatter, eating vigorously and starved of love, and I tried to make it up with the aged Swede. But my Swedish was limited to salutations, valedictions, requests for the time, the time – or some of it – and the word *omöjlig*, meaning impossible. But soon it was *omöjlig* to talk at meal-times and, for that matter, other times, because the Bombay contingent was becoming drunker and drunker and singing loud brave songs, like Christians being taken to the lions. I soon found this contingent not uncongenial and myself drank loudly with them at the bar and in various cabins after closing-time. The morning of disembarkation at Bombay was very drunken – much champagne and no breakfast – and in the cabin to which I had been invited (the bar closed, its stock under seal) corks exploded in *feu de joie* and the world was, as on my sister's poker-work blazon, one of froth and bubble. To this cabin came at length a card from Mr Raj. The message read: 'Do not answer, then. Or perhaps you are ill or dead, in that case not to be blamed. But I know such love to be possible and I have told her so. Your father is well. Weather very wet and cold.' The picture on the card was of Blenheim Palace. Somebody, seeing this, said:

'Home of the Churchill family. Good old Winny. "Their finest hour," he said, nineteen-forty that was. I was one of the first of the few.' He was bald now, all rugger fat, and his eyes filled with tears as he saw in imagination the lost mess-mates. 'Finest hour,' he repeated, 'and look at me now. Selling laxatives to the Wogs. Oh God God God.' He began to cry. A fierce man with very lively eyebrows, having read Mr Raj's message several times, looked up at me fiercely from the bed where he sat, and said:

'Why didn't you answer him? The least you could do, damn it. What did he want to know, anyway?'

'About Platonic love,' I said. 'Whether it was possible.'

'It's not possible. Everybody knows it's not possible. It's been proved by somebody or other not to be possible.'

'Is that what I should have told him?'

'You can still tell him, damn it. No such thing. Quite impossible.'

'*Omöjlig*.' A cork cracked, flew, foam frothed the carpet. 'Tell him that. What you said. If he wants a woman there's only one way to have a woman.'

'There I would disagree,' said an upright scholarly-looking man, very fair, a salesman of veneers. 'There are many ways. At least three hundred and sixty-five, according to some of the Hindu experts.'

'Yes yes yes yes yes yes, we know all about that, we've all been in India, we've all read the bloody books, but there's only the one way really, I mean, however you get down to it. I mean, all this mooning about and thinking it's spiritual and what have you, that's only being shy or something, or scared of it, like all of us when we were kids.' The fierce eyebrows danced like moustaches. 'Tell him,' he said, 'to get on with it.'

'I'll send him a cable,' I said, 'telling him that.'

'Yes, you do that thing. You ring the bell there. You get a cable form and send it off and tell him that one thing.'

An hour later flushed and unsteady people sang and swayed down the gangway, some, in their slow progress, embracing now one side, now the other, of the stair-rail. Two nuns came at the end, a black rebuke to all. All were swallowed by the grim Bombay and, beyond, the grim India that lay behind the grim customs-sheds and warehouses. And a cryptogram, that at the time seemed most ingenious, was on its way to Mr Raj: 'Can Oriental People Understand Love. Are They Innocent Or Not. Not Only Women.' Waking up thirsty in the late afternoon I regretted it but hoped that Mr Raj would puzzle some meaning out of the nonsense: surely Ceylonese culture was too earnest to go in for acrostics. But probably Mr Raj would show my cable to somebody, perhaps to my father, who was used to brooding over lines of type. I groaned, good old irresponsible Denham, middle-aged business-man fond of his joke.

To the shipping agent at Colombo came, and then came to me, a picture post-card of Colombo – a nice touch. Mr Raj said: 'I have, after much puzzling, deciphered hidden meaning. Much helped there by Indian post-graduate student of English Literature, he believing that Shakespeare was really a different man of different name. How wise you always are, Mr Denham. Western culture teaching us that both body and soul important.' (Here, because of the exigencies of the post-card, the writing became minute.) 'Will take advice, but must not hurry.'

We moved now to the East Indies and I, becoming bored again, began to snarl at a rather complacent Dutch business-man about the horrors of Dutch rule in the East, and, more particularly, about the seventeenth-century massacre of the British at Amboyna. There we were, under the fans of the lounge, neighing and barking respectively at each other, ordering drinks in strict alternation, hating each other like brothers, history like snow covering the stones we had thrown at each other, while the great Eastern islands crawled past and men were put down to home or exile at tiny ports whose names I cannot now remember. And then came Singapore. This time, for some reason, there was no card from Mr Raj, but there was another man I had met in Colombo that time of settling Wicker in, and he brought news of home. This was only indirectly news about love.

13

I never quite know what to think of Singapore. (The *Koekoek* gave me a day to come, yet again, to this conclusion.) Singapura means lion-city; prehistoric, myopic, Sanskrit-speaking visitors having spotted a mangy tiger or two in the mangroves. Sly Malays sometimes call it *Singa pura-pura*, which means 'pretending to be a lion'. That, I think, is about right. It is a profoundly provincial town pretending to be a metropolis. It is a town full of pretending. The new Chinese rulers pretend that their coolie forebears were not workless immigrants, happy, in blue trousers, to dig and build for the kindly British, but the original lords, whipped into servitude by red-haired invaders. Banning American pornography, juke-box pop-tunes, naughty films, Singapore pretends to be highly moral. Its hotels pretend to *haute cuisine*, its buildings to architecture, its white women to *chic*. Only in the mean streets, where rich low life pullulates, is there no pretence. There, among thugs and whores and shark-fins and opium, one can relax, having really arrived in the city. But they pretend that is not the city.

I had lunch in the grill room of a hotel much admired by Somerset Maugham – *Châteaubriand* which I twice sent back, first, because it was cold, second, because it had been re-heated. I was loud with the head waiter about it and refused to pay. At the table behind me a group of white men – jumped-up commercials pretending, too late, to be the ruling class – tut-tutted, and one flowery-hatted woman said. 'Where does e think e is?' Now I myself am a commercial but I make no pretences: all I wanted was a steak well-cooked and hot. I said to this woman, 'Ah wuz thinkin ah wuz in Zoo Resterong at Belle View Manchister, missis, but food's better thur an animals as more manners,' a silly thing to say, not at all dignified. Then I left. I went to a cinema to see a film in Hindustani: it was about two rival Persian kingdoms, in each of which there was a ruler who had deposed his twin brother, and the rulers themselves seemed to be twins, an impossible situation, unless that was merely the effect of the bad lighting. So I went to sleep, waking up to find the plot now enriched by the addition of twin sisters who had arrived, each separately and unbeknown to the other, to fall in love with the twin usurped, or usurpers, it was hard to tell which. After two hours the plot really began to settle down and thicken, so I left. I drank in the Adelphi Hotel for a time, and then I went to seek my evening meal in Bugis Street. It was there, with no surprise, that I re-met Len.

The Chinese shop was filthy, but the food was good. I chopsticked away happily for a time, with a bottle of cold Carlsberg, and then became aware of another white man, alone at a near table, austerely dining on plain rice and a fried egg. The man gloomily nodded and said, 'Colombo, that's where it was. The Mount Lavinia Hotel.'

'That's right,' I said, 'just before Christmas. Len,' I added, to show that I really remembered. Len brought over to my table his rice with the fried egg bleeding on to it, and asked for another glass of water, really cold this time. The face of an El Greco saint, I had thought, but this time I could be more specific. El Greco, yes, but one of the men cringing from Christ's whip in the Traders in the Temple picture in the National Gallery. Those men all look good men – thin and hard-working, bearded and philosophical –

and one can see no money, no goods. Anyway, Christ has no real right to be there, because, through the arch at the back, you can see the palaces of the Grand Canal in Venice. In that picture a lean man looks up to heaven, an empty basket on his head, and Len had that man's face.

'How's business?' I asked, pincering in some fried pork.

'They're watching more,' he said. 'I saw a couple at the airport in London, big men with overcoats on. But we shall manage for a bit longer. Another year, say, and I might be able to retire.'

'Retire?'

'It's the same as anything else, the way I see it. We're all entitled to a bit of leisure. We do our duty, one way or another, giving people what they want, which is all that trade is, or art is, or religion is, the way I see it, and then we're entitled to do what we really want to do. The same as yourself.' He took a spoonful of rice and a tail of the fried egg, and washed it down gloomily with water. Outside the hot cheerful quacking world went by.

'And what do you really want to do?' I asked.

'Well, I had thought of going in for a study of religion and so on. I've never really had much time for that, and yet, funnily enough, it was religion that made me take up this job, in a way, that is.'

'You mean the opium of the people?' I asked.

Len became smaller, more hunched, hissing, eyes afire. 'Not so loud,' he said. 'You don't know who's listening. Him, for instance.' He shouldered in the direction of a Chinese boy of seven or so, a loud naughty boy in striped pyjamas, laughing with tooth-stumps, refusing to go to bed. 'They're all round, Everywhere.'

'I'm sorry,' I said.

'I've always said you were straight,' nodded Len. We both looked askance at the 'always', which had settled on my little dish of fried salt, but we let it go. 'But you can't be too straight with those that can't understand. No,' he said, 'it was religion in a different way. You ever heard of a writer called Graham Greene?'

'I once had lunch with him,' I said, 'in the Café Royal. It was Friday, and we both had fish.'

'Interesting,' said Len without interest. 'Very interesting. But it's his books I was thinking about, not the man himself. It's the same as Shakespeare and Bacon in a way, if you can catch my meaning. Well, I read his books as they came out, and still do, and it seemed to me he was saying that you could only get close to God if you really got down to the real dirt, so to speak. Not,' said Len, 'that I altogether hold with the way that God made the world or runs it, for that matter, but it struck me that He's about all there is, and He was worth a closer study, so to speak. Anyway, I'd been in insurance before, quite respectable. But these books made me see that that wouldn't do. That doesn't lead you anywhere near to what really matters – you know, sin and punishment and ultimate reality and all that caper. That leads you to all your life in a semi-detached and pottering about the garden on Saturdays and cold meat for supper after the boozer on Sunday night. That takes you away from anything that's worth having. So I got out. The wife cut up rusty at first, but now she thinks I'm doing sort of liaison work for a toothbrush firm. A bit vague, but you don't have to make things too clear to women.'

'Will you have a cigarette?' I said, having finished my meal.

'They're a substitute,' said Len, shaking his head, 'a substitute for getting nearer to the real thing.'

'And what is the real thing?'

'That's what I've got to find out,' said Len. 'But I think it's something to do with justice. I don't mean doing right, you know, not being just and all that lot, but like a kind of one thing balancing another.' His face showed great suffering as, over his cold mess of egg and rice, he tried to make himself clear. 'But if you don't do anything, there can't be any balance. It's as though we're given a pair of scales and we've got to use them. Now, if you put nothing on one side you balance that with nothing on the other. That's like just coming home from the insurance office and having a go at the garden. But if people do wrong, well, then, there's something heavy on one side of the scales, and then you get the punishment, and then the scales are being used, which is what we're here for, the way I see it.'

'So people have got to do wrong, have they?'

'The way I see it. If they do nothing, what are they here for? If they do good, well, that's supposed to be its own reward.'

'How about heaven and hell?'

Len shook his head in doubt. 'I don't know yet. That's something I hope to find out when I retire. But it seems to me that you can't have a pair of scales with one pan in this world and the other in the next. That's where I part company with God. Not really, I mean, because I still don't know enough about Him, but with God as they show you Him in church and Sunday school and these Cecil B. De Mille films and all that caper. No, people have got to be taught, the way I see it, and they've got to be taught here and now. That way everyone of us is a little bit of God. That's what God is, perhaps. Just all of us.'

It was not, of course, strange any more to be listening to a racketeer talking theology in a filthy Chinese food-shop in Bugis Street, Singapore. Len's favourite author had shown us that the divine image, however twisted or misunderstood, could appear on a beer-mat, lurk like a rebus in a calendar nudescape, be the circular sticky stain of a

Guinness glass, show red in a broken-bottle wound. His merely talking about God make me hungry for whore country, the ship not sailing till dawn. I suggested that we two go to a particular cabaret I knew, there to sit under low-powered glamourising bulbs with Chinese hostesses. I thought, biting my cigarette-holder, of how exasperating Chinese girls were, flat-breasted and delicate-limbed, with doll-fringes and porcelain smiles, seeming to offer so much different from—from what? From Englishwomen? But I had never slept with an Englishwoman. Yet English-woman, I thought, must be the same, because all the others were the same. And then I thought sourly of the girl I had once slept with, presumably – from her enclitics – here or north of here, who had said to me, 'Mr Denham, you come quick-lah. You very heavy-lah.' To hell with all women.

'No, I don't think so,' said Len. 'There may be a next world for men, but I don't think there can be one for women.' With a start I realised that I had damned them aloud. 'Now, it's a funny thing, but you'll perhaps remem-ber telling me when we met in Colombo,' said Len, 'telling me about something that had happened to you when you were in London. I thought of that a lot, strange to say, though it was none of my business, really, but we'd had a drink together and that made you my pal, and in any case there's always this question of justice.'

'Yes?' I said.

'You paid her beforehand and then she just walked out, through the bathroom or some way. I forget how you told me it happened. I think there was a bedroom on the other side. Now, were you right to want a woman like that and pay her for it? That's neither here nor there, it's no real question of right and wrong. Ethics,' said Len heavily, 'per-haps don't really come into it. That's something I'm keeping for my retirement. But the same thing happened to one of our lot.'

'Your lot?'

'Yes, yes,' said Len impatiently, 'it's a bit too complicated to talk about, really. Just take it that it was one of our lot, which it was. Well, he met her off Hampstead Road – Robert Street or William Road or somewhere, though why the hell she was round there God alone knows, though perhaps He doesn't know and that's something for my retirement – and it seems she was all right, talked a bit slash as he put it, and they went to a hotel not too far from Euston Station. Well, she charged him five quid in advance and then went into the bathroom, to get ready as he thought, though why a woman has to get ready in the bathroom is something, again, that God might or might not know. Anyway, he was there, stripped off as he put it, and waited, and then he got off the bed and found the bathroom was locked. She'd gone all right, five quid and all, and this one of our lot didn't really like it. He talked about it later on as a bit of a joke, though you could see he didn't really take it that way. Five nicker is five nicker, as he put it, using his own language so to speak. I thought about you at the time, not thinking we'd meet again, and it seemed to me that it wasn't right she should get away with it. It might have been the same one that you had. Although with everybody nowadays it seems to be something for nothing, no sense of justice.' Len called for more water. Without thinking, I said, 'Have this on me.'

'All right,' said Len, 'just water, that's all. Now then, we waited, three of us, including the one who'd paid his five quid for nothing. We did four nights. The others began to say that we ought to give it up, a waste of time, but I said there was the question of justice. I spoke pretty strongly about it, as you can guess, and they said we'd look one more

night. We did look one more night and saw this one somewhere round about Drummond Street. I can,' said Len, 'tell
you exactly when it was. It was two nights before I flew out
here. That's just a week ago.

'What did you do?'

'What did we do? Well, this one of our lot said he'd be
satisfied if he could just get his five quid back. But, I said,
that couldn't be right. That just cancelled out nothing for
nothing. There was the question of punishment. So we got
her into the car and took her back to the office.'

'What office?'

'It's not really an office, but we call it that. We've got to
call it something, stands to reason. We got her there and
told her what we were going to do. She started crying then
and said she was only doing what she was doing because of
her boy friend. When he'd got started properly, she said,
it would be all right. She we asked her what he was doing,
and she said he was a printer, but of course we didn't believe
that. If I could have got hold of him I'd have punished him
too, because I don't think there's any worse crime in the
world than living off a woman. So I told her that what was
going to happen to her was going to happen without any
hard feelings on anybody's part, it was just a question of
justice. Then she changed her tone, and you'd got to hand
it to her. I've never heard a mouthful like that from any
woman, and what made it worse was her speaking so
refined. So then she was punished.'

'How?'

'You wouldn't be interested. Nothing permanent. I mean,
that wouldn't be right. You only want permanent injuries
for the big stuff. You oughtn't to ask that question anyway,
because it's the question of justice that matters, not how
it's administered. It's a matter of something nice and sharp,
something they'll remember all their lives, but it needn't

last all their lives. Last long enough, though, keep them out of mischief for a bit. So, in a way, as you are, in a sense, my pal, you can say that you'll get a bit of personal satisfaction out of justice being done.'

'Yes, yes, cut out the bloody theory.' Len looked hurt. 'What did you do then?' I asked. Where did you take her? How much did you knock her about? You smug little swine,' I said, 'trying to be God.'

'There's no need to talk like that,' said Len, with dignity, but glinting with danger like the dangerous street outside. 'You've got to keep your emotions out of things like that. And you say to cut out the theory. Yet it's only the theory that really counts.'

'I think I know the woman,' I said. 'I'm pretty sure I do.'

'I shouldn't be surprised if you did,' said Len. 'It might well have been the same one as put it over on you before. If you really want to know,' he said, 'we gave her a stiff brandy and one of our lot took her in the car near where she said she lived. Somewhere not too far from Baron's Court or Earl's Court. I forget where exactly. She was bleeding a bit from the mouth. A couple of teeth is as good a punishment as any. She was crying, too, this one of ours said, all the way back in the car.'

'How,' I said, Denham the plump middle-aged businessman becoming dangerous, 'would *you* like a couple of teeth knocked out? For, by Christ, if you don't get out of my sight this minute I'll do it.'

Len shook his head in wonder. 'I don't see why you should want to do that,' he said. 'It isn't as if I've done anything wrong. I just put the balance right, that's all. If you did that to me I'd have to do something of the same sort to you. And so it would have to go on. But I couldn't let it go on. You'd have to learn about justice, too. Anyway, as far as I'm concerned, you're still my pal. And that's why it's not right for you to talk to me the way you did, the way I see it. So we'll just forget it, I think, which is the best way. I've got to go nqw, anyway, but don't think I'm going because you said to me to go. What you said was not the words of a pal, but I'll shake hands with you to show there aren't any hard feelings.'

'Go on, go,' I said. 'Get out of my sight.'

'You shouldn't have said that,' said Len. 'Now I'll have to wait a couple of minutes just to show I'm not going to take any orders.' He waited a couple of minutes, the fire of justice in his eyes, myself just sitting there, staring back. Then he nodded, got up, paid at the cash-desk and stood for a minute at the door, loud hot Bugis Street behind him, this time looking like El Greco's lasher, not the lashed with the empty basket on his head. It's obvious, I think, that the basket is empty: there's just no sense of weight about it. Then Len, scourge of erring humanity, nodded again and went out. That was the last I saw of him.

14

It was as if this so unviolent tale of violence shocked England to silence so far as I was concerned. There was no message from Mr Raj or from my father at Hongkong, nothing waiting when we arrived at Yokohama. Between China and Japan I wrote a brief letter to Winterbottom asking if everything was all right, London being a big place where, conceivably, there might be more than one swearing prostitute of refined speech with a printer boy friend trying to get started. I had forgotten Winterbottom's address, so I enclosed the enveloped letter with a brief message to Mr Raj, asking him to stamp and post it, also asking how things were. Disembarking at Yokohama, I found Japanese weather cool and clear, a sharpness in the air but a promise of the cherry blossom season soon. I travelled the twenty-one miles to Tokyo by train, was met at the magnificent station by Archie Shelley, who handed car and driver over to me and then was on his way, he having many dinner engagements between then and his going on leave. The firm has its office and show-rooms in Marunouchi, but my house is in Deninchofu, a house of wood, paper and glass on stilts, surrounded by a delicious garden with dwarf pines and little bridges.

The two female servants were there to greet me – '*Yoku irasshai mashita, kange*' – and also Michiko San, who was not a servant. Like her not-yet-ennobled namesake, she was a girl of the people, mission-school-educated, a tennis-player, a smart wearer of Western clothes. How far what Mr Raj called love entered into our relationship I don't know: she was what I wanted, that's all I can say. She's gone now and I refuse to be sentimental about her; I still see her like in Yoshiwara, the Asakusa district, other places – delicate untemperamental women who seem to belong to a different race from the men, women who spoil one for assertive Alices and Imogens. Anyway, this story is not concerned with my private life. All I will say now is that, kissing Michiko, I suddenly with a shock saw that the curve of her cheek was not unlike the curve of the cheek of my sister Beryl: more and more that dull Midland town and its suburbs was threatening to swamp the wide world.

We dined that evening at the Hanabasha and were home and to bed early. The next day the pleasant routine of my public life again – the office in Marunouchi with my efficient Japanese underlings, meetings with business friends, the sense of the pulse of a clean modern city round me, then home to my wooden house with its sliding paper panels, shoes off for that exquisitely clean floor, cold Japanese beer, quiet talk and dalliance with Michiko. Then, quite soon, England started to roar in again by air mail. First came Winterbottom's letter:

'. . . A terrible thing happened to Imogen. She came home covered in blood, beaten up by people, crying and crying. She'd done nothing wrong really, it was them she picked up or who picked her up rather who were wanting to do wrong and it seemed only right to both of us that she took their money. This sort of thing happening we never expected. She went to bed and cried and cried and wouldn't get up and wouldn't eat anything for days. I was distracted as you can guess, and all this was a pity as I think I've really got started at last. As you know there's been a newspaper strike so I got the idea of listening to the

B.B.C. news and printing a kind of one-page newspaper. It was only what people could hear for themselves on the wireless but they seemed to think it was more true somehow when they saw it printed on paper. And I got some of the news wrong, not being able to take down in shorthand, and I put down there was another war coming very soon, which people believed. I gave this to the pubs and the shops round about for them to sell and now I've been getting a bit better known.

'But she's gone off now. Imogen's gone off back to her father. Now here I am in London and the reason why I came here in the first place was this running away with Imogen. So I'm not here now for any reason any longer, except that I think I'm getting started and she left me the money. Now Alice has been writing to me to go back to her, but how can I? The firm wouldn't take me back. Me running off in the way I did and having no references I don't see how I could get another job there. So here I remain. I still haven't got my winter overcoat but spring looks like being early this year, some of these last days being quite warm for the time of the year. I hope everything is going all right for you in Japan. I miss Imogen, being here on my own, and I still love her, even though she's left me. But she did look a mess, four teeth out, poor girl, wearing a scarf round her face when she went off back to her father.'

I finished this letter written in a peculiar script of Winterbottoms' own invention, rather like an illiterate's tongue-out copying of print. Perhaps Winterbottom wanted to show that, even when he was using a pen, he was still a printer. Then I looked out at busy Marunouchi, delicate snow blossom drifting from a sky made of delicate metal. All this Winterbottom business did seem like comic puppetry, very remote from the clack of the Japanese typewriters next door and the real flesh-and-blood Michiko waiting for me at home. And then, opening the next letter, I heard the voice of Mr Raj filling the office and knew that, whatever else one might say about him, Mr Raj was real. He had sent no flimsy blue air-letter form but a fat letter with a half-crown stamp on it, as full of meat as one of his curries:

'Dear Mr Denham,

'Well, still dear Mr Denham, despite your inordinate laziness hardly to be cancelled out by expensive cablegram, I have obeyed your behest and sent the letter you sent to the gentleman for whom it was intended, the circular with his address still reposing in your father's very full rack of letters. The copulation you suggest I have not yet achieved, but have strong hopes that this will not be much longer delayed, as the lady whom I am now emboldened to call Alice to her very face, shows some small affection for me and even asked myself and your father, who remains still a very good man, to tea with her in her house. In return I suggest to your father that we ask her in to eat a really good curry, bigger and more delectable than any I have so far made, and he thinks this to be a good suggestion. So this suggestion will be fulfilled, perhaps this very coming Sunday. The fact of my now living with your father has made people accept me more willingly than before, and only two nights ago I was sitting with your father in the Mucky Duck, as I am now emboldened to call it, together with his friends, with whom I have myself played golf, and they talked about foreign people as black bastards, in my presence, as though I were not myself black, and even asked my opinion about these black foreign people. So when I drink in the Mucky Duck with Alice (my pen almost blushes as with red ink to write the name so boldly) there is now nobody who dares to say "Look at that black man with that white woman." They take all for granted, Mr Denham. So I have much to thank you for. But then you are a man who has been to many countries, as witness you now in far-off Japan, and how are things there with you, Mr Denham? You are not a man who would regard a man of any colour as any other than his own brother.

'Now here our friendship emboldens me to say that once I told you a lie, albeit a white one. You will remember that short time ago that seems already an age, Mr Denham, when we first met in Colombo. I then said to you that I thought perhaps you were the Mr Denham who had been my old teacher in Trincomali. Well, in Trincomali there was never any such man! No, my teacher there had been a Mr Susskind, an American. I used this simple device of harmless lying to get to know you better, especially as I found out from a letter sent to you where you lived in England and I myself was going there. I had indeed seen you around, and thought to myself that here was a man who was really a man and would be a friend to me. And so it has worked out, Mr Denham.

'My work continues, and in a questionnaire I have given to people to fill in I have asked many relevant questions about people's ideas of race and what are the important differences between the races of the world, and so on. Various people I have asked to fill in this form have been insulting, but I am now proof against insults, Mr Denham, normally asking these questionnaires to be filled in in quiet places, such as public lavatories, where insults can be swiftly and painfully dealt with, though with no animosity. Lately I have found the gun I borrowed useful too, though still it has not been loaded, and at empty pistol-point some people in lavatories or in lighted doorways have been asked, or indeed persuaded, to give honest answers to the questions I ask. Thus scholarship is able to proceed, and difficulties must be smoothed out as best they can. The weather is a little more warm now, and there is a hope of spring coming early, not, of course, that I have seen an English spring yet, but poems read in school in Trincomali were full of daffodils and similar flowers, and also of lambs skipping, which on our streets here, I think, we are unlikely to see.

'And it is appropriate that I am in love, Mr Denham, for spring, so I have read also, is the time when in England it is a duty to be in love, so there I will do my duty. Love, therefore, must proceed apace, along with my work. Your father says he will not write, as he has little to say except his love for you, but will leave the writing to me. I assure you that if his health ever shows signs of impairment, I have Indian and Ceylonese medical friends who will be more than happy to minister to him, so you are never to worry. Also I have replenished stock of brandy, small stock it is true, in the cupboard, so it is always there for emergencies. Well, now I close, asking you to write soon and *at great length* and knowing you are my friend, as I am yours and will always be. Amen, as your father's friend the bloody Christian would say! Not that he is any longer a friend, for he does not like me but I do not care (he would not answer questionnaire sensibly) and he no longer comes to the house.

> 'Very very sincerely, Mr Denham,
> R. F. Raj.'

I should, I know, have felt suspicion at my father's curious silence. It was unlike him not to send at least a brief dayfather's scrawl, his aromatic self breathing up in coughs from the old man's laboured penmanship. But for some weeks after my receipt of this letter from Mr Raj I had my own troubles in Tokyo, and these were not business troubles either. They were to do with Michiko San.

God knows I have nothing against America, Americans. As far as the eastern seaboard is concerned, the thirteen colonies, I can't see America as anything other than a fine clever country that has been a little naughty but can have any time, as far as I am concerned, full dominion status. I mean, I don't accept the Declaration of Independence. I have never told any Americans this, naturally, but in my business and social dealings with these fine super-fatted people I have always assumed that they and I are much the same, and I have got on well with them accordingly. At the time of Michiko San's trouble it was unfortunate that I was on the point of achieving a most diplomatic live-and-let-live arrangement about colour television with an American firm. But in Tokyo there is a sort of small America called Washington Heights, where the families of a couple of thousand or more U.S. Air Force men live, and, to quote *Time*, have never had it so good. These men were, still are, fine super-fatted men, their wives alluring for the most part but too aware of it. They were, before the time of Colonel Johnstone, most irresponsible, with provocative buttocks that would make a man groan and clench his fists, gin on their breath at all hours, their children neglected. The younger ones responded to this neglect by, for the most part, spectacular but not really viciously bad bad behaviour. Those of school-age merely tore up the school buses, smoked in public chimneyly, pitched peach-pips at people, little more than that. But some of the older teenagers fancied themselves men, of the race of the makers of the not-sufficiently-punitive A-bomb, and devised punishments more gratifying. It was unfortunate that Michiko San should be chosen for punishment.

I went down to Yokohama, unwillingly, to witness one of the last rugby matches of the season, the rugby cup having been donated by my own firm, and, finding it too late to return to Tokyo after the junketings, spent the night in the Tunnel (very clean, most unvicious, the very act like a surgical operation). When I got back to my house (it was week-end) I found Michiko in bed distraught and weeping, the servants butterflying or cho-cho-ing about helplessly. Michiko, in such distress, had forgotten much of her English, and it took some time to discover what had happened to her. She, foolishly, had gone to see friends the night before, had walked some way from somewhere in the dark, had been attacked by teenagers of Washington Heights (O Heights, O Washington, O Liberty) and, as far as I could find out, near-raped. As always, curiously, happens, this was the beginning of the end of whatever our relationship was. She was hardly to blame, nor I. American teenagers, in their strange way, can hardly be blamed for anything either: chocolate malts (Jumbo ones) and juke-box trumpets shut ears and eyes to morality. (They were only kids, in a strange country, their fathers doing their duty for democracy etc.) It was the thing that happened, that has to happen sooner or later, that is better for coming from the outside. It meant that she didn't want me, nor did I want to touch her, though I felt anger, compassion and pity and other cognate emotions. And in seeing people and demanding some kind of justice, in letting off hot air on social occasions with Americans, I dissipated much energy, wrote no letters home, opened, as a matter of fact, no English-stamped letters either, unless they were typewritten ones. And I made myself unpopular in certain circles, for what, officially, was Michiko San to me? In a sense, my rumblings about justice, my occasional whisky-fed snarls did the house no kind of good. And then, of course, I came home one day to find, as I took my shoes off at the door, something strange – the colour television still and silent, and Michiko not there any more. I ranged the district in the car, toured Tokyo with growing lack of hope, returned to a late and silently-served dinner quite hopeless. Next day I received a cable.

You have been more patient with this inept story-teller than this inept story-teller has had any right to expect. You have had no action, you have had merely J. W. Denham on leave, eating, drinking, unjustifiably censorious, meeting people, especially Mr Raj, recounting, at the tail of the eye, almost out of earshot, the adultery of small uninteresting people. Now, God help you, you shall have all the action you need. The cable, of course, said that my father was dying. It did not come from Mr Raj, it did not come from my sister in Tunbridge Wells, it came from that great Shakespearean, sniffer-out of death and of life, Ted Arden. The cable said, with admirable clarity: 'Dad dying. Come home quick.' Alliterative, you see, poetical, but none the less urgent.

Cable Rice in London? Nonsense. I looked carefully, my hands on the smooth desk trembling, at Mishima, my chief assistant. He was intelligent, competent, no doubt, with peering myopic eyes that had pored systematically, when he was a student travelling home on trams, at the longest words in the English language ('Floccinaucinihilipilification,' he would say, 'is manifestly of more letters than antidisestablishmentarianism.') Could he be trusted? He could be trusted. But the firm's rule stood, like one of those bloody thumped Red Sea commandments: 'Thou shalt have, as firm's ruler, none other than a European, nay, not even for a day.' I said to Mishima:

'I have to return to England. Immediately. Arrange a

183

plane booking, please, for tonight if possible. If not to-
night, certainly tomorrow morning.'

'Trouble, sir?'

'My father's dying.'

'Oh, I see.' His father had died, so he said, though I
did not believe it, along with his mother and three aunts
and uncle at Nagasaki. 'Right away, sir, I will do that.'

'You'll take over in my absence.'

'Oh, I see.'

'I'll be away a week at the most.'

'Oh, I see.'

He returned from his telephoning as from a trip to the
tobacco kiosk: the regular brands were not available –
no BOAC, no QANTAS, no KLM, no –

'Yes, yes, yes. What?

He named a new Scandinavian airline that had a first-
class seat available. That would do. '*Tack*,' I said, distraught.

15

Before take-off that same evening I cabled Ted Arden –
'Arriving London 18.00 Sunday. Leave message if any
change.' – knowing that he was bright enough to know
how to leave a message at London Airport. I took with
me to read the wad of unopened personal mail from England, all of which, as I now saw, was from Mr Raj.
Mishima was swift, darting, efficient, bowing courteously
with no signs of gratification when I handed over all the
keys to him. The aircraft waiting was a fine new DC-8,
the hostesses too blonde, big and Nordic to be true. I
was surprised to find the first-class cabin almost empty.
'Why?' I asked the goddess called Miss Björnsen. 'At
Singapore,' she said, all smiles, 'you see. Very great surprise.'

Singapore was nine hours off. I was fed and wined mas-
sively – viands for Vikings in high hall hiccuping; seafood
salt with savour of seabrine thwacking throat with thriv-
ing wine-thirst – and I wondered that I had such appetite,
my poor father dying. But, of course, he was in another
world, nothing would come home to me till I came home
to smell and feel England and know it, temporarily at
least, real. Distractedly I thumbed through Mr Raj's
letters: there were references to my father's great health
and I was not to worry if he became ill; Mr Raj had shyly
kissed Alice Winterbottom in her own doorway and not
been repulsed; the spring advanced along with the thesis

and the collation of answers to the questionnaire. I slept from Hongkong on, was awakened by clicks of safety-belts and a blonde smiling Fricka or Frigga above me, telling me that this was Singapore, an hour for re-fuelling, light refreshments would be served. And then came Miss Björnsen's great surprise. The airport was full of armfuls of orchids and teddy-bears, the flash of lights of worm-eaten Chinese photographers, the smiles of milling men of hideous handsomeness, and the core or cynosure was a face and body I had seen once or twice on the cinema screen—a female film-star with expensively tousled hair like corn-syrup in colour, no lipstick on those lips that had been kissed publicly how oft, a free trade-show of bosom cunningly high-hoisted, no stockings. 'Her name?' I asked a middle-aged woman fellow-passenger.

'You mean to say you don't know who that is?'

'No, no, I don't.' And, seeing her mouth harden at my brusqueness, 'Sorry. I've got a lot on my mind.'

'That's Monique Hugo.'

'Oh, French.'

'Yes, French.' And, as if to prove to the gaping Singaporeans that France was what they had always been told it was, Mlle Hugo fell into the arms of a long-haired young man and kissed and was kissed with hungry open mouth. Lights flashed like tiny orgasms, some people cheered, a champagne bottle cracked open.

'She's been making a film here,' said my informant. 'Location shots, rather. They're going to finish it off in London. She plays the part of a French spy in Japan for the Americans.'

'Why?'

'I don't know why,' said the woman huffily. 'That's what it said in the papers.'

And now Mlle Hugo was kissed gluily by other men

and more lights flashed, and then a precise Chinese voice loudspeakered that we were all to proceed to the aircraft. Warm in Mlle Hugo's glory we proceeded, in flowers and lights and kisses, the air like an oven, smiles and smiles like meringues. The smiling Nordic goddesses at the top of the steps, greeting with smiles Mlle Hugo and her loud or handsome entourage, suddenly seemed to shrink, to hand over all they had of numinous to this tarty-looking little minx with no lipstick. The first-class cabin became a bower, soft, perfumed, but also steely with the sharp eyes of executives who spoke authoritative American, bringing out from zipped flat cases typewritten sheaves, preparing, while their star reposed, her hand soft in the guitar-hardened fingers of the long-haired young man who, I noted, had a guitar in the luggage-rack, to go into airborne conference. Me they seemed to resent. One, whose seat was next to mine, said:

'I wonder if you'd mind taking that seat near the front there. We just want to get together for a little while, one or two things to discuss.'

'I would mind,' I said. 'I paid for this seat.'

'Oh, come now, Be co-operative. We've a lot to get through.' And, by God, he tried to lift me out by the left arm.

'Don't try to push me around,' I said. 'This isn't Washington Heights.'

'Sure it isn't, and nobody's trying to push. Okay, if you won't you won't.' And so I stayed there, a scowling unphotogenic enclave in their hieratic polity. From then on I had the impression of deliberate persecution. The guitar-player took down his guitar, tuned it loud and long, and began to sing a French song which I might, at another time, have appreciated for a certain Gallic toughness under the conventional mush:

'Tu es mon
Violon
D'Ingres . . .'

Readers interested in the private lives of great stars may like to know that Mlle Hugo snores slightly when dozing, picks her nose covertly, scratches her head. We had a tumultuous reception at Bangkok, though it was the middle of the night, and then, on the long leg to India, Mlle Hugo played the moon to my sour Endymion. She came over and sat by me and said, finger in mouth like sweet innocent little one, *'Allo'*.

'Hallo to you.'

'Ow far you go?'

'London.'

'Ah. I go there too.'

'That's nice for London.'

'Comment?'

'Oh, come off it,' I said. 'You know English well enough. Reserve all this ingenuous little-girl stuff for your fans.'

'Comment?'

The executive who had, off and on, been sitting next to me, returned from the men's room smelling of after-shave lotion. 'Keep away from him, honey,' he said. 'He bites.'

'And wouldn't you bite if your girl had been raped by American teenagers and you'd just got a cable saying your father was dying?' I shouldn't have said that; I should have been calm, cold, English. Now I was going to get sympathy; I'd have to watch my tear-ducts.

'Gee, why didn't you say? Gosh, I'm sorry. Anything we can do to help?'

'Your fathair,' said Mlle Hugo. 'Your father dyeeng? My fathair dead too. In thair *Résistance*. Shot by the Jairmans.' And she let her smoky eyes get moist ('register grief'); and then ('now let's see some tears') let us see some tears.

'Aw, come on now, Moneek,' said the shaved executive. 'That's just not true. You're getting sort of mixed up with that last movie you made.'

Anyway, Mlle Hugo, in the capricious way of goddesses and great ladies, had decided that she had taken a fancy to J. W. Denham, fat business-man who had lost his Japanese mistress and was in the process of becoming an orphan. The guitar-playing young man looked gloomy and strummed funereal chords, so that another executive, who seemed to have been built around a pair of incredibly heavy spectacles, said, 'For Christ's sake.'

Admire, for Christ's sake, Denham at Calcutta, Delhi and Karachi, Mlle Hugo on his arm in the hail of photographers' flash-bulbs. Are we perhaps wrong to sneer at these whipped-like-cream, spun-like-sugar crackly crunchy products of the shiny mythopoeic machines of our age? Every brown girl, far more beautiful than she, who gaped at this avatar at the airports where she was fêted, showed in her teeth a hunger for unifying myth, while, in the council-chambers inland, the statesmen strove for disunity.

Monique, as I was now to call her, returned to her hard-fingered younger man for the Middle East leg, and, with his hard fingers, he fed her pieces of toast towards Cairo, and she drank coffee from a big cup, hands cupped around it, big smoky eyes looking at me from over the rim. Off and on we all dozed; off and on men went to the men's room to shave and return with glassy chins in a mist of shaving lotion. In full light, approaching Rome, we fed off schnapps and Smørgasbørd, and Rome greeted half-drunken smiles (Denham, in the newspapers of Italy, bound for his dad's death, smiling and waving for the photographers like a man who has achieved large triumphs). And so on to London, and at London Airport the ultimate glory of television cameras wheeled up to the steps, the screams of a distant fan-club, the approach of a bright young man with a microphone who said:

'Welcome, Miss Hugo, to London and the first live airport interview in ATA's series *Meet The Stars*. Tell me, Miss Hugo, what kind of a trip did you have?'

'Oh, very naaaeece.' And all the time, by God and for Christ's sake, this unlipsticked spun sugar held on to Denham's arm.

'And how did you like Singapore?'

'Oh, very naaaeeece.'

'You, sir, are, I believe,' (this was to me) 'Mr Nussbaum?'

'I,' I said, 'am Mr J. W. Denham, business-man from Tokyo, whose Japanese mistress was near-raped by kids from Washington Heights and who has now come to England to witness his father's death.' That was the fault of the bloody schnapps. God forgive me, but I am at least being honest, I am at least blushing as I set this down. Suddenly there seemed to be a rapid regrouping, skilfully directed by somebody used to managing crowd-scenes, and I found myself cast down from the plinth I had shared with the goddess, an ordinary man on the outer circle. A clear-voiced, clear-complexioned ground hostess was leading me, with others, to the disembarking passengers' waiting-room, and there another hostess standing in a kind of pulpit called my name. I went up to her and she gave me, smiling, a message in an envelope. I fumbled the slip of paper out and read: 'Dead. Ted.' There was the Shakespearean touch again, the later clipped style of *Antony and Cleopatra*. I sat down. My father was dead.

I told myself not to blame Mr Raj just yet. Mr Raj was

at least there to look after him. He might have died a
month, a week earlier if Mr Raj had not been there. He
was not a young man; he had long outlived McCarthy and
Black, my friends whom the war had killed. Seventy was
a reasonable age to die. But I felt mean that I had not been
present for the last few words, the conventional blessing,
the rattle and the rictus. People like the family about them
when they die. Had Beryl been there? I doubted it, but
I would soon know. I would soon know everything.

This was Sunday. There was, I thought, a midnight
train I could catch, but I felt I needed a night's sleep.
Tomorrow morning would do. I dozed in the bus to Victoria. Next to me was an American gentleman, his wife
and daughter seated across the aisle. Desperately he
dredged the dull journey for sights of historical interest.
My dozing head lolled on to his shoulder and I awoke.
'That's all right, son,' he said, smiling. 'You sleep it off.'
At Victoria I got a taxi and was driven to my Italian
widow's little hotel in Bloomsbury. She was there, her
reading glasses on, *Oggi* on the table of the breakfast
room. She now had a budgerigar in a cage, a bird of blue
smoke colour. It twittered madly. There also, with no
surprise, I saw Winterbottom.

'*Buona sera, signora,*' I said. 'Have you a room for me?
I'm sorry I couldn't let you know I was coming. My father
was dying, I was told, and now I'm told that he's dead.'
I looked at shabby Winterbottom. He was not well. His
beard had grown considerably, but he had now to match
it the feverish Cristo-look that the peasants of New
Mexico had remarked in D. H. Lawrence.

'You said he was dying,' said the widow. 'You told that
to all the world on the *televisione*.'

'I saw it,' said Winterbottom. 'I saw it in the pub. About
two hours ago. I knew you'd come here so I came here.'

'I'm dead beat,' I said, sitting down. 'It was a very tiring journey.'

'I can see that. Yes, it must have been.' Winterbottom then, in his dirty raincoat, began to bite his nails. The widow said:

'*Numero otto*. A double room. The only one free.'

'That will do very well,' I said. 'How are things with you?' I asked Winterbottom.

'They took it from me,' said Winterbottom. 'This chap did, I mean. I couldn't pay him any more money, and he wouldn't wait. The printing press, I mean.'

'And where are you now? God, I'm tired.' I was, too. The world seemed full of twittering budgerigars. 'Could you,' I asked the widow, 'send out for a small bottle of brandy?'

'It seemed,' said the widow, 'from the *televisione* that you had enough brandy.'

'Oh, God, was it as bad as that?'

'I'll go and get you something,' said Winterbottom, 'if you'll give me the money.'

I looked again at Winterbottom and suddenly thought that a large bottle of cold English pale ale would suit me as well as anything for a nightcap. This was strange: I so rarely drank English beer. 'Come on,' I said. 'We'll go round the corner. God, I *am* tired.'

The pub round the corner was called the Anchor. It was full of swearing men, a West Indian tart, a trembling lecturer from the university who drank tomato juice, trembling. On the walls were photographs of the Royal Family. 'Just one,' I said. 'I honestly think I'm too tired to sleep.'

'I'd get these,' said Winterbottom, 'honestly I would, but I can't. I feel really ashamed, but I did my best. Honest. I'm just not intended to be successful.'

'How's Imogen?'

'I honestly don't know. I just haven't heard. And, in a way, it's a good job she hasn't written. This one opens everything, absolutely everything. *That* jealous.'

'Which one? What? You forget I've been in Japan.'

'Jennifer,' said Winterbottom, bowing his head in deep gloom. Then he tried to wash down the name like a pill in his half of mild. 'It's the one I'm living with now. I can't remember properly how it started. It was when Imogen went back. This Jennifer was in a pub, you see, and then she came home with me. She said she'd cook me some sausages. And there it is. Very jealous,' he repeated. 'And talks, you know, refined, like Imogen used to.'

'You are a bloody fool, aren't you?' I said. The light ale, warm and flat, was going down badly: that vision had misled me. I ordered brandy and soda. God, I was tired.

'Oh, yes,' simpered Winterbottom. 'And, look here, I'm really very very sorry about your father. That's one of the things I came round to say. You know how I got here tonight?' Pride stirred in him. 'We were both in the pub together you see, and then this television thing came on. So I said I knew you, and she said she didn't believe it. I said I was just going to the gents. The gents is in the yard outside, you see. Well, I dashed like mad for the tube. I don't think she's got any idea where I've gone to. But there'll be a hell of a row when I get back.' He giggled.

'What are you living on?'

'What can I live on? Her, chiefly, I suppose. She's got a small pension, you see. And then there's her alimony.'

'How old is she, in the name of God?'

'Old? Oh, older than me. A lot. But, oh, not all that old, really. And she's very smart. But she's very jealous.'

'You,' I said, 'are going back to Alice.'

'You know,' he said, in wonder, 'that's what I thought. I though that you could see how the land lay and let me know.'

'You'd better come back,' I said, 'before it's too late. Before Alice gets tied up with somebody else.'

'But that Jack Brownlow's already married. He'll never get a divorce.'

'I'm not thinking of Jack Brownlow,' I said.' Never mind who. You should never have started all this, you're not cut out for it.'

'It was she who started it, she and Jack Brownlow.'

'Never mind who started it. You've committed the great sin against stability and you see now what a bloody mess you can land into when you do that. You know,' I said, 'I think I'd better go and get some sleep. I'm just about dropping.'

'Look,' swallowed Winterbottom, 'if I go back there I'll never get out again. She'll make sure of that. When are you travelling?'

'Tomorrow morning.'

'If,' swallowed Winterbottom, 'you could lend me the train fare—'

'Lend lend lend,' I said. 'Give give give. What the hell would you do without me?'

'And if I could stay the night with you—'

'Yes,' I said, my eyes shutting. 'And I lend you my razor and a clean shirt.'

'You'll get it all back, you will honestly. It shouldn't be too hard for me to get my old job back again, not really. I mean, it isn't as though I've done anything really *wrong*, is it? Anyway,' said Winterbottom proudly, 'I am admitting that I made a bloody fool of myself, aren't I?'

I almost fell. 'Come on, now,' said the vinegar landlady. 'Don't know when to stop, that's what's the matter with some of you people. Get home while you can still walk.'

'I'll look after him,' said Winterbottom eagerly. 'Don't worry. I'll see that he gets back all right.' He led me, tottering, out. People sneered at me, me, who had been embraced that day by a goddess.

16

For, I thought, travelling next morning to the Midlands through spring in England, we had had enough chaos. Let the death of my father be balanced by the re-birth of a marriage. Winterbottom sat opposite me, the nervous bridegroom in a clean shirt, clean-shaven. He had spent part of the night at the wash-basin, taking off his beard with my nail scissors and my razor. I had, meanwhile, slept as dead as my father. Now I wondered what exactly had to be done about this death. There were the questions of burial, newspaper notices, official registration of the event. Did not one also have to organise a sort of festive meal, mainly of ham and tongue and strong tea, the chief mourner joking bravely in black as he offered nips of whisky round? And then the matter of the will and pro- bate and disposing of the Holman Hunts and Rosa Bon- heurs and the small library that was really a typographical museum. And his ties and his shirts and his overcoats. I examined lean Winterbottom, shabby in his first-class corner seat. He should be given some of those.

When we arrived, Winterbottom and I stood for a moment on the platform, hands in our pockets in irreso- lution, my luggage beside me, Winterbottom with no lug- gage. 'Did you,' I asked, 'ever get your winter overcoat?'

'No. It'll still be here, I suppose. It is a bit chilly, isn't it?' Yes, I thought, and if everything was being left to me, it was a good thing it was chilly. How soon after death did decomposition set in? When had he died? I got the image of the body racing back to the simple chemicals it was made of, the cold, almost like a soul, restraining it, making it hang on to identity for a little longer. Mr Raj, presumably, would here be helpless, knowing nothing of undertakers (did Hindus still cremate?) and the tolling of the one bell by, surely, the eyeless Selwyn. I had expected Mr Raj to be there waiting on the platform, but he was not and that, I realised, was as well, all things considered. A panegyric on that dead good old man, then perhaps one on the living, her beauty and, now, amenability. No, we didn't want that. Winterbottom said:

'I shouldn't have come like this, not really. I should have given you a chance to explore the ground, so to speak, find out how she'll take it.'

'She'll take it all right, but wait till this evening. An afternoon will be enough time for breaking it gently. This morning you'd better go and see your old boss.'

'I daren't, I just daren't.'

'Of course you dare. How long did you work for them before?'

'Six years.'

'Six years and never a hard word?'

'Only once or twice.'

'They'll take you back. Damn it, you've only been away since Christmas. Apologise humbly, say you've been a fool.'

'Which I have.'

'Which you have. Tell them that you've gained a lot of experience in London.'

'Which I have, in a way, but not in that line.'

'Never mind, they'll take you back.'

Winterbottom nodded, unconvinced. Again and again he fingered his new clean chin, unconvinced, the bold London Winterbottom, that had lasted so short a time, gone for ever. We walked up the stairs, Winterbottom letting me carry both my bags, and out of the station. He was swallowed up by the busy Monday town, fingering his chin, and I called a taxi.

The driver, a hale warty man in his sixties, was inclined to inquisitiveness, evidently, from his accent, a South Wales immigrant. Stranger in these parts, was I? On a visit, then? Had relations here, was it? My dad, was it? Dead, was he? There was a pity, now. He sighed and nodded with a sort of satisfaction at somebody, not yet him, being dead. Married, was I? Thinking of getting married sometime or other, then? Should be married, man of my age. After the gasworks, the cricket-ground, the neo-gothic municipal baths – all bathed in weak spring sun – came the dull suburb which the same sun made seem flat, cardboard, not a necropolis, but something that had never lived.

'This is it, then?' said the driver, stopping. 'No blinds down. No blinds to come down. There is the modern world for you, disrespectful. Curtains is not the same thing, no matter how you look at it, isn't it?' He handed out my two bags and took his money, reversed cheerfully into Clutterbuck Avenue and was off townwards again, back towards life. The pre-human deadness of the suburb this forenoon was remarkable: limp shirts and nightgowns, that no one could ever have worn, fought each other feebly on the lines. There was not a dog, not a cat to be seen on the clean pavements like mortuary slabs, not a bird to be heard. I stood outside my still father's house, realised that I had no longer a key (curious that all my keys should be in the pockets of Asiatics) and would have to knock. I knocked and nobody answered. Where was Mr Raj? At work, perhaps, on race relationships. Perhaps lunching early. No sense of a house of the dead came to my second knock – the Rosa Bonheurs and books and carpets retained vestiges of my father's life, tobacco smoke in the folds of clothes. I knocked once more, and now I feared that the corpse that was no longer my father would wearily rise and come down and open the door, coughing a noiseless welcome. And the whole street was deserted. Frightened, I picked up my bags and almost fell down the shallow stone steps. A bag in each hand, I started to climb Clutterbuck Avenue, panting, seeking sanctuary in the Black Swan or Mucky Duck, a Flayer's ace.

I entered the public bar, where two very old men drank very slow pints. One of them, suited and bowlered, had the grey lost look of the long-retired; the other was wrapped in dirty cerements, including sacking leggings, and smelt of horse-dung. Behind the bar was Veronica, her hair in curlers, her thin body in flat sweater and toreador pants. She looked at me exophthalmically, recognised me, then went to call up the stair-well: 'Edward! He's come.' To me she said, 'He's not frying the fish today, he's cooking it in a casserole in the oven.'

'Brandy, please,' I said. 'Tell me what happened.'

'Martell's?' She looked at me with no warmth. Then, drawing the brandy, she said, 'It's been such a worry for all of us. You've no idea.'

'When did he die?'

'Yesterday morning. Just as the bells were ringing.'

'I'm sorry. But I couldn't help being in Japan.'

She handed me my glass, looking at me as though she thought that I could, in fact, help it. And then there was the stage-galloping-horses sound of Ted hurtling down the stairs, and then, wiping his hands on a tea-towel, he appeared. He said:

'Ello, me duck. Am I glad to see yer!' He shook hands in hearty condolence.

'I couldn't help being in Japan,' I said. 'Somebody's got

to work there, when all's said and done.'

'Japanese,' said Veronica.

'And I'm very grateful. You know that,' I said.

'It was nothing,' said Ted. 'Yer dad was a customer. A landlord's got a responsibility to his customers.'

'I can't get into the house,' I said. 'I've not seen him yet. I've not seen anybody yet. I've no idea what happened.'

'Well, yer see –' Ted scratched his chin, unshaven yet. The sound was of a match striking. Then he drew himself a little arf. 'Lovely that,' he said, having drunk. 'In real good condition.' Veronica said:

'While you're down here I'll go and lie down for a little while.'

'Do that, me duck,' said Ted, with loving eyes, his nose twitching. 'Me poor old duck. The old trouble,' he explained to me, as he watched her go off. Then he said:

'I adn't seen yer dad in ere for a few nights, and some of is pals was asking where e was. So I asked this black bugger that yer dad's ad living there, and e said that e was not too well and ad been staying in bed for a few days, but that nobody wasn't to worry. I asked what the matter was, and then this one says that it was just a bit of over-eating, that's all, nothing to worry about. Anyway, me and one or two others, two of those that yer dad used to drink with, went round there, and this black bugger wasn't too anxious to let us in, so to speak. Anyway, e couldn't really stop us, and we go upstairs and there's your dad just about snuffing it, and there's a couple of other black buggers around the bed, only blacker than this one that was living with yer dad, and they say that they're in the medical profession and everything's going to be all right. Well, I didn't like the look of that so I ring up Doc Forsyth that attends the wife and asked im to come round and ave a look. E comes round and e talks about gross neglect, them being is very words, and e plays ell. E plays ell about you, too, not making provision for yer dad, as e put it. And that's another thing,' said Ted. 'What's all this about you shouting the odds on the telly last night? I didn't see it, but there's plenty as did. What's all this about you raping somebody or something?'

'Didn't anybody try to get in touch with my sister?' I said. I started to mottle and tremble with shame.

'Ow could they, me duck? Nobody found any letter from er in yer dad's ouse, nobody seemed to know er address except yer dad, and e was past giving anybody's address except the one e was going to.'

'You could have got the police to broadcast an SOS,' I said. 'Please,' I said, 'I'm not finding fault. I'm very grateful as you know.'

Ted shook his head in great sadness. 'Nobody listens to the wireless any more, me duck. It's all telly now. Though,' he said, 'it's a wonder they didn't see and ear you on the telly. Every bugger else seems to ave done. You saw im, Arold, didn't yer?'

'Yis,' said the old man in filthy cerements.

'Anyway,' said Ted, 'we thought it was quicker to get old of you, distance meaning nothing nowadays. It doesn't strike me that this sister of yours is much good. Doesn't seem to ave written to yer dad at all.'

'And what did he die of?' I asked.

'Art failure,' said Ted. 'Though, of course, that's what everybody dies of. That's what it says on the death cersti-ficate, anyway. Doc Forsyth said that yer dad ad been overloading is stomach. Shouldn't ave been let, e says. Too many people there, blackies too, as knew nothing about it trying to put im right. And they put im right all right,' said Ted vigorously. 'Right in is bloody coffin. At least, that's where e'll be this afternoon. I give old Jackie Starbrook the key. E's undertaking the job. That, I suppose, is why e's called an undertaker,' mused Ted. 'Funny, never thought of that before. And Mrs Keogh's done the washing and laying out.'

'I'm very grateful,' I said again.

'I've got a list of what you owe,' said Ted, always practical. 'I'd no idea them cables cost so much. And the phone call to London Airport. It's a good job yer gave me yer address before yer went away. That black bugger would never ave give it. E didn't want yer back. E said yer'd play ell with im.'

'Where is he now?'

'Around, I suppose,' said Ted vaguely. 'E's been carrying on, or trying to, with that wife of that one that went away with that other. E seemed very keen on er when e was ere the Saturday before last. Taking advantage, in a way, e is, there being so many West Indian niggers about going around with white women. Nobody seems to think nothing of it these days. I feel a bit sorry for im, in a way. Like kids they are, really.'

'I'd better go,' I said. 'I'd better see about the funeral and the funeral tea and whatever else has to be seen about. There's so much to do.'

'We can do yer a tea ere,' said Ted. 'I don't see why not. We've got a catering licence. Three and six a ead I reckon we could do it for. I can't do fried fish, much as I'd like to, because of the difficulty of keeping it ot. Besides, yer've got to ave am at a funeral. Am, tongue, fancy cakes. A bit of trifle if yer like. Whisky in the tea extra, of course. Yer can buy a few bottles ere.'

'But,' I said, bewildered, 'who do I invite?'

'Oh,' said Ted, 'is pals. We was all is pals, really. Is pals would appreciate it. There's nothing like a good funeral tea for putting new art into people.'

17

In the dark brown dining-room of his vicarage the vicar resumed his hearty lunch of cold underdone beef, hot mashed potatoes, thick bloody beetroot slices. He drank, sighing, beer which he poured from an ox-blood-coloured jug. He offered me some. In the corner of the room his golf-bag leaned, ready for the afternoon. He said:

'I needn't tell you, Denham, how bloody sorry I was to hear about your father. I didn't have a chance to see him before he died. I didn't even know he was bloody well dying.' He forked in some bloody beetroot which went down like an oyster. 'I'd stopped coming round to pick him up for golf because that Indian you persuaded your father to have living with him became really bloody offensive. And your father never came to church. An old-fashioned rationalist, as you know. These quaint old substitutes for faith. Still, he was a bloody good man.' He cut beef vigorously and chewed with strong, though middle-aged, teeth.

'In what way offensive?' I asked. On the wall opposite me, in full churchy light from the window, was an eighteenth-century print of a leering parson fumbling fat whores. This fast-munching vicar had, poor man, a silvery saintly face. Even his appetite seemed to be a desperate act. He, too, was a victim of modern England. He gulped and said:

'Oh, he sneered at Christianity, you know, and said how much better Hinduism was. How Christianity could not embrace the world of plants and animals. He said that the Church didn't know the meaning of love.'

'I see.'

'Anyway, Wednesday will do very well for the burial service. Luckily, this is an easy week for me. Bloody easy week,' he emended.

'I can't,' I said, 'quite understand. Mr Raj never seemed to me to be the sort of man who'd be gratuitously offensive. And he isn't, as far as I know, a very orthodox Hindu.'

'He seemed peculiarly possessive about your father. I did notice that, the two or three times I called. As though he wanted your father all to himself. But why? Surely the bloody man's got a father of his own?' The final tiny parcel of beef, beet, potato, blessed by the last of the mustard on his plate, went down. He rang the little bell that stood by the beer-jug.

'He's been ruled paternally by the British,' I said, 'for a long time. Now he wants to get his own back. I don't mean revenge, not revenge. He just wants to be a father. And you get in the way because you are, in his muddled mind, what he'd call a padre, and that makes you a sort of rival father. Will that do for an explanation? Perhaps it won't.'

'I know all this bloody Oedipus business,' said the vicar, with a most gentle belch. 'If you want to take the father's place you've got to kill the father first. You don't turn the father into a son. It's all bloody nonsense, anyway. We just didn't take to each other, that's all.' A girl with an open mouth, fat cheeks, a new perm, brought in pudding for the vicar and took away his well-cleaned meat-plate. *'A pudding servant girl, pudding to follow.'* Who had written that, quoted that, said that? Of course, Everett. And he was a man I had to see this afternoon. The vicar shook sugar over his pudding.

'Wednesday, then,' I said. 'Thanks very much. And who do you play golf with these days?'

The vicar looked at me, pudding spoon in his hand, and, to my shocked horror, his eyes filled with tears. 'I knock around on my own mostly,' he said. 'Nobody wants us these days, nobody. They don't want us on Sunday, they don't want us on Monday. People only want us when they're bloody born and when they're bloody dead.' He put his spoon down on his plate and then he pushed the plate away. Then, thinking better of it, he pulled the plate towards him again and ate his pudding with desperate appetite. 'They say the church spire interferes with their bloody television reception,' he said. He wiped his eyes with his free hand.

'Wednesday,' I said again. 'Good-bye.' I got out as quickly as I could, hearing him say, 'They don't want us at all, bloody people.'

These words of the vicar drove me to a large brandy at the pub by the bus-stop for town. I hadn't yet eaten. I downed another double brandy as the landlord called time, saw the bus coming and ran out for it. Hazy, but not quite vertiginous, I re-enacted parts of my past life with my father till I was put down at Corcoran Street. Off Corcoran Street was Markham Street. In Markham Street were the offices of the *Evening Hermes*. I asked a ruminant girl for Mr Everett. Soon Mr Everett came out. 'Yes?' he said, as though he didn't know me. He didn't ask me in.

'I merely want,' I said, 'some information. The address of my sister Beryl in Tunbridge Wells.'

'Oh, it's you, is it?' Everett added, to the five stave-lines of plastered hair on his scalp, a kind of frowning alto clef on his forehead. 'I've got some reason for disliking you but I can't at the moment just think what it is.'

'How is Imogen?'

'You had something to do with that, didn't you? Didn't you? Wait. You shouldn't be here. You should be in Japan. Japan,' said Everett, and then, to my surprise, began to quote one of his own, or Harold's, or John's, or Alfred's poems:

'Rice-paper land, O lotus-footed,
Whose tiny trees are tiny-rooted,
And cherry-blossom bells tinkle over the lakes
And old Fujiyama shakes and quakes.'

'Oh, God,' I said. 'No. That is not it at all. My girl was raped by teenagers from Washington Heights. That's the picture I've brought back with me. And my father's dead.'

'Yes,' said Everett calmly. 'There was something on one of the commercial television networks about that. About both of those things. Imogen,' he said, 'will recover. She's lost four teeth. Just now she looks as she used to look when she was losing her first ones. But those came out naturally, of course, for the most part. These later ones, apparently, were knocked out.' He began to shake and quake.

'Come on,' I said. 'We'll go to the Hippogriff.' I took his arm. 'I want to see Alice, anyway.' And then I realised that I'd better not say why I wanted to see Alice. And that Winterbottom had better be kept away from Everett for a while.

'I'm all right,' said Everett, shaking himself free. 'I'll come with you. Trudy,' he said to the girl who chewed and chewed, 'get my hat like a good girl. I don't really need a coat, do I?' he said to me. 'That's a smart suit you've got on,' he said, fingering the material. 'You're supposed to be a rich man, aren't you?'

'If you mean the Collected Poems,' I said, 'as you know, I'm quite willing—'

'Oh, to hell with the Collected Poems!' cried Everett. 'Thank you, my dear,' he said to the girl who had brought his hat, 'thank you so very much.'

Calmly he said, as we walked towards the Hippogriff, 'I'm really quite glad you've come to see me, you know. I knew your father. I think your sister would be rather pleased if I wrote a little something about him, wouldn't she? When is the funeral?'

'Wednesday afternoon.'

'I'll be there. I shall be so sorry to see Beryl and Henry under such sorrowful circumstances. Sorry and glad. I believe they must be doing rather well, must be very busy. I wrote to them, you know, but they haven't yet replied.'

'What's their address? Nobody's been able to tell them yet what's happened.'

Everett stopped at once and took from his inner pocket a stuffed wallet. He shuffled a mass of visiting cards and paper-scraps clumsily, saying under his breath, like Dr Johnson, 'Too too too.' At length he found what I wanted. 'Here you are,' he said.

I called in at the Post Office, which was quite near the Hippogriff and, Everett looking aimlessly at the ceiling as he waited, I sent off a telegram. There were no other relatives left alive, nobody except my aunt in Redruth, and she was too old to manage the journey. Beryl could write to her later. The rest of the mourner-guests would be told by Ted (three and six a head, wasn't it?) so there was no need to put an announcement in the paper. The rest of the mourner-guests would, I assumed, be the entire clientèle of the Black Swan or Mucky Duck.

We descended into the Hippogriff, knocked, were examined by a new face, were admitted. Behind the bar was Manning. 'Where,' I said to Everett, 'is Alice?' 'Where,' repeated Everett like a parrot, 'is Alice?'

With miraculous timing, right in on his cue, a jowled man on a bar-stool, evidently from his voice a risen market-stall salesman, began to sing:

'Alice, where art thou?
In the cellar bathing bow-wow.'

'She's got the day off,' said Manning. 'Gone to Stratford with her boy-friend. Here you are, sir.' A fat back by the bar was given whisky. In the twilight, I now noticed, a young couple were dancing, arms round neck, waist respectively. Yet the juke-box was silent. The silent newspaper reader in the shadows I remembered from my first visit was still there, squinting in furious concentration. Everett and I sat down to pale ale and a bowl of cocktail onions. From the darkness of another corner arose to the sight a West Indian with a guitar, not the West Indian I remembered.

'I see you looking,' said Manning, quick. 'Had to get rid of the other one. He got too mournful. Songs about death and God and his mother and so on. Drove the customers up the wall,' said Manning, 'drove the customers out.' He added potato crisps as a relish to our cocktail onions. I began to eat my lunch greedily. Everett said, dreamily:

'You know the story, I suppose. You know what happened to her.'

'I know.' I grimaced at the pale ale, warm, flat, but decided to stick to it; it would keep me off drinking.

'How could you know?' said Everett with energy. 'How could you know when you've been in Japan?'

'The news was waiting for me in Bugis Street, Singapore,' I said. 'And it was confirmed in Tokyo.'

'Oh,' Everett seemed deflated but not surprised. 'In some ways it's perhaps for the best,' he said. 'It's brought her back to her father. A father needs a daughter in his old age.'

'You're not so old.'

'Oh, yes, very old. Not many years off sixty,' said Everett. 'I've had a fuller life than most. I've lived life to the full, being a poet. But she doesn't like men, really. She only likes her father. She's back to what she used to be, quite skinny, you know, with those teeth out. And not going to the hairdresser. We're happy together, yes, happy.' His hand shook on his glass. 'Very happy, just the two of us.'

'She'll get herself a denture under the National Health,' I said brutally. 'She'll get herself a hair-do before she goes to see about that. She'll be interested in men again. You can't stop these things.'

'Oh, no,' cried Everett. 'She hates sex. She told me so. She's always pretended to like it, because liking it means you've grown up. But she's never grown up, really. It was all a façade, you know, something superficial, a skin hiding her real self. This, I assure you from the depths of experience, from the depths of a father's heart, is the only possible true and lasting relationship with a woman. Yes, yes, yes.'

'No, no, no,' echoed the market vendor from his lonely stool. He was not trying to be offensive. Everett ignored him, saying:

'You've never had a daughter, so you can't possibly know. To whom did Shakespeare turn, worn out by physical lust and the shames of a player's life? Not to his wife, who soon, anyway, became his widow, but to his daughter. A wonder, a lost one, a sea-change child. All those things. Now,' said Everett, 'I enter, I hope, on my last phase. A poetry more rarefied, perhaps, full of mature wisdom, an old man's benediction for a sinful world, a poetry calm in resignation.' He extended his arms in blessing. 'A poetry which says that none of us really has a right to an answer.'

'An answer to what?' I said.

'An answer to all the questions that ultimately become one question, and that question it is not easy to define, though we all know what it is.'

I looked carefully at Everett. Everett looked ecstatic up at the ceiling. I didn't really think that Everett was mad, any more mad than the vicar and Ted Arden and Selwyn and the non-TV-watchers of this modern England. Everett seemed, at last perhaps, after much searching, to have found something that would serve to hang the garments of action on. A storm-tossed daughter had sailed home; a storm-tossed poet had sailed home. Ship and harbour were one. It was time for me to leave now, surely? Surely I had other things to do? But I couldn't think of any, except this last duty to the living Winterbottom which could not, anyway, be fulfilled at the moment. The dead were not really the concern of the amateur. My father was probably now being hammered home with skill, the likeness of a man soon to become a child's chemistry outfit. Ted would be thinking of how much ham to order and how many loaves would have to be cut up. The very professional language for the dead awaited the poor bloody vicar's trained voice. The bereaved son, the amateur, had leisure now to think of the awful thing he'd done – coming home without asking permission, even though he'd paid his own fare, leaving the Tokyo branch of the firm in the hands of a man who would, quite possibly, abscond with the million-odd yen that were still in the safe, not yet paid into the bank. Oh, well.

'Wednesday, then,' I said to Everett.

'Oh, yes,' said Everett. 'And I shall write a little obituary poem on the death of a craftsman. It can appear on Saturday, can't it? Wait,' said Everett, 'don't go yet. Wait.' He took out of his pocket, trembling, his glaze-covered journalist's notebook, and began to write in pencil. The West Indian struck up, but Everett, in a fine frenzy, didn't seem to hear it. The West Indian sang:

'It was towards the end of the Second World War
That the atom bomb fell on Hiroshimaw.
Though some folks call it an international crime,
Yet it showed the progress of these modern times.'

And so on, several stanzas of trite folky Caribbean observations on the achievements of the white man. I ordered beer for Everett and brandy for myself, while Everett, in furious concentration, thought and wrote, his lips mouthing silent sounds, rhyme-rows, his pencil occasionally sketching rhymes in the smoky air. When the singer had done and the juke-box had, with a soft slow tune, brought the embracing dancers to their feet again, Everett said: '*Epitaph on a Printer*. Listen:

'He, who did not originate the Word,
Yet brought the Word to man when man was ripe
To read the Word. But that ill-bound, absurd
Book of his body's gone. A mess of type
That death broke up reads greater nonsense now.
Now God re-writes him, prints him, binds him, never
To fail or be forgotten: God knows how
To make one copy that is read for ever.'

'But that,' I said, 'could just as well be *your* epitaph.'
'It's for your father,' said Everett. 'I'll put that in on Saturday.'
Leaving the Hippogriff, I looked into the coffee-bar next

door, half-expecting that Winterbottom would be there, biting his nails, waiting to hear from me, his herald to Alice. But he wasn't there. I thought that now was the time for me to go home. (I'd left my luggage at the Black Swan; I could pick it up first.) My father would surely by now have been reduced to the status of something merely still in a coffin. There was nothing to fear. I would never see him again, alive or dead.

18

I collected my bags from the Black Swan, just opening, and also the front-door key to my father's house. This had been returned to Ted by old Jackie Starbrook, undertaker, and was a token of work completed. I walked down Clutter-buck Avenue quite briskly, bravely, swinging my bags. A corpse in a coffin, the lid nailed down, couldn't con-ceivably get out. A coffin was merely a piece of temporary furniture less capable of offence than a piano (which mice can play in the middle of the night) or a gas fire (which can leak) or a television set (which, once switched on, is hard to switch off). Nevertheless, my heart knocked as I opened the front door. A coffin, after all, wasn't sound-proof. Supposing I heard groans from inside it, supposing I heard a muffled moan to be let out. I dropped my lug-gage in the hall and spent two minutes looking in unease at the shut door of the front room. If he did moan that he wanted to be let out, I couldn't do anything about it, could I? There were no tools to prise the lid off. Besides, if I kept quiet he might not hear me. I tiptoed into the dining-living-room, into dimness made by the closed cur-tains. I switched on the light. And, even if he did hear the sounds of a man walking about, as long as I didn't speak or cough or sigh he wouldn't know who it was. And anyway, damn it all, he'd had his life. It wasn't fair of him to want any more, not after the expense and trouble.

I sat by the electric fire, smoking. I heard nothing from

the next room. At last, bold, I got up, set my shoulders and walked to the front-room door. I pushed the door open and, inevitably, it gave a ghost-film squeak. I switched on the light. The settee and easy chairs had been pushed towards the window, leaving space for trestles. On the trestles sat the coffin. Very bold now, I knocked on the coffin-lid. There was no answer, nobody at home. Then, in a spasm of unfilial impiety, I switched on the television set. In a few seconds life flooded into the room. It was a variety show, girls kicking, a handsome low-browed man singing. I switched off, and the sound and the vision heeled over into silence and blankness, into death. Death was the fact in this house, powerful, palpable, even when I went back to the other room to read. For, when I tried to be absorbed in *Barchester Towers*, the characters and the locale seemed to shrink to something desperately galvanic on a television screen. I looked round the room, which seemed different. Had death made it seem different? No, it wasn't death, it was Mr Raj. The room seemed to smell of Ceylon – rancid, aromatic. On the table was a table-runner, I now noticed, of Ceylonese design. And, with a real shock, I saw that the Rosa Bonheur was gone. In its place was a Ceylonese moonlight scene, hideously vulgar. And I saw that there were books of Mr Raj about – *Race and Racialism, Elements of Social Psychology, A First Book in Sociology, The Bhagavad-Gita,* a volume of artistic nudes. And on the mantelpiece, unframed, was a photograph of Alice – Alice in a woollen dress looking common, the innkeeper's daughter. I smelled for traces of my father, but nothing seemed left. His own books were there, true, but they were a rather cold record of professional achievement, locked in a case that, I supposed, was never unlocked. But it wasn't just a matter of possessions; it was as though the house bore no real stamp of his having lived there — there was no after-flavour of my father, no echo. I went into the kitchen to get something minimal to eat: a tin of American spiced sponge-meat hid, a genuine exotic, among the jars of condiments and curry-stuffs. I ate some of this meat (eating meat in a house of the dead always suggests, somehow, eating the dead) and drank water. Then, fidgety and nervous as a dog left alone, I worried about Tokyo. Mishima, my chief assistant, now left in command. That cash that should have been banked. Mishima's occasional clipped factual reminiscences of war in Nagasaki: never a complaint, never a micrometric movement of lips or eyebrows to indicate what he felt towards the allied authors of outrage on Japan. Mishima, quiet and swift-moving at midnight, loading the type-writers, comptometers, the varied expensive stock of the showroom, on to a lorry. Mishima away, never to be seen again. I felt the more nervous because I knew that, sooner or later, real noise, real intrusion of the outside world, must shatter the dead quiet in telephone peals. A telegram would be telephoned through from Beryl in Tunbridge Wells. Rice, having seen my brief television appearance, would, having tried furiously to get me all day on the tele-phone, try once again. I tiptoed out into the hall and to-wards the telephone. As I reached out to lift the receiver and thus immobilise the hated instrument, the hated instrument rang. Instinctively I answered it.

'Yes?'

'He got the stuff,' came a whisper. 'The question now is where to store it.' In delirium I fancied that this was one of Mishima's friends reporting success and the end of Den-ham, but wrong number, wrong exchange, wrong city, wrong hemisphere. Such things were possible, anything was possible. Think of poor Imogen in Bugis Street.

'Yes?' I would hear more.

'That is Fred, isn't it?' Agitation, doubt. 'Hallo, hallo. What number is that, please?' I rang off, trembling. The coffin in the front room creaked, I'm sure it creaked.

I went back to the electric fire and switched on the radio. It said, plummily:

'. . . and also in transit. Whether this problem can really be reconciled with problems which, because of a certain superficial similarity'—here it sibilated horribly—'are regarded, with no attempt to demonstrate precisely why, as cognate problems, is a question which can only be answered when a great deal more research has been done into the conditions in which such a problem seems likely to arise.' The volume rose all the time and I tried to quieten a voice that, I really thought, might waken the dead. But the bakelite knob came off as I turned it—it was a decrepit pre-war radio—and rolled on to the floor. 'Certainly,' roared the voice, 'we can feel proud that something, however little, has been achieved in the direction of clarifying the nature of the problem—' I killed the radio at its root (the switch of the plug by the skirting board), being frightened of touching other knobs on the instrument itself, and then, on my knees and panting, fumbled to find the round of bakelite which had dropped to the floor. It lurked, among swatches of fluff, under the armchair. I started, with difficulty, to rise again, and then, with no real surprise, heard a male voice high above my buttocks, a voice of the East, Mr Raj, saying:

'And so, Mr Denham, you were praying for the repose of the soul of that good old man, now unhappily deceased, your father.' Authentic Raj, but not quite the relaxed Raj I had known. He must have entered, using the key that was once mine, under cover of the shouting radio. I got to my feet, turned, and there he was, the little feminine gun in his hand, a raincoat on, a gangster in milk chocolate.

'What did you see in Stratford,' I asked, '*Hamlet* or *Othello?*'

'So you knew I had been in Stratford, Mr Denham,' said Mr Raj. 'But, then, you know so many things. You are almost, if not quite, omniscient.'

'Put that gun away,' I said. I never dreamed, in all my life, that I would ever say that to anybody. I'd never even said it on the stage. For that matter, as an adult, I'd only ever acted in two amateur productions: once, in Kuala Lumpur, as an attendant in *Tobias and the Angel*; once, in Kuching, as the Italian singing-master in *The Critic*, nobody else at the time speaking any Italian. 'Put that gun away,' I said, with remarkable professional smoothness, all things considered.

'Oh, yes, Mr Denham,' said Mr Raj. And he put it away. 'I feared, hearing noise and seeing lights, that somebody had broken in. I have heard of body-snatchers, Mr Denham. It is a good thing that I recognised you from the size of your bottom, if I may use the term, because the gun is loaded.'

'Well,' I said, 'you seem to have made a fine bloody mess of things. Take your coat off. Sit down. Make yourself at home. Although, perhaps it ought to be you telling me to make myself at home.'

'This is your home,' said Mr Raj seriously, 'more than it is mine. I do not think I shall stay here any more.' And he sat down on a dining-chair, keeping his raincoat wrapped round him.

'I don't know whose home it is,' I said. 'For all I know it may have been left to my sister Beryl. It's not mine, anyway. This house, this suburb, this town, this whole damned country mean nothing to me any more. There's no link left.'

'I know what you are thinking, Mr Denham,' said Mr

Raj. 'You are thinking that it is my fault that your father died. You are thinking that, after all the promises I made, I have let you down and your father down and, perhaps, myself and my race also down. And I never wrote to you, Mr Denham, about how well or ill your father was, because I thought that I and my friends of medical ability could make everything all right with nobody knowing anything, and I thought that it was not right that you, in far away Japan, should be unduly worried.'

'But I *was* worried. It was so unlike my father not to drop a single line. Oh, why were you such a bloody fool?'

The light of fire without its heat in the eyes of Mr Raj. '*You* are bloody fool, Mr Denham, if you will forgive a black man using the expression to a white man, to think that I should want to kill your father—'

'Nobody said anything about you *wanting* to kill him,' I said. 'You just neglected him, that's all. Grossly, or shamefully, or something, according to the doctor.'

'That, Mr Denham, I must most strongly and heatedly deny. Your father lacked nothing. I treated him better than my own father was ever treated. If my father could have eaten the food your father ate he would be alive to-day. Your father was very well looked after; perhaps, when one considers so many weighty historical factors, better than he deserved.'

'What do you mean? What had he done wrong?'

'It is not a question of what he personally had done wrong, Mr Denham, but of what people of his generation had done wrong by their ignorance or tyranny. He was there, your father, in my power—'

'Oh, don't be so bloody stupid,' I said.

'All right, Mr Denham. What was to prevent me poisoning your father? He was an old man, he would have died soon anyway.'

218

'But, God Almighty, why should you have wanted to do that? You didn't hate him, did you? You, the big anti-racial man, had nothing against him because he was white, had you?'

'Oh, I loved your father, Mr Denham, that good old man.' Mr Raj washed his hands with air and fixed his sight on the upper bar of the electric fire. 'But sometimes, when he slept and snored in his ignorance of me and my people and so many other peoples, sometimes my love could have meant my putting hands round his throat and seeing him dead there. I say this to you to prove that I did not kill him. He had the best of medical attention when he was very ill. My medical friends came and tried many things on him. They were glad to.'

'I bet they were,' I said. 'A nice white lay-figure that couldn't fight back. That was going to die soon anyway. That was, despite all your bloody talk about us all being brothers, fundamentally the enemy. It won't work, it just won't work at all.'

'What will not work, Mr Denham?'

'This pretence of us understanding one another. Such a bloody small planet, and one half can't understand the other half. I've pretended as much as anyone, but they all let you down.'

'Who let you down, Mr Denham?'

'You,' I cried angrily, 'you and you and you. With your Western clothes and your fine English vocabulary and your pretence that race hatred is something that white men invented. Pretending that you can be trusted.'

'I see, Mr Denham,' said Mr Raj, rising. 'We are not your equals, then?'

'Oh, that's nothing to do with it. You're different, that's all, but you pretend to be the same. When you use words like "love" and "equality" and "brotherhood", you delude us into thinking that you mean by those words what *we* mean by them. And when you talked about devotion to my father — *that good old man*' (I mimicked his high pitch) '— you might well have meant the sort of love a man has for a pig that he's fattening for the slaughter. I'm not blaming you,' I said, tired already, 'I'm blaming myself.'

'I thought you were very different type of man, Mr Denham,' said Mr Raj, 'different because you had travelled in many lands, lived with races of many different kinds. And now I have to listen seriously to what you have to say for those very reasons. And love, you would say, is not possible between the black and the white? Well, I have wondered much.' He sat down again, on a different chair, abruptly. 'Haply for I am black,' he said.

'It was *Othello*, then?' I couldn't be heated very long.

'Oh, Mr Denham, it is not just to see plays that you go to the town where Shakespeare was born. It is spring and the river and love and the swans. Sweet swan of Avon,' said Mr Raj, 'what a sight it were.' He stood up very suddenly and dramatically and drew the little pistol from his pocket. 'Mr Denham,' he said deliberately. 'If you will not forgive me for my failure, then somebody must die.'

'Oh, God,' I said, 'don't be a bore. We've got a full coffin in the next room. One death at a time, please.'

'Either you or I must die, Mr Denham. One death is never enough. You must die for not forgiving me. I must die for not being worthy of forgiveness.'

'Have you been drinking, Mr Raj?'

'A little,' said Mr Raj. He counted solemnly on his fingers with the muzzle of his gun. 'A little whisky in a public house in Stratford. Then some good wine at a Trust House were we ate. French wine, very good. Then tea at a place called, very strangely, the Black Swan. Then she would not stay any longer. She would not walk with me to distant fields to carry out your advice, long ago given, of copulation. She insisted on coming back by train very early. So I brought her back and she said she was going to see her father and mother and I was not to accompany her. So I went out lonely to drink beer, having now little money left. And then I walked about here, scene of the crime, and saw lights on. I think I have not drunk enough,' said Mr Raj. He opened the sideboard cupboard and took out half a bottle of Martell and a glass. 'You will join me, O untrusting and hating Mr Denham?' he invited.

'If you call me those things,' I said, 'certainly not.'

'Very well, then,' said Mr Raj. 'I must drink alone.' And he did, a full glass of raw brandy. He wiped his mouth delicately on his gun. 'I have failed to make contact,' he said, 'failed, failed, failed.'

'Oh, shut up about failure,' I said. 'Who the hell hasn't failed?'

'So you admit it?' said Mr Raj. 'You admit that I have failed? Inevitably, I suppose you must. And your father is now in his coffin, you say, and the coffin is next door in the next room? Ah, well, that is a chapter closed. And to-night you resume your old bed, which, by fortunate chance, has now clean sheets on it, and your father's bed is not for use, it bearing on its mattress marks of the dead and the incontinence of the dead.'

'I'll sleep down here,' I said, 'in this chair. I don't mind.'

'You are trying to pretend, Mr Denham, that things are as they were, but you know that they are not. You must not talk of others pretending when you yourself pretend so much. I shall find a bed elsewhere. It was only devotion to your poor old good dead father that prevented me from finding a bed elsewhere.'

'You fell over yourself with gratitude, as I remember—'

'Oh, yes, I was grateful. I had nowhere else. But this

221

house became very soon, in effect, my house, Mr Denham. I took your father to my bosom, not me to his.' Mr Raj frowned at his phrasing, then shook his head impatiently. 'I was in charge and control. I cooked and made the beds. Soon the cleaning woman, seeing what she termed a negro living in this house, would not come any more, for she said that negroes were, being black, inevitably dirty people. So I did all, Mr Denham, without complaint. Now I can go elsewhere. Contact must at last be forced to be made.' He held the brandy bottle up to the globe light, squinting at it. 'This,' he said, 'I shall finish. I bought it for your father, but he will not need it now.' Disdaining the glass, he drank straight from the bottle. I admired; I said:

'You've learned a lot since you came to England.'

'Oh, yes,' gasped Mr Raj, lowering the bottle. 'My English has improved, I think. Though you would maintain, perhaps, that I do not use words with right meaning. Well, there we shall see.' Suddenly Mr Raj began to swing his arms, as in grotesque fast marching, the bottle in one hand flashing, the gun in the other. He gritted his teeth and showed me the white completeness of the double row. He frowned, so that his upper face was all creases. Then he crashed into a sort of shouting rhythmic rhapsody of which the elements were English words, language reduced to what my father's body was swiftly being reduced to: simple senseless elements laid side by side, unbound into a totality of meaning. I said:

'Shut up. Shut up.' I had heard enough nonsense that day. 'Shut up.' Then the telephone rang. Mr Raj collapsed into coherence, pointing the bottle at me, saying:

'If you answer that, Mr Denham, I shall be forced to shoot you.'

'Oh, bloody nonsense. Let me get out.'

'No, Mr Denham, you are not to listen to vile slanders.

You are not to listen to people saying I am to blame for everything.' The telephone double-burred urgently, and I could not get past armed and raincoated Mr Raj. I said again:

'Let me get out. I must answer it, you silly bastard. It may be my sister.' I was no longer frightened of any further intrusion of the real world; the real world in a raincoat blocked my way, mad as a hatter.

'If it is your sister,' said Mr Raj, 'you are certainly not to answer. You will tell her in vile terms that I am to blame, thus spreading this vile slander yet further.' And he stood in the narrow doorway, ready to shoot me with the brandy bottle, the gun limp in his other hand. I tried to butt him out of the way with my right shoulder, but Mr Raj stood fast. 'No, Mr Denham, it is not to be. Soon the telephone will cease its importunities, and then the dead may be at peace once again.'

'You silly bloody fool,' I said. 'How dare you do this to me in my own house. I'll have the bloody police in on you.'

'Now,' said Mr Raj, 'you talk in the manner of bloody clergyman. Bloody bloody bloody. I forgive you for that, for you have lost all control.' I said:

'You bloody stupid black bastard.' The telephone, as if shocked, ceased its ringing.

'So,' said Mr Raj, 'you too have also thought of me as black man and hence ignorant, like stupid singing West Indian negroes in the town. All right, Mr Denham, I have done enough for you. Now I get out. So I am not worthy of white sodality also you will be saying? That is neither here nor there. We do not have to *ask* any more, Mr Denham, because, Mr Denham, now we *take*.' Mr Raj looked down at his right hand, saw what it held, smiled in a large radiance, then dropped the bottle gently to the floor. 'Stupid, yes,' he said. 'Black also. But bastard not.

My also stupid and not very prepossessing brother in Gray's Inn can give you whole family tree. There is no bastardy in my family.' He walked towards the front-door under the hall's dim light. Through the ghastly stained glass of the door shone a street lamp's beam. Mr Raj turned before opening the door. 'Many things, Mr Denham,' he said, 'but not bastardy. A good-sounding word, bastardy, like Portuguese or like thundering of small Portuguese cannon, bastardy.' And with that word as his good-night or good-bye, he nodded, quite amiably, and went out. He closed the door carefully behind him and then, as an afterthought, pushed something through the letterbox. It ponked tinnily on the floor – his, or my, key. Then he went down the steps, carefully, I did not attempt to go after him. Poor Mr Raj, despite everything. He would be back next day, contrite, to collect his books and clothes and table-runner and Ceylonese curry-stuffs. Contact, eh? I had always known that there was no real contact, except briefly in bed, over a shared bottle, across counter or desk among white stucco colonial houses. Thank God I had never been committed, as salesman in Africa or Asia, to any philosophy of ultimate identification through closer and closer and deeper and deeper contact, over which to grow, at length, grey with frustration. That had been left to the old-before-their-time, ill-paid colonial officials, the new not-so-ill-paid intellectual missionaries of organisations bearing initials like easy chemical formulæ. But I had never had, never would have, any cause to be dishonest with myself, to be, at last over the brooding bottles of the disappointed, ready to strike tables and bar-boys through frustration. There was just this man, J. W. Denham, buying and selling, alone and content to be so, except in work, play, bed, his shadow moving over exotic backcloths like the Bank of America's man-on-the-spot in the *Time* and *Life* advertisements, content to live in his guts till – let that day be distant – he join his father, though not through the door of a grave near an inglorious suburb.

But, if that contact was impossible, was there other? There didn't seem to be here. The TV-watchers were zombies, the others were mad, and both thought myself mad. But here you had to pretend contact, listening, saying yes to what you couldn't understand, grinning like an ape at catch-phrases hurled across one like tennis-balls, cause of loud laughter, the small change of their own traffic of contact. And if I said, 'That reminds me of a curious custom they have up-river in the rather backward state of Rama-rama –' (Oh, yes, and where's that?) 'You see, when the time comes for a man to enter the married state, they cut curiously-shaped marks in his –' (Oh, yes, there was something like that on the telly. Yawn, and aimless eyes round the room, looking, in vain, for the real thing, the telly.) 'And the women are, you know, really beautiful. So graceful, so, you know, essentially feminine.' (Oh, yes, blackies, aren't they? And, tell me, is it true that Chinese women are made, you know, a bit different like from, you know, ours, you know. 'Cause one chap – ha ha – told me – ha ha – cut on the slant, you know, ha ha.) Oh, let the funeral soon be over, and the ham and tongue tea, and get me back to where I know there's no contact and I don't have to pretend.

Mishima said, 'I have cleared everything out of the stock-room and sent the money in the safe to a friend I have living in Korea. Now all that remains for you, sir, is to commit hara-kiri. I have brought the knife and, as you will see, the process is perfectly simple. It is by far the best thing to do.' Then my father came in, coughing, saying, 'You'll find some sausages in the kitchen, lad. We could have those fried. Lie less heavy on the stomach than all this curry and rice and whatnot. That's what did for me. Liked it, but stomach couldn't take it.'

'All right, all right,' I said, 'forget it,' waking up from my tired doze to hear knocking at the front door. 'Somebody go and stop that filthy row. It's not my job, after all. Why pay a dog and bark yourself?' I sat upright suddenly, guilty at dozing off when, surely, I should have been looking after something, and realised that the knocking had been part of the odd bits of dream. Then I heard real knocking, so perhaps the dream-knocking had been real too. This was Beryl, arrived at last. My watch said just after eight-thirty: it wasn't all that late. 'Coming,' I called, as I moved towards the third spasm of knocking.

Beryl was just going to knock in my face as I opened the door. 'What the devil's happened to your clothes?' I asked. Then I saw that it was, though a woman, not Beryl. Mrs Winterbottom in disarray, dressing-gown round her shoulders, and looking wild-eyed. 'Come in,' I said, 'take it easy. You'll catch cold out there, dressed like that. I said I'd see you first, but you weren't there. And I don't know where he went to. But, after all, he is your husband. He has a perfect right to come and see you, hasn't he? I mean, none of this is my fault.'

'He's shot him,' she said. 'Inky's shot him. He's shot poor little Billy.' *Nobody cared to shoot poor Billy*, my brain started to say, a line from some poem or other, some ruthless rhyme or other. Ruthlessly rhymed, shot, rimshot, Ruthless Ruth or other.

'Come in, quick,' I said. She was ready to start howling it to the street. 'Quick.' I got her inside, closed the frontdoor, and then she crucified herself against this door, starting to bay, at bay. 'Come on in, have some brandy, calm down, we'll go back together.' I pulled her down the hall like something heavy just delivered by van-men, into the living-dining-room. No brandy, of course, Raj drank all, but small flask of whisky. This I put to her lips, like an air-nozzle against a flaccid tyre. She spat, spurted, squirted, trying to sigh air of grief and shock out. 'Come on,' I said, 'take some.' She howled instead. 'Come,' I said, gripping her fine wide shoulder, 'you'll wake my father.' I didn't mean that figuratively, I really thought, not yet used.

'He shot him, Inky shot him, he's dead. Dead on the bed.' That echoed something, London Airport, why? Dead, Ted. Of course.

'Where is he now?' I asked foolishly.

'They're both there. Both there when I left. Nobody would come. I knocked next door. But everybody was listening to the telly.'

'Watching the telly, you mean.' Oh, bloody Denham, are you mad like the rest of them?

'Nobody would hear, nobody would come. Somebody shouted me to go away. Because of the telly.' She howled. The body in the coffin grunted, disturbed, turned over.

'Come,' I said, brave Denham. 'We'll go back together. Wait,' I said, less brave Denham, 'I'll ring the police.' Oh, Denham, Denham, don't, for God's sake, get mixed up with the police, you who should be in Tokyo, a murder case, vital witness. 'The police,' I said. 'As far as I remember, it's 999.'

I dialled, asking Alice, 'What's the number of your house?' She stood, her hands limply buttoning herself, Hecuba, permed hair all over the place, just by the place under the stairs where the fuse-boxes lay hidden.

'Eleven, Clutterbuck Avenue. Eleven,' she cried. 'The only place with a light on. The others are all looking at the telly. He sold the telly,' she howled.

'Police?' I said. 'I'd like to report a murder. Eleven,

227

Clutterbuck Avenue. Urgent,' I said, perhaps unnecessarily. 'The wife, I mean widow, of the victim says that the murderer's still there. Armed, desperate. Please hurry.'

'Pull the other leg, mister,' said the police-voice. 'It's got bells on.'

'You bloody fool,' I said, for the moment identifying police and killer. 'There's a dead man at Number Eleven, Clutterbuck Avenue.'

'Yis, and there's a toilet-paper in our lavatory. You've been seeing too much telly.'

'For God's sake,' I said, 'let me speak to the desk-sergeant.'

'He's just gone round the corner,' said the voice. 'I'll tell him when he comes back, but there'll be trouble, mister, if you've been pulling our legs.'

'For God's sake,' I repeated. 'Number Eleven, Cl –'

'I've got that,' said the shamelessly unbuttoned, tea-drinking voice, 'I'll let him know.'

I put down the receiver. I said to Alice, 'You'd better come with me. You can have my father's overcoat.'

'No, no,' she cowered. 'He might kill me too.'

'Or me,' I said. 'All right, you wait here. Don't go into the front room, there's a coffin there. You've been frightened enough.'

She began to bash her knuckles against the kitchen-door, howling. 'Oh, Billy, Billy.'

'All right,' I said. 'Try and be sensible. I shan't be long.'

I went out, hatless, overcoatless, into the nippy spring-night air, with a Muslim moon and a few stars that twinkled as for a poem by Everett, and turned into Clutterbuck Avenue. What poor Alice had said was true: in every front-room window was a weak blue glow, shadows absorbed around it. Where the front room was completely dark, there, one had to assume, the television was in the living-dining-room. Nobody seemed interested in real life, which, in this instance, of course, was real death. I palpitated as I approached Number Eleven, recognisable from its lights, all lights on. I didn't fancy going in alone. But this was a peak televiewing hour: nobody must be disturbed. The Black Swan and Ted? He'd done, was doing, enough. Then, I thought, perhaps the arrival of strangers would upset Mr Raj unduly. He might say, 'So you are betraying me into alien hands, a very unkind act, Mr Denham,' and still shoot me first. I would go alone, brave, and nobody should ever know about it officially; my name must not be disclosed to the press, for I was still officially in Tokyo.

The front-door was closed. I did the only thing one could do: I knocked. A raincoated shadow through the stained glass, calm steps, approaching. Mr Raj opened to a gap of three fingers' thickness. He set an eye of some suspicion to this chink. Then he said, cheerfully, 'Ah, Mr Denham, so it is not good-bye so soon, after all. Come in, sir, come in with pleasure.' Thank God, I thought. Nobody really ever murders anybody; people just die. Hysterical Alice, silly perhaps merely punched-on-the-jaw-and-flat-out Billy, Mr Raj having meant no real harm. But Mr Raj said, 'Come upstairs, Mr Denham, and view the *corpus delicti*.' He seemed rather pleased with this technicality, as though the commission of the crime were well worth the opportunity of using it. He did not close the door. 'You go first,' I said. Mr Raj said:

'Oh, no, you, please, first, Mr Denham. You always first. The white man before the whole world.' And Mr Raj amiably waved his dainty pistol, bowing me towards the stair-foot. I began to mount, leaden. Then, to show I was not afraid, I jauntily ran up, like a healthy man singing to the lavatory after breakfast. 'In this room, Mr Denham,' said Mr Raj. 'Or should I perhaps now call it a tomb? Room, womb, tomb,' he added. 'English is really a remarkable language.' On the double bed, rumpled, I presumed, by love-making, naked Winterbottom, undressed for the act of reconciliation, lay face downward. Naked, I thought. Very convenient for everybody. 'There,' pointed Mr Raj, with pride. 'There, just behind the ear. Not very much blood, as you see. What they would, I think, in the world of violence and professional murder, call a clean job.'

'Why did you do it?' I asked.

'Oh,' said Mr Raj, 'I came to seek my due. Yes, it was my due, after so many preliminaries of wooing and courtship, which, I believe, are the correct terms to use, Mr Denham. The door at the front was not open, but the door at the back was. The door at the back nearly always is, Mr Denham. Why it should be so, I do not know, but it is a thing I have noticed. Perhaps English house-breakers only like to make their break-in by the front. Perhaps to do so at the back is *not cricket*, Mr Denham.' Mr Raj laughed boyishly, swaying. 'And then, Mr Denham, I went cautiously upstairs. All lights in the house were on, Mr Denham. Perhaps this man had pursued her from room to room. But from this room I heard, with all lights on, noises of what one might term gratification. I see a stranger possessing her bed, Mr Denham.' Mr Raj saw it again, vividly, in the dressing-table mirror. His eyes were very large. 'So, Mr Denham, I shoot the seducing stranger. I am, after all, a man of some passions.'

'You realise it was her husband,' I said. Dead Winterbottom had an unburst boil on the back of his neck, I noticed, a mole on his left scapula.

'A stranger to me,' Mr Raj said, 'a total stranger, Mr Denham.'

'And now what do you propose to do?' I asked. 'The

police will be coming soon, I should imagine.' I had to make that qualification. I could not really imagine swift squads rushing up, screaming justice, in this suburban land where murder was for the telly.

'They will hang me, do you think, Mr Denham? My intentions were not, of course, really murderous. I was, in a way, trying to protect. And I did not know this man, I certainly did not know him. This man,' he added, almost with proud affection, almost ready to stroke the corpse. There was in Mr Raj's eyes the look of a man who foresaw a handsome rug made of the pelt of his victim.

'You were jealous,' I said. 'Jealous, and perhaps puritanically disgusted.'

'So it was to you she came first, Mr Denham,' said Mr Raj. 'In what terms,' he said eagerly, 'did she speak of me?'

'She didn't say much. Something like "Inky shot him dead." '

'Inky,' said Mr Raj, smiling. 'Her name for me. An allusion to the ink that is invariably on my studious fingers.' He held out his studious fingers, neither inky nor bloody. Inevitably Mr Raj added, 'Murderer's fingers. And what, Mr Denham, would you do now in my position?'

'You can't do anything till the police arrive. Then I should call your brother in Gray's Inn. You're entitled to a lawyer.'

'My brother,' laughed Mr Raj, 'would love to be a judge so that he could put on black cap and condemn me to death. But he has not the brains to be a judge. He hates me, Mr Denham, hates me for superior intelligence and, also, because of more prepossessing appearance.' I fancied I could hear a car, a car of some power, turning a corner. I said:

231

'There are other things you can do. A lot depends on what you want out of life. Whether you think it's worth hanging on to through all the humiliation and whatnot of a trial and newspaper reports, the juicy Sunday paper meat of the corpse-chewers, reading in bed.'

'But what would you do, Mr Denham?' asked Mr Raj, smiling almost foolishly.

I looked down at poor Winterbottom again, another printer with his type broken up, sinner against stability grotesquely punished. I rubbed my tired eyes, thinking of starvation in India and corpses ten a penny. 'You really want to know what I would do, if I'd done what you've done and were standing here above my handiwork?'

'Oh, yes, Mr Denham. I am, when all is said and done, still here to learn from the West.' He smiled, attentive but relaxed, not sober yet.

'I'd walk out quietly to the back garden, put that gun to my head, and pull the trigger. I'd do that before the police came and all the horrible irrelevant business started. That's what I'd do. But that doesn't mean that you've got to do it.'

'No, there is never any compulsion,' said Mr Raj. I could now hear another car, coming round another corner, another powerful car. Was it coming here? With loud brake-shrieks it answered that it was not merely coming, it had arrived.

'They're here,' I said. 'It's too late now.'

'Oh, no, Mr Denham, never too late. The garden is not really necessary, is it? I mean, it is not like some dirty thing that you have to do, like going to the lavatory, is it?' There were people coming up the stairs, one pair of light feet, two pairs of heavy, a voice calling thickly:

'Who's up there? No funny business, mind.'

'Now,' said Mr Raj, seeing blue bulk on the landing, 'as forces of law and order are coming to apprehend.' He put the neat lady's pistol to his right temple and squeezed the trigger, with a delicate milk-chocolate finger. Just before he did it, he winked at me with his left eye, as though the whole thing were a joke, really; which, for a Hindu, perhaps it was. When he fell on to Winterbottom, I was able to see for the first time the picture on the bedroom wall – a small reproduction of 'The Last Watch of Hero' which made it seem more vulgar than, perhaps, it really is. Hero-Alice, waiting with classic anxiety for her weekly lover, Leander-Jack Brownlow perhaps, to swim the stormy straits for a night of Pimms No. 1 and love. There's been nothing of that about any of them, nothing heroic or leander-like, just silly vulgar people uncovering the high explosive that lies hidden underneath stability.

19

Life had to go on, and life for me meant my father's funeral. The police had certain questions to ask me on Tuesday; the *Evening Hermes* sent one senior, one cub reporter to interview me; poor Alice, sobbing, one presumed, in the home of her parents, was seen tearfully in a smudgy photograph allegedly saying, 'I loved him'; there was nothing to report from partially edentate Imogen. From Beryl came a telegram: 'Phoned twice no answer heartbroken cannot leave shop Henry not well am writing love.' In black, in church, I wept as the vicar's voice purged of blood, fluted, to its stock response of sniffs, the noble cadences, the irritable gnomic rhetoric of Paul in the burial service. Then my father's golf-friends and I marched, with the coffin-load, to the smell of fresh earth of the plot my father had bought, where my mother already was. The ghost of Mr Raj whispered, 'Mr Denham, this Christian custom of burial is far inferior to Hindu ceremonial of burning, which is more cleanly and also more symbolical. Look now, that bloody vicar is about to say something.' And indeed the vicar said, 'Ashes to ashes, dust to dust.' I remembered that I had once seen a priest in Spain smoking at somebody's graveside. I was dying for a cigarette myself. How sane people were in Europe! That was my answer, of course, if I ever wanted ultimate contact: Europe, of which Ireland and Wales are a part, and not England, England being alone and mad, or American and mad.

At the Black Swan, people who had not been able to come to the funeral had managed to come to the tea. There were many tables on trestles, many people in Sunday clothes sharp-set. I was looked at by many with admiration: a man, from far mystic and dangerous Japan, who seemed associated with more deaths in the space of a day or so than anybody there remembered. It was a fair trio: natural causes, murder, suicide; and round all three glowed savoury unsavoury lip-smacking harmonics – slow poisoning (them foreigners not to be trusted), lust and jealousy (read about them things in Shairkspier at schiool). And here was the great Shakespearean himself supervising the setting-down of the funeral meats, the natural shine of spring salads, the nursery gleam of jellies and blancmanges and coloured cakes. By my side stood Everett, shaking only slightly, disappointed that Beryl and Henry Morgan could not be present. Indeed, I was the only relative there, and I was officially in Japan.

'Am and toongg,' said Selwyn, clanging this latter like a bell. He, bless him, had tolled the one bell only. 'Yer got ter ave am and toongg, mister, cause dead expects it. Ah knawww, bein born betwin nart and deeeeh, abaht dead, what dead wants and doozent want. Respeck, they wants, lahk this ere.' Selwyn protested a bit too much, because he. like everybody else present except Ted, felt a certain guilt: it was not fair to be sitting down to a spread like this with so many deaths on our hands. But soon, cups of warm whisky-bristling tea inside them, they would feel that, damn it all, it was a funeral tea after all: they weren't just there for a good time. Selwyn said, nudging me:

'Am wettin on, mister. Moosent kip me tahkin.' And he went off to join Cecil. Both wore white jackets. Cedric seemed reserved for something greater, being dressed in black trousers, green bum-freezer, as on waiting-on nights

235

downstairs, and a sort of chain of office on his chest. This frightened me somewhat. I said to Everett:

'Has he been made mayor, or something?'

Everett looked round and said, 'No, no, apparently the mayor wasn't invited.' But everybody else seemed to be there. I began to compute, feverishly, so many teas at three and six a head. Then in came Veronica, queenly in black, and I felt mean and grubby. She, O regally delicate-row-of-pearls-pearled satiny dignity, recalled the lowlier from their furtive low jokes and all to order. 'Right, me ducks,' said Ted, 'yer'd better all get sat down. You ere, Vicar, and Mr Denham ere and Mr. Whatsit ere, and me and the wife ere, and the rest of yer where yer like. No rushing now. Plenty for everybody. And this,' he warned, 'is a solemn occasion.' Only Ted could have got away with that. They all nodded, feeling no sense of a rebuke.

I was at one end, Veronica at the other, next to me Everett and an old old man of fair appetite. I had never met him before. But everybody ate well except Veronica: there is nothing like death for promoting what Hopkins called tasty lust. The ham and the tongue were dipped lustily in mustard and A.1 Sauce and champed away at. Cecil slugged unmeasured whisky into everybody's tea, except, of course, Veronica's. I saw a couple of cases of it by the merry fireplace. I was certainly doing everybody proud. When whisky had been served all round, Cedric, who nevertheless had his own place and plate, revealed his chosen office as that of toastmaster. He stood and said:

'Madame, Your Reverence, and gentlemen, the chief mourner and donor of the feast wishes to take tea-and-whisky with you. He requests that you remain seated.' Everybody, cup raised, looked towards me solemnly, and I nodded from side to side, raising my own cup for a good funereal swig. There were hearty lip-smackings and then the talk grew livelier though still subdued. Selwyn came round with more tea in a massive brown pot. 'Ere yar, mister,' he said to me. 'Al live arf empty fer whisky ter goh in.' When he had passed on to other hearty mourners, strangers to me, the old man at my right nodded, champed, dripped, and said:

'One of the nobility he is, by rights. Selwyn there. Disinherited by his dad. Whole family a bit touched.' He touched his temple, nodding. Then he whispered the name of a noble and well-known family in my ear. Taking his mouth away, he gave me a fair gale of whisky. 'Cut off without a shilling,' said the old man. 'In bloom of his youth.' Then he resumed eating.

The jellies and blancmanges and fancy cakes were regarded as mere fripperies, toys for ladies and vicars. Veronica, however, would eat nothing more, and most was left to the vicar, who spooned large wobbly helpings of yellow shivery and white shaky. And the poor sweet-toothed man could not say, 'Bloody good this is,' because he was seated next to a lady. And nobody really believed his bloodies, knowing them not to be sincere. But in the middle there was one old man, older even than my neighbour, who slopped toothlessly away at the nursery treats, the squelch of his spoon on the wall of the jelly on its dish, as he sought a new helping, echoing vulgarly, so that somebody guffawed. 'Right,' said Ted in fire. 'Stop that, Elkin Matthews, if you don't mind. This is a solemn occasion.' He bowed to Cedric courtlily, saying, 'I apologise for asserting your function, Mr er.' Cedric said, 'That is quite all right, I assure you.' A solemn occasion. Tea came round again, and Selwyn called:

'If anyone wants whisky withaht tay, e can ave it. Raht. Plenty bottles bah faaaahplehs.' Selwyn then flashed his sightless glasses round the guests ending at me, saying,

Aaaah, mister,' and filled up what cups asked for filling. Then Cedric stood and said:

'Madam and gentlemen, I have pleasure in calling on His Reverence the vicar to propose the health of the deceased.' People hear-heared and settled comfortably for boredom, some searching in crevices of molars with matchsticks for odd threads of ham. These, found, were looked at seriously and chewed up with finicking rabbit-teeth. The vicar said:

'Mr er, that is, ladies, or madam, and gentlemen. Your toastmaster, inadvertently or not, spoke with great aptness in asking me to propose the toast of one whose health, by the very nature of things, can no longer be one of the body but only of the soul. He has put off the body and will never see it again. The body is like an overcoat one loses. One will never need it again in the fair weather of the hereafter. There it is never cold, there it is——' He realised what he had said and gulped. Selwyn, flash-quick, flashed:

'Ah abaht rezzy reckshoon of body? Aaaaah.' The toastmaster flashed back, banging with a tea-cup as gavel. 'Order now, please order.' Somebody, tooth-picking, lazily said:

'All right, Selwyn, one singer one song if yer don't mind.'

'And so,' said the vicar, 'we toast his spiritual health, which is another way of saying that we pray that his soul be gathered up in Abraham's bosom, which is another way of saying that we trust he is reposing now in heaven, in the sight of the angels and saints, to whose company may he soon be admitted, and under the loving eye of his one eternal and heavenly Father. Amen. Now,' said the vicar, more briskly, less professionally, 'let's see more of you at church. This is as good a time as any to say that there are too many of you who only turn out for occasions like this, the mere rags and bones of religion, and neglect your more essential duties. I know who comes, and I know who stays away, and I want to see more——'

'He called on thee for a speech,' said an incredible leprechaun of a man, 'and not for a commercial.'

There was a little more gavel-banging and then Cedric called on Ted to say a few words about the deceased. It seemed as if I was to be completely ignored, but I didn't mind much. Ted said:

'I knew im, she knew im, e knew im, we all knew im.' After this paradigm, which impressed his hearers, he paused. 'E was a customer ere. Not perhaps one of the best customers. Not like Roger Alliwell ere oo drinks whisky to the tune of near one bottle a day, which is good for the ouse and, as far as we can see, does imself no arm. But e was a customer, loyal to the ouse, regular in attendance, and that's all we ask of any man or woman for that matter. Well, now e's gone. We're sorry e's gone. You're sorry e's gone. I'm sorry e's gone. And we can't say much more than that. Now the question is: as e gone to a better place? I don't know the answer to that, nor do you, nor does she. Perhaps e knows,' said Ted, shrugging towards the vicar, 'because it's is job to know. But the rest of us don't know. Right. But I say this. E done is best for all. Never a ard word come out of that man's art. Right. Well loved e was and for all is faults we would love im still, if e was still alive. But e's dead now and we wish im all the best in is new destination. And I can't say no fairer than that.'

Veronica burst into the muffled applause by saying, 'Opening-time, Edward. I'll go down and open up.'

'But all the customers is up ere, me duck,' said Ted. The vicar said:

'I'll take my leave at the same time, if I may.' Everybody stood up for the lady. The old old man next to me said:

'Who is this here funeral for, have you any idea?'

'He's dead now,' I said. 'It doesn't matter.' The lady and the vicar gone, the men sat down again and sighed the relief of men among men. The whisky came round again, some drinking it mixed with cold stewed sweet tea, deadly, and the second case was started. Cedric chafed as toastmaster with none to ask to speak except me, and me he would not call on. But Cecil growled a whisper to him and Cedric nodded. He rose and said:

'Gentlemen, I now call upon Fred Allen for a hymn.' There was reverent applause and then Fred Allen, a young rosy man with wings of his open-necked shirt flat-ironed on to his breasts, stood to sing, in a fine clear untrained tenor:

'Call us to Thee, O God,
   But bid Thy children come
To greet Thy blest abode
   And our eternal home.

'We are but feeble worms
   That tremble at Thy word,
Whom yet Thy love informs
   Though not Thy goodness, Lord.'

There were, of course, other verses, all with bad Wesleyan rhymes, so that even Everett grew solemnly exhilarated. After this hymn, which nobody could, out of reverence, applaud, but to which all sang Amen, an older man was bidden arise to sing badly 'The Holy City'. And he cried breathlessly, before the last chorus, 'Altogether, now,' so that everyone told Jerusalem to open its gates and sing Hosanna in the highest, and nobody could say that there was any infraction of prescribed solemnity. After this, one of my father's golfing friends rose to sing that only God could make a tree, in a curious perpetual wavering, perhaps hard to achieve and worthy of applause. To one, like myself, who had been a student of literature, it was fascinating to see the delicate process of secularisation. Soon we had 'Keep Right On To The End Of The Road' and, shortly afterwards, by a natural modulation, 'Roamin' In The Gloamin'.' Then what could be more natural than a solo from a genuine Scot, one Jock Macintyre, who gave 'I Love A Lassie'? Then there was 'I Belong to Glasgie' from everybody, and by this time Cedric, who had taken more whisky than was right, had already gone very green with his chain of office dangling in dejection.

At nine o'clock, when my whisky cases were empty, Cecil got up to growl a song of the early Victorian era:

'A sailor is a bastard when he comes ashore,
When he puts down his bottle it's to pick up a whore,
He woos sweet young maidens and swears that he'll wed,
But he sails off in the morning while they're still in bed.'

There was a rollicking chorus of too-ra-lays, and old men opened at each other, leering, lubricious mouths pegged with but few teeth while they sang. When Selwyn started some occult half-intelligible ditty which was, nevertheless, from its gestures and clumsy step-dance seen to be clearly obscene, there came a call from below, 'Edward! Customers!' Ted said, with great presence of mind:

'It's time we joined the ladies.' So downstairs we all went, but not before somebody shouted:

'To the donor of the feast!' Then everybody raised the dregs of his whisky to Ted, who, modestly, truthfully, disclaimed such hospitality. 'Im,' he said, pointing vaguely to me, but nobody would really believe it. Oh, well, England, I thought with satisfaction, just as ungrateful as Asia. But Everett had taken a great fancy to Ted. 'Remarkable man,' he said. 'Such personality. He reminds me most strongly of somebody.'

We had a jolly evening below and, after so much whisky, I actively enjoyed some warmish draught beer. At closing-time Ted said:

'Stay on for a bit. A little arf. You and im together.'

'You know I'm off tomorrow evening. Back to Tokyo. A lot to do tomorrow morning.'

'If you've got yer cheque-book andy,' said Ted, 'yer can pay me what you owe me, can't yer, me duck? Just wait till closing-time. It's last orders in a minute.'

Tonight Cecil and Selwyn were not on duty. They played a game of darts with men in cloth caps, only one of whom had been, cap and all, one of my funeral guests. Selwyn showed himself brilliant at required doubles, swift at subtraction when calculating the score. Him I would never see again. I felt sorry. I would never again have any call to come to suburban England, to provincial England. Why, then, to metropolitan England? I began to plan leaves in wine-skin countries, snow-capped schnapps countries. Where should I eventually spend my tired retirement? There was, of course, only one vague answer, a vague picture of a dead England, by the sea and yet all deeply rural, boozy and squiry, haunch-of-venison, wenchy, Hollywood's English dream. That would do to place, while I was still young enough, my decrepitude and eventual death. Till then, wine and bad drains and downy upper lips for my leaves.

At closing-time Selwyn said:

'Ah ave ter goh ome, mister. Ah av wahf and nahn

childer. Morst on em in bed, boot soom wettin oop fer ther dad.'

'I'll never see you again,' I said. But he wouldn't shake hands; he danced gravely backwards, laughing 'Ho ho ho', then saying:

'Al see yer again, mister. Ah knawww. Ah knaw oo al see and oo al not. Niver dart that.' Cecil shambled after Selwyn like a man who had wet himself, but this was because, I knew, he had secreted one bottle of my funeral whisky in the back waist-band of his trousers. Soon Veronica gave me her hand in dignified farewell, suffering me to kiss her lightly-powdered cheek, then (headachy; me poor old duck) off to bed, leaving just three of us: Ted, Everett and myself.

'Which would e like to see, me duck,' said Ted eagerly, 'me guns or me old man's books?' He seemed to have taken a liking to Everett, but it was me he addressed.

'I personally,' I said, 'have no wish to see any guns, thank you very much. Incidentally, the police have, in their possession, a little weapon which might interest you.'

'So that's where the bloody thing went to,' said Ted, striking hammer fist on anvil palm. 'Well,' he said. 'I've thought back and I've thought back, but I couldn't think ow or when or oo. Anyway,' he said, 'it's ad some use, that's one thing. None of the rest of them as.' He looked carefully at Everett. 'I don't think I will bring them down to show yer,' he said. 'After all, yer never know, do yer? I'll bring down me old man's books.' And, shushing himself so as not to disturb Veronica, he went daintily upstairs.

'Remarkable man,' said Everett, 'reminds me of somebody.' Ted came down with an ammunition box and he spilled books and dust and a smell of old apples on the bar-counter. Everett looked them through with little interest.

A Book of Prayers for Working Men
Blind Before the Mast
Herbert Henry and Revivalism in Flintshire
Marine Engineers' Association: Transactions of 1891
Simple Class Singing for Board School Teachers
Great Thoughts from Wilhelm Meister
Cocytus: Rationalism in Decline
Works of Tom Paine, Vol. III
The Complete Richardson

Then he picked up a small quarto book, older than the others, no title, of course, on its spine, opened it and said, 'My God'.

'Something wrong?' asked Ted.

'Wrong? Look at this.' And he showed Ted the title-page. Ted read it frowning, lips fumbling. He said:

'I see what yer mean, me duck. Spelling's all wrong. But me dad said they never could spell in them days. 1602,' read Ted. 'Very old. Wait.' He moved back, fearful. 'That means it's been through the Great Plague and the Black Death. It's full of germs. Throw it in the fireplace, quick.'

But for once Ted was ignored. Everett and I were equally excited. It was a play, *Hamlet*, but *Hamlet* in a form which, if the date did not lie, was earlier than any known. The pirated quarto of 1603, bad money, had, contrary to Gresham, been driven out by the authentic silver of the quarto of 1604. This find in the Black Swan put the composition and production of the play forward to 1602 or earlier: or was it a version of that *Ur-Hamlet* on which Shakespeare had based his own work? I said, all the dead except this ever-living one forgotten:

'Look for the *To be or not to be* speech.' I breathed hard; Everett panted. Everett said:

'See.' I read, horrible wooden type on sick yellow crinkled paper:

'To die or to liue I theres a poynte
Is it more worthie the mindes paines to endure
Or with brawling canon fighte the troubled ocean
And stoppe all striuing hence –

'Piracy,' I said. 'Some other bad stenographer taking it down at a Globe performance. Before the blessings of Pitman and Gregg descended. Charactery, I believe they called it.'

'Astonishing,' said Everett. 'Look,' he said to Ted, 'may I take this away?'

'Yer can keep it, me duck, for all I care.'

'Nonsense. You'll have all the libraries in America clamouring for this. This'll make your fortune. Good God, incredible.' And Everett saw, in the clock above the bar, another book, not yet published, certainly intrinsically superior to the one he now held in his hand, if less likely to cause a stir among scholars. That book of the poems of Everett might, he was thinking, be handled in just this way a century or more hence, in a pub if there were pubs, after closing-time, which there would certainly be if there were pubs, taken from a box of books brought down breathing of dust and apples. 'Ten per cent,' said Everett. 'Is that a deal?'

'Fifty per cent if yer like, me duck. We'll go arves. Which reminds me: oo'll ave one little arf more before we go to bed?'

20

How much of that last episode you believed, I don't know and don't care. Of this final episode you'll believe less, of that I'm certain, but please don't begrudge poor old whining Denham, back in Tokyo, his modicum of fantasy. Besides, I'm doing a certain homiletic good in showing – with however fictitious an example – that rewards come to those who never sin against stability, who don't play around with the fire of marriage, whose life and marriage are both solidly secure and not without excitement and interest, chiefly because their work means something to the community and to themselves. But see below.

The day after the funeral I flew back by jet-plane, knowing that everything at home was being taken care of – Beryl written to about her duties; the bank confirming its executorship of the will; Mr Raj's possessions with the police. (His body was also a possession, destined, along with books and clothes and condiments, for his Gray's Inn brother.) Only one thing of Mr Raj's I kept, something that nobody else was likely to want.

I arrived in Tokyo in fear, but I found everything in order, Mishima having proved efficient, perhaps too much so, for the rest of the staff smiled and bowed when I walked into the office. And so things went on quite calmly. I had no personal letters from England, except from Rice, who said that he had heard from certain sources, by roundabout means, that my father had died, this apparently having been announced for some reason on a television programme, not that he watched television himself, and some fool or other had got hold of the foolish idea that I myself had announced my father's death, manifestly impossible, me being in Tokyo and hardly, anyway, likely to appear on British television. I should, said Rice, have cabled for permission to fly home, for this could quickly have been granted, and my loyalty to the firm in remaining in Tokyo when my heart must have been well-nigh broken with sorrow at my father's death was greatly appreciated by one and all.

So that was all right.

Months later I was sitting in my office, and a clerk came in to announce two visitors. I sat writing, waiting for them to be shown in, ready to perform the big executive trick of breaking the surface of absorption like a swimmer, then coming forward hearty with outstretched hand. But while my head was down to my work I heard a known voice say:

'Well, me duck, never thought yer'd see us ere, did yer?'

They were both smart, touristy, Ted with a movie camera strapped to him, Veronica a vision in white with pearls that were not Mikimoto.

'I never expected,' I said, 'but I'm delighted all the same. Have you come into some money, or do post-war publicans always do this?'

'A world tour,' said Veronica, in her lady's voice, to which Ted inclined like a serf, 'thanks to your friend Mr Everett.'

'That *Amlet*, me duck,' said Ted. 'Yer remember that? Worth a packet it was, and oo would ever ave thought it? Ad our names in the papers, we ave, although not in the good uns like the *Mail* and the *Mirror*. Small papers that we aven't ever eard of, but still there it is. Never expected all that fuss, did we, me duck?' he said to Veronica. 'And it's been bought, the book as, by somebody called Folger or something in the U.S. Dollars we was paid in. And old Everett got ten per cent, so e's bringing is poetry book out now. So everybody's appy.'

'Do sit down,' I said. 'We'll go out for a drink in a minute. Does this mean that you've retired?'

'Oh, no, me duck,' said Ted, very smart in his palm beach suit and tan shoes, a frivolous touristy hat on his knee. 'Just a oliday, that's all. And a bit put away. It was a nice little bit we got, but not as much as all that. Was it, me duck?' he said to Veronica.

'I'm very pleased,' I said. 'Do you know, I'd forgotten all about that curious find of ours. It was the night of the funeral, as I remember.'

'Looking a bit fatter,' said Ted, nose twitching. 'Isn't e, mé duck? But that's a contented mind, they say.'

'And what's the news back home?'

'Oh, Cedric's looking after the Swan, Selwyn and Cecil to elp im. And that Alice Winterbottom thinking of getting married again. Got over it quick, she did.'

'Who to? Jack Brownlow?'

'Nawwwwww,' scoffed Ted. 'Im? No, the bloke she works with in that club. Thinking of starting a pub somewhere. Business arrangement more than anything, as far as I can see. Love, she says, she'll never marry for love again.'

'And Everett's daughter?'

'Yes, queer little bitch she is. Came in the pub with er dad. Regular e is now.'

'Oh, she's pretty,' said Veronica, 'and quite smart. I should say her teeth are false, though. An awful little flirt.'

'You mark my words,' said Ted. 'She'll get erself into trouble one of these days.'

We went for lunch to a restaurant which specialised in fish dishes. The fish swam all round the room in glass tanks and you chose what you wanted by pointing to it. Ted was delighted, Veronica disgusted. 'Me poor old duck,' said Ted.

'The old trouble?' I asked.

'I'm a great deal better,' said Veronica, 'thanks very much.'

I took the afternoon off and drove Veronica and Ted back to my house. Veronica was fascinated, Ted hardly interested. While Veronica wandered round my garden, Ted and I talked. Soon the talk became Ted's monologue.

'Shakespeare,' he said. 'I know that book wasn't written by im, but e's been a lot in my mind lately. Partly because if e adn't lived nobody would ave taken the trouble to make a book like that, and we wouldn't ave ad this money. But we're entitled to it from im in a way, yer know, because e'd always made all sorts of promises to the Ardens, yer know, an Arden being is mother, as yer may or may not ave eard. Always going to play up at the Ardens as a kid, and very fond of is uncles and aunts. Always said e'd make a big name and leave money to the Ardens, because everybody said e was more of an Arden to look at than a Shakespeare. And the Ardens and Shakespeares couldn't never really get on, yer know. And the funny thing was young Will, as they called im, couldn't stand is dad. Real Arden e was. Ran away from ome because e couldn't stand is dad.'

'How do you know all this?' I asked.

Ted gaped at me. 'Ow do I know? It's in the family, passed down. It's true, true as I'm sitting ere in –' He paused, amazed. 'Japan,' he said. 'I'm in Japan. Never thought as ow I'd be in Japan.' One of my two servants brought more cold beer for us, took out a glass to Veronica in the garden. It was a gorgeous flowery day. 'Bloody marvellous,' said Ted. 'Like on the pictures.'

'Tell me more,' I said.

'Funny,' said Ted, 'the way this interests people. There was professors taking it down in a book back ome. Came round to the pub, they did. Very interested in Selwyn they was, too.'

'Carry on.'

'*Or-then-tick* they kept saying,' said Ted. 'They said ow there was no proof it was *or-then-tick*. I told them I didn't give a bugger whether it was *or-then-tick* or not, it was the bloody truth. Well, anyway, yer know what was Will's downfall?'

'Women?'

'One woman,' said Ted. 'And she was a black woman. E wrote a poem about er avin black airs growing in er ead and e said they was like black wires. Joking, I suppose, but a queer way of joking. It never does to joke with a woman.' He looked out: Veronica was still enchanted with the bird-loud garden, its bridges and dwarf trees. 'This black woman of is,' said Ted, 'ad come on a boat from Africa. Well up in the world she was, daughter of a chief or something, and she wasn't made into a slave but was taken into some-body's ouse and made a lady of. And this poor bugger fell for er, ook, line and sinker. Mind you,' said Ted, 'I've eard about these black women, ow they'll practically do it for yer, and once you ave one yer don't want anybody else. Although,' said Ted, 'I wouldn't mind aving one of these two little Japs that you've got ere. Anyway, about this poor bugger Will. This black woman, yer see, was taken off to the West Indies as a sort of companion like for some lady of this family she'd been living with oo'd taken a real fancy to er, and she, the white one that is, ad ad to marry some bugger oo was going out to the West Indies or some-where as a sort of governor for the place, it aving been taken from the Spanish or somebody. Well, Will's broken-

250

arted. Is art's so broken e can't write proper any more, not the stuff e used to write, full of fun and whatnot, making everybody piss themselves of laughing. E writes all these gloomy things what everybody switches off now when they come on the telly. And e daren't go back to is wife. Yer know why?'

'Why?' Ted came nearer and whispered:

'E'd got a dose. This black one ad given it im.'

'No.'

'Yes. Oo's telling the story, you or me? Anyway, e gets so ill they ave to send im back to Stratford, is nose fair dropping off. Nobody likes the plays e writes, so e makes no money. So e lives off is son-in-law, what was making good money as a doctor. And all the time e goes round saying e's got three thousand quid a year, and people owe im thousands more, and all that caper, till everybody gets fed up listening to im. Sometimes people takes im in the local, gives im the odd pint, and tries to shut im up when strangers come in, because e talks like e's crackers. Last stage, yer see,' said Ted, pointing skullwards. 'Goes to the brain then. Some of is plays is mad, quite early on, people spending their lives trying to work out what e means. And that thing e wrote for is grave, ravings of a madman about cursing is bones or something. And look at the way e made out that will. Treated is wife shameful, but I do believe, and the ole family believes it, that e didn't even know er for is wife in is last days, poor bugger.'

'Extraordinary,' I said.

'Yes,' said Ted. 'It's always been believed that e let down the Arden blood, the Shakespeare being so piss-poor that nothing could ardly let that down. My grandmother wouldn't ave is name mentioned in the ouse. I'd better go out to the wife,' said Ted. 'She's not been so well, poor old duck, I don't want er to think I'm neglecting er.' He rose, saying, 'Will is really a terrible example for everybody, showing what appens when you leave the wife of your bosom and go off ooring after other women. So you'd better watch out,' he said to me. 'All these foreign women. Not that they're black, of course. And then, of course, you're not married.' He poked me in the stomach in play. 'I wish other people would take note of Will Shakespeare's story,' said Ted, 'before they start running off to London with other men's wives, or just on their own, ooring.'

That night we visited various places where well-shaped and scented, though completely naked, Japanese girls came to sit on male knees. Veronica was not greatly amused. Then, before midnight, they had to be driven to Yokohama to spend the night on board their ship, which was due to sail eastwards before dawn. I didn't go with them; I sent them with my driver. I was feeling tired, I said. But I had genuinely been glad to see them.

I looked at myself in the mirror before bed. Going bald and jowlish, teeth stained with tobacco-tar, belly big with self-indulgence, chest narrow, legs stumpy, disgustingly hirsute everywhere. But the body doesn't matter, the body's only something you use. It was the eyes I didn't like, the unloving mouth, and the holier-than-thou set of the nostrils. I went, naked, into the small study next to my bedroom, where I had been working on this story, and read, naked, scratching, through the nineteen clipped fascicles. Had I really clarified anything for myself? Of course not. The mess was there, the instability, but I wondered now if that sin against stability was really the big sin. What I did realise quite clearly was the little I'd helped, the blundering or not-wishing-to-be-involved plump money-eyed man on leave inveighing against sins he wasn't in the position even to begin to commit. For surely that sneered-at suburban life was more stable than this shadow life of buying and selling in a country where no involvement was possible, the television evening, with the family round, better than the sordid dalliance that soothed me after work? (What work? I didn't make anything; I wasn't even an ice-cream butcher, a John Bull printing outfit printer. I didn't dispense a Shakespearean radiance in the public bar.) And adultery implied marriage and was perhaps a nobler word than fornication or masturbation or – never mind. If poor bloody innocent little Winterbottom had died, and striving Mr Raj (a man who had come too soon for the blending, as they were all coming too soon), surely it was something that they invoked the word Love? Even the word was better than this emptiness, this standing on the periphery and sneering.

I read through the first fascicle again. Smug, wordy, pretentious, but let it stand. Let it all stand, we're not here for entertainment. And I knew that I would retire soon, able to afford it, and where I'd retire. And so I *would* see that great prophet Selwyn again. And others. And be less of a fool next time. And I knew who I thought I'd ask to marry me, but she'd probably say no. Perhaps if I exercised a little, took off some of this weight . . . I couldn't believe that she'd really disliked me; she hadn't been indifferent enough.

Under the fascicles in the drawer I had placed Mr Raj's only extant piece of formal prose. My poor dear Mr Raj. I read it through again, though it was now very late, but the passage itself is not very long. It's just a beginning. I append it here, giving Mr Raj the last word.

In considering the all-pervading contemporary problem of racialism, we have to realise that it is not sufficient merely to counter the depositions of the racialists with the stark facts of the ethnologist and anthropologist. This, of course, has its value, not to be gainsaid, but racialism arises in the hearts of the common people and it is not really necessary for the racialist of a fascist, or communist (though there rarely found) or plutocratic state to do more than focus the jet of hatred on one sect or other that has met with the dislike of the ruling class or which it is convenient, for various reasons of an economic or other nature, to subdue or even, in certain extreme cases, to exterminate. Of course, these forces are not solely directed against a race; sometimes it is a religious sect that meets with the displeasure of the ruling caste, but the technique of arousing hatred is much the same.

The capacity of people for hatred can never cease to astonish. This is especially so as it would seem that man is by nature gregarious and that he has created a world which is, in effect, founded on love under various other names. Trust is love, credit is a form of love, reliance on the police force or army of a state is also a form of love. It is easily understandable, of course, that love within and for one group must, of biological necessity, imply quite contrary emotions to those elements outside the group which seem likely to threaten (even when this appearance has no basis in fact) the well-being and security, nay the very existence, of the group. We see this clearly when kittens in baskets hiss and spit, though they are blind and have not been taught the nature of fear or of hate, at a quite friendly dog which sniffs near the basket. All this is understandable and biologically necessary. But what cannot be understood is why man, in being forced by economic necessity, as well as being gently persuaded by the increasing shrinking of the globe through aeronautical advances, to think in terms of larger and larger groups to which he must give allegiance or, in a word, love, is increasing his capacity for hate.

Here one is tempted to lay down one's pen and smile

pityingly and in lack of comprehension. A spring English day compels the heart to greater love of nature and of one's fellow-beings. The heart in particular expands to the presence of the loved female, and wonders why she too will not love. Love seems inevitable, necessary, as normal and as easy a process as respiration, but unfortunately